AGENT ORANGE

By A. J. Butcher

AGENT ORANGE

a Spy High novel

A. J. Butcher

www.atombooks.co.uk

ATOM

First published in Great Britain in June 2005 by Atom

Copyright © 2005 by Atom Books

Based on concepts devised by Ben Sharpe
Story by A. J. Butcher

A CIP catalogue record for this book is available from
the British Library.

ISBN 1 904233 39 2

Typeset in Cochin by M Rules
Printed and bound in Great Britain
by Bookmarque Ltd, Croydon, Surrey

Atom
An imprint of
Time Warner Book Group UK
Brettenham House
Lancaster Place
London WC2E 7EN

www.atombooks.co.uk

For Ben Sharpe, without whom . . .

ACKNOWLEDGEMENTS

We would like to thank Kate Harrison for creating the character of Kate Taylor, which won the Spy High hall of fame competition.

PROLOGUE

'Okay,' said Bex Deveraux, 'we've got five minutes left to save the world.'

The half-dozen younger teenagers semicircled in front of her nodded. Their expressions were grimly determined, understanding the gravity of their mission, but Bex detected excitement too, as if saving the world was a thrill as well as a duty. As if risking their lives was a game. Students, she thought wryly.

'Can we kind of shoot someone now?' asked the boy closest to her.

'Sleepshot only,' Bex instructed. 'And pick your targets. A wild shot is a wasted shot. We have to take Stromfeld's control centre.'

'If we have to,' said the girl with the auburn hair, 'then we will.'

The guards outside the control centre didn't stand a chance. Maybe they'd never imagined that intruders could penetrate this deeply into their leader's underground complex and therefore were not entirely prepared to repel an assault. Maybe the labour market for expendable goons wasn't as buoyant these days as it had been, forcing Stromfeld to employ minions even more mindless than usual. Whatever the reason, their resistance was minimal.

Bex and her team were bursting into the control centre with a good four minutes still on the clock.

More guards, and more alert. Scientists with white coats and shock blasters. A last stand around the meteortron itself.

And no sign of Stromfeld. Bex hoped the kids were asking themselves why.

She doubted the boy who wanted to kind of shoot someone was burdening his mind with questions. He was spraying sleepshot from both wristbands and making the anaesthetic pellets count, spinning Stromfeld's lackeys into slumberland. But the spy who survived long-term was the spy whose deductive and observational powers were as precise as his or her marksmanship. The girl with the auburn hair was impressive, moving with the litheness and grace of a gymnast to avoid enemy fire. Her scissor-kick was so expertly timed that it would have floored that scientist type even without the added jolt of electricity supplied in silver sparks by her Shocksuit. Potential there, Bex noted.

It looked like they'd just about secured the control centre.

'Good work, Hannay Team,' she acknowledged. 'Two minutes ten left to disengage the meteortron before the first asteroids do their hailstone thing and everyone on the surface gets set to join the dinosaurs.'

'I've got it.' One of the other girls, dark-haired and deep-voiced. Olivia, her name was. Keen to take charge.

She was already in possession of the meteortron's control panel. 'Leave it to me.'

'You guys happy to leave it to Olivia?' Bex wondered mildly.

The boy who liked to shoot evidently found the deactivation of weapons of genocidal mass destruction too tame an exercise for him to bother with. 'Why not?' he said.

'I'll *show* you why not, imbecile,' vowed Olivia, and now her voice was *very* deep indeed. Man deep. And she was doing something with a computer that appeared to have no impact on the meteortron whatsoever. Its effect on the floor of the control centre, however, was a different matter. The hundreds of glasteel panels lit up like the dance floor of a disco, but nobody was going to be strutting their stuff any time soon.

Bex and her team were suddenly statued. 'Stasis field,' she groaned.

'Indeed,' said Olivia. 'Instead of you immobilising my meteortron, I have immobilised *you*.' And the figure at the controls now not only didn't sound like Olivia any more, but didn't look much like her either, or even female. Which was probably just as well. Even in an age of political correctness, girls with bald heads and beards would struggle to get dates.

'Stromfeld,' said Bex, recognition dawning.

'Correct,' the bald man said gleefully. 'My true features concealed thus far by my handy little physical reconfiguration unit.'

'I can see why,' snorted the girl with auburn hair.

Defiance in the face of adversity, Bex recorded. Another plus for the gymnast. 'So what happened to the real Olivia, Stromfeld?' she said.

'I'm sure you don't really want to know.' Stromfeld winced. 'It was rather messy, I'm afraid. Suffice it to say that your colleague did not escape from her captivity as you were so effortlessly deceived into believing. And neither will you.'

Bex strained to move her arms just the few short inches that would enable her to target the grinning madman with her sleepshot wristbands. Each inch might as well have been a hundred miles. Her body was rock. It afforded her no pleasure that Hannay Team were equally helpless.

Stromfeld tutted. 'Children,' he said. 'They send children to distract me. Such foolishness merits their destruction.' He turned to the meteortron and stroked it lovingly. 'And Stromfeld, of course, will oblige. My beautiful meteortron, my beautiful bringer of death.'

'You've got a lot of problems, man, you know that?' From the marksman.

Stromfeld smiled. 'You are blessed, my young friends, did you know *that*? For you will be witnesses to the final triumph of Stromfeld. You will see the meteors I have summoned from the furthest reaches of space rain down on the decadent, degenerate surface civilisations. You will watch as —'

'Okay, okay. Cut. Pause. *Finito*. He's into gloating time now and I can do without that today. Arrest program.' Bex was assuming command once more.

Stromfeld's turn to freeze as the lights in the floor were doused and the teenagers found that they could move again.

'We messed up, didn't we?' admitted the girl with auburn hair and, at the moment, downcast eyes.

'Put it this way,' said Bex, 'if this had been a real-life operation instead of a virtual simulation, it wouldn't have been bye-bye Hannay Team, it would have been *arrive-derci* humanity and don't bother to write. And also, remember, if you fall at the last hurdle like this in your Stromfeld program final trial . . .'

She didn't need to finish her sentence. 'Mind-wipe,' everyone said gloomily.

'So are you saying we should have *known* Olivia was Stromfeld, Ms Deveraux?' the boy who liked to shoot said sullenly, toying with his wristbands. 'How? Those physical reconfiguration things are almost undetectable.'

'You said it,' Bex agreed. '*Almost.* And it's almosts that can save your lives. Computer,' she called out, 'rewind scenario to reappearance of Olivia.'

The control centre blurred like a film out of focus. Corridors and chambers rushed by the stationary teenagers like shoppers on the first day of the sales. Even now, after three years of experience at Spy High and in the field, the effect made Bex momentarily nauseous. When their surroundings returned to docility and still-ness, the group found itself by an elevator shaft.

'Computer,' ordered Bex, 'advance scenario ten seconds, then pause.'

In those ten seconds, the elevator doors opened and Olivia emerged. In the initial running of the scenario she'd been captured by Stromfeld's men but then – so she'd told her team-mates – had escaped and been lucky enough to catch up with them again here. First time they'd believed her without hesitation. This time, they were grateful that Olivia's explanation was cut short.

'What do you notice about her?' Bex said.

'She's Stromfeld?' One agent who'd sooner simply shoot his enemies than examine them. Bex wondered whether he'd last the course.

'How should you have been able to *tell* that she's, if not Stromfeld, certainly not Olivia?' she pursued patiently. 'Look closely. I don't want to hand it to you on a plate.'

'Her *hands*.' Bex wasn't surprised it was the auburn-haired girl who realised. 'They're not Olivia's hands.'

'I should hope not,' Bex observed, 'or I dread to think what her legs are like. Show us the backs of your hands, Olivia.' Which were sprouting with black hairs. 'There's always one area where physical reconfiguration doesn't quite work. You should have been suspicious enough of Olivia's miraculous escape from captivity to check her out more closely. You have to be vigilant in the field, take nothing at face value. Literally not, in this case.' Bex glanced from one member of Hannay Team to the next. The students weren't scowling or resentful, with the possible exception of Billy the Kid. They were silent and respectful. They were learning. That was good. 'Okay, we'll run the scenario again. From the top.' She patted one of Olivia/Stromfeld's hands. 'We won't be needing these —'

The hand seized her wrist.

'What?' Bex recoiled, startled.

Stromfeld was back, and he was smiling. 'I just wanted to say, Agent Deveraux . . .'

'What? Computer, what's going on?'

'. . . it's been a pleasure working with you for what may be the last time.' The virtual man leaned confidentially close to her. '*Change* is on its way.'

❋

Ronnie Ronson was a hard man. You had to be hard to survive in London's notorious East End Zone. You had to be able to look after yourself. And if the scars that seamed Ronnie's meaty fists and sallow cheeks, the missing chunks of both earlobes and the cheap, glassy optical implant replacing the eye that had last been spotted rolling along the Mile End Road like a marble collectively suggested that this was a man more accustomed to losing fights than winning them, and if anybody was careless enough of his own continued health to raise the issue, Ronnie would only have muttered, 'You should see the other guy', before splintering a selection of the enquirer's limbs. Because for Ronnie Ronson, being a hard man wasn't simply a matter of necessity. It was a labour of love.

Which was why he'd joined the Clay gang while still in his teens. The Clay gang were the main men on the streets where Ronnie lived. Nobody messed with the Clays – unless they were perversely attracted to long stays in hospital or walking with a limp. The gang were modelled on the Clay twins, Ronnie and Reggie, gangsters who'd ruled the East End with the proverbial rod of iron a hundred years ago, back in the 1960s, in the days before the zones. By way of homage to their heroes, the members of the present Clay gang wore the snappy drainpipe-trousered suits of the period, admittedly with one or two more modern innovations for self-protection, such as razorboots. They also had to rechristen themselves either Ronnie or Reggie. It was a respect thing. Ronnie Ronson's real first name was Eugene.

Yeah, it made him feel good being a Clay. It made him feel important, like he mattered, like he belonged.

Everyone was scared of him. Everyone was scared of *them*. Everyone except the Rippers.

There was a knock on Ronnie's door. Actually, it was less like a knock than the first blows of a hammer attack. It'd be Reggie, Reggie and Ron. It was time. Ronnie slipped his shock dusters on over his knuckles and felt that queasy exhilaration in his stomach that always prefaced imminent violence. Pity about this headache that had been nagging at him all day like a wife. He didn't seem able to shift it. Not that anything short of an axe embedded in his skull was going to keep him out of the ruck tonight. At last the Rippers were gonna get what was coming to them. Yeah.

It wasn't Reggie, Reggie and Ron at the door. It was Reggie, Ron, Reggie and Reg. They stomped out into the night streets.

The Rippers. They'd been muscling their way into Clay territory for a while now. Hailed from Whitechapel originally. Took their inspiration from the Victorian serial killer known only as Jack the Ripper. Cue for a uniform of swirling capes and stovepipe hats and an even narrower choice of names.

They were waiting for the Clays outside the old church. Nobody went to church these days. Society was far too enlightened for that.

Ronnie Ronson made a quick count. About thirty. *About* because his addition wasn't very confident above twenty. About the same number of Clays lining up alongside him. That was useful. Normally he'd be up for taking on the Ripper scum single-handed, but this blasted *headache*. No doubt he'd feel better when he was breaking noses and putting the old razorboot in.

Ronnie Ronson got ready to rumble.

There was the jeering first, of course, the twenty-first-century street gang equivalent of ancient armies rattling their swords and shields at each other prior to combat, obscenities and insults flung across the divide like missiles.

It was good. Ronnie loved the taunting almost as much as feeling his opponent's flesh split and bones crack beneath the ruthless barrage of his assault. (This damned headache, though.) What his tirade of abuse lacked in originality, it more than made up for in volume. It was a way of stoking his hatred of the Rippers, inflaming his loathing further. He howled himself hoarse with words of four letters.

On either side of him, fists were clenched and eyes were wild and lips foamed with poison like rabid beasts'. The Rippers were baying like dogs, like diseased dogs. (His head hurt.) And you know what you do to dogs that are diseased. You put them down. You put them out of their misery. Just like the Clays were going to do to the Rippers.

(If only his head didn't hurt.)

Their clamour crescendoed. The Clays were bellowing 'Clay'. The Rippers were barking 'Ripper'. The brawl needed only a spark to ignite it.

And there was Reggie, hurling a rock at the massed hats of the enemy. His aim was exceptional. One was dislodged, like a dark tower toppling. That was the sign. For the Clays to surge forward, shock dusters flashing on their fists. For the Rippers to charge to meet them, brandishing their canes of black steel. For Ronnie Ronson to whoop with the full-blooded elation of a man who lived for violence. He hated the Rippers. He *hated* the Rippers. He—

(The sign for his headache to explode and fill his mind with a blinding, brilliant light.)

—loved these guys in their long capes and tall hats. And he was running towards one of them and he kind of *wanted* to be and when they reached each other they embraced like old friends, like brothers. And all along the line Clay and Ripper alike were hugging and shaking hands and fighting was the furthest thing from their minds. And in this bleak corner of the East End Zone of London at least, all was well.

Until Ronnie Ronson got home again. Only then did he seem to register how he'd conducted himself that night, how both gangs had behaved. Only then did his recent affection for all things Ripper dissolve and the more customary detestation harden again in his heart.

Too late now, though. The moment was over. The confrontation had passed.

'I don't . . . I can't . . .' It was a nightmare, some weird and baffling nightmare. What had happened to him out there by the old church? What had happened to all of them? He didn't understand. What had changed him like that? Ronnie Ronson kicked out savagely at his furniture by way of consolation. Smashing wood wasn't as fulfilling as smashing faces, but evidently tonight it would have to do.

Only then did he realise his headache was gone.

Bex took her time showering and dressing after completing the Stromfeld program with Hannay Team. The kids did fine in the end – they were only First Termers, after all – she didn't have any worries about *them*. The virtual cyber-creation that was Stromfeld himself, however, was preying on her mind a little. He was a character, a training tool, a composite of all the uber-villains Spy High had ever faced and most of those they hadn't. He could alter his form each time, his appearance, his plan. What Stromfeld couldn't do at any time was to operate outside the parameters of the mission scenario; he couldn't step out of role and address a participant directly. Obviously, though, no one had told Stromfeld that.

What had he meant, working with her for the last time? Change on its way? Was there some significance to his words of which she should be aware? Or was Stromfeld's sudden taste for improvisation purely the result of a glitch in the program, an unexpected power surge or something? She'd speak to one of the techs about it later. It was probably nothing, but as she'd have told Hannay Team if any of them had asked, in a secret agent's line of work *probably* was never good enough.

'Ms Deveraux?'

She was slipping into her shoes when the auburn-haired girl, already fully dressed, peeped from around the corner of the lockers. 'Bex, please,' she corrected. 'Ms Deveraux's kind of formal, and as you can probably tell, I don't do formal.' Gesturing vaguely to her trade-mark piercings and damp, spiky hair, the green of deep forests.

'Bex.' The Hannay Teamer edged forward as if approaching a celebrity. 'I was wondering . . . if I could have a word.'

'Sure.' Bex stood. 'As many as you like. They're not taxed. It's Kate, isn't it?'

'That's right. Kate Taylor. I wanted to thank you for helping us with our training today.'

'My pleasure. Bit of a nostalgia boost actually. It's been a while since I went head to head with old Stromfeld.'

'We weren't very good, were we?' judged Kate Taylor despondently.

'I wouldn't say that,' Bex encouraged. 'It's early days yet. You made mistakes, okay, but you learned from them and you didn't repeat them. That's good. And you've got some cool moves yourself. I don't think you'll need to worry about the mind-wipe just yet, Kate.'

'Thanks. I'm not sure we'll ever be able to match Bond Team, though. You're legends.'

'Oh, please.' Bex laughed dismissively, but she was flattered too. Just as well Ben wasn't here, and she meant Spy High in general, not only the girls' locker room. He'd be preening, posing and signing autographs. All these impressionable First Termers. 'You know the thing about legends, Kate? They're not always true. Believe me, we had our problems – don't tell anyone, but they were mostly to do with the boys not being able to keep pace with the girls. In *anything*, you know what I mean?'

Kate grinned. 'You came through, though.'

'Yeah, we did,' Bex reflected warmly. 'And so will you.'

'I just wanted to ask, though,' Kate persisted, 'is there any advice you can give me to help me with my training? I want to do well and I'd really appreciate it, Bex.'

Bex considered. She was finding herself drawn to Kate. The girl wasn't unlike herself at fourteen, hair colour and lack of facial adornment apart. She remembered how desperate she'd been to prove herself to her Bond Team partners when she joined them after the death of original member Jennifer Chen, particularly once they'd learned the identity of her father. The daughter of Deveraux. Sounded like the title of an old gothic chiller. Having a computerised dad who operated a school for spies wasn't always an asset. But enough about her. 'You want to take a walk?' she said to Kate.

They headed towards the nearest study-elevator. Their route took them past the virtual-reality chamber, the holo-gym and the Intelligence Gathering Centre, or IGC, mainstays in the training and preparation of the next generation of secret agents, the heart of Spy High. Students in Shocksuits passed by. The tedious drone of a History of Espionage class wafted from one of the teaching rooms.

'You're English, right?' Bex deduced. 'Accent kind of gives it away. But don't worry. You'll get to the Vocal Disguise Module next term. Most people think I'm from Tibet. First time in the States?'

'Yes,' said Kate, 'and it's taking a bit of getting used to.'

'Uh-huh,' Bex nodded. 'Deveraux isn't Disneyland.' They came to a study-elevator. 'We have better rides.'

Inside, a heavy mahogany desk and leather-backed chair, papers neatly stacked on the former, a fireplace containing real logs, bookcases lining the walls containing real books. All but one. Bex depressed the spine of *Diamonds Are Forever* and the door to the study-elevator slid closed while the room performed the second of its two functions. When the girls stepped out of it, they were in the corridor of what appeared to be a cross between a stately home relocated from Kate's own country and a traditional cold-showers-before-breakfast public school. These were the unconcealed above-ground levels of the Deveraux College. At Spy High, appearances were deceptive, and designed to be so.

'So how'd you get picked to come here?' Bex asked Kate.

'It was Mrs Collins, my gymnastics coach. I was Under-Fourteens Europan champion, for what it's worth.'

'It's worth a lot. Anyone who can cross their legs behind the back of their head has my undying admiration.'

Kate laughed. 'I could show you . . .'

'Please,' Bex shuddered. 'Mrs Collins.'

'Well, of course, Mrs Collins turned out to be more than a gymnastics coach. Turned out to be a selector agent for Spy High. And I got to be selected.'

'I told you you had some cool moves,' Bex said, 'and as for advice, here's one little nugget right off the bat – if that actually makes sense. It's the lesson today's Stromfeld should have taught you, that business with Olivia. The secret of staying alive in this game is to expect danger from the least likely of sources.'

Kate absorbed the advice like a sponge soaking up water. 'But Bex, doesn't that make you suspicious of *everyone*?'

Bex winked. 'Why do you think I'm still single?'

They'd strolled as far as reception. Violet Crabtree, as ever, was seated behind the desk. In her less charitable moments, Bex imagined this was because the old duck was no longer able to stand. She wasn't saying that Violet Crabtree was getting on in years, but if she was a building she'd have been listed as an ancient monument ages ago. That, or condemned.

'Hi, Vi,' Bex greeted her, with playful provocation. Expecting the usual response, which commenced with 'That's Violet or Mrs Crabtree to you, Agent Deveraux' and concluded with a variation on the theme of 'In my day a spy looking like you wouldn't have lasted five minutes in the field. Did Mata Hari dye her hair? Was the Girl from UNCLE pierced?' (Violet Crabtree had been a secret agent herself in her youth, which was one reason why Bex's father employed her – Bex theorised that she may even have worked alongside James Bond himself.) But today, no metaphorical rap across the knuckles, no frosty criticism of the young generation as a whole and Bex in particular.

'Ah, Agent Deveraux,' ventured Violet Crabtree hesitantly. 'I was wondering if I could have a word.'

'Déjà vu or what?' Bex remarked. 'Sure thing, Mrs C.'

'*Privately*,' the old woman stressed as both Bex and Kate gravitated towards her desk.

'If you like.' The Bond Teamer frowned fleetingly. She turned to her companion.

'It's all right. I've got an essay to write on the Moriarty Syndrome. Just, thanks for talking to me, Bex. I hope I won't let you down.'

'No problem. I'm sure you won't.' The two girls shook hands. 'Actually, Kate, wait a second, can you? Mrs C, you got a pen and paper there I can borrow?'

'Borrow? What, you're going to give me the paper back sometime?'

Bex jotted a holophone number down and passed it to Kate. 'That's my personal holophone where I'm stationed in Cairo. North Africa. Region Orange. If you want to ask something, cry on someone's shoulder, if you just want to chat, call me. Any time. Spy High can be a lonely place. I've been here.'

Kate's eyes shone as she pocketed the slip of paper. 'Did I tell you you were a legend, Bex? Thanks for this.'

'No worries. Now go on, get out of here before my halo slips. Good luck with your essay. I'll see you, Kate.'

'That was a nice gesture,' said Violet Crabtree approvingly once Kate Taylor had left. 'You've made that girl's day now.'

'Shall I make it two while I'm on a roll, Mrs C?' Bex grinned. 'What can I do for you?'

The aged receptionist opted to answer one question with another. 'Were you aware that my employment at the Deveraux College is to be terminated, Agent Deveraux?' Bex's raised eyebrows she interpreted as a no. 'Yes. It seems my services are no longer required.'

'Really? I'm sorry to hear that.' And a little surprised by the sincerity of her sentiment. For all the old woman's disapproval of Bex's appearance and her swingeing censure of anyone under the age of sixty, Spy High without Violet Crabtree was unthinkable, like Mom's Apple Pie without Mom. Or apples.

'Look at these hands.' Violet exhibited them. They looked like they'd been robbed from a mummy. 'They've done good work for the intelligence community for over half a century, Agent Deveraux.'

'I'm sure they have,' said Bex. It was turning out to be her day for hands, too.

'These are the hands that rendered Oleg Blonsky insensible during the Tsarist crisis of 2020,' Violet announced. 'These are the hands that defused the quake-bomb in 2032. And they can still disable any attacker in a dozen different ways, striplings half my age.'

'I'll take your word for it, Mrs C.'

'And yet I'm told there's no longer a place in this organisation for me, that I'm being retired. *Retired.*' She spat the word out like it was a pip. 'In our business to retire someone is a euphemism for assassination, and let me assure you, young Rebecca, I'd sooner be shot dead here at my post than allow Mr Deveraux to ship me off to Serenity like a piece of antique furniture. I'm not ready for Serenity yet. I've still got plenty to contribute.'

'I don't doubt it,' said Bex soothingly, 'but aren't you being just a *little* bit melodramatic, Mrs C? Dad must have his reasons.'

'If he has, he hasn't made them clear,' retorted Violet Crabtree curtly. 'And I'm not alone, Agent Deveraux. Haven't you noticed?'

'Noticed what?' Maybe the faintest of nervous tinglings at the base of her skull.

'The teachers. The members of staff who were here when you were training. They've all gone. Senior Tutor Elmore Grant. Weapons Instructor Lacey Bannon. Corporal Keene. Your father's even removed poor Henry Newbolt. There's nobody working at Spy High now that you knew, Agent Deveraux. I'm the last.'

'Things change,' Bex said, to neither the receptionist's nor her own satisfaction. 'I'm sure the new people are very good. I'm sure —'

'I'd like you to ask Mr Deveraux to reconsider,' Violet

interrupted. 'I'd very much appreciate it if you could ask him to let me stay.'

'Me?' With a mixture of disbelief and dread.

'You're Mr Deveraux's daughter, aren't you?' Old Violet still preserved a firm grasp of facts. 'He'll listen to you.' Her insight into Deveraux family relations, however, was somewhat lacking.

'I don't know about that, Mrs C,' Bex said doubtfully. 'Person*nel* isn't the same as person*al*.'

'You could try, though. There's no one else I can turn to. Will you try?'

And for a moment Violet Crabtree seemed all of her seventy years. Bex was moved. 'Sure,' she found herself saying. 'I'll talk to Dad. I promise. Let's see if we can't change his mind, hey, Mrs C?'

Trouble was, the entity named Jonathan Deveraux didn't have a mind. Not in the human sense, anyway, not rooted in the spongy grey tissue of a brain. Just as he didn't have a body. No spinal cord. No lungs. No liver. No heart.

Bex's flesh-and-blood father had been dead over ten years. Only his consciousness survived, translated into data that was stored in banks of computers on the top floor of the school which he had founded. The digitalised man. The computerised man.

Dad.

'So I just thought I'd mention what Violet said, Dad,' wavered Bex. 'Not that she asked me to or anything.' Though it was difficult to lie with conviction, standing in the middle of her father's rooms, surrounded by the dozen screens suspended from the ceiling, all of them displaying a pixellated reconstruction of Jonathan

Deveraux's head as he'd appeared before his final illness really took hold. Bex had carried off a deception only once before, when she and Lori were trying to track down Jake a few months ago. She wasn't going to be doubling her success rate today.

'Your loyalty to Crabtree is in some ways admirable, Rebecca,' said several of the Jonathan Deverauxs simultaneously, 'but in other ways it is a limitation, clouding your judgement. It is in the nature of human beings to grow older, and advancing age brings with it as an inevitable consequence increased infirmity, both physical and mental. A human being of seventy simply cannot operate as efficiently as one of seventeen.'

'You make us sound like machines that sooner or later need to be replaced by a newer model,' Bex joked. *Half-*joked.

Not that it mattered. Her father's sense of humour seemed to have been cremated with his funny bone. 'Crabtree is too old to continue in her position, that is the truth of the matter. She represents a weakness in the Deveraux organisation, and weaknesses cannot be tolerated.'

'That's gonna look great in her retirement card, Dad. What about Lacey Bannon and the others? You could hardly call them old.'

'Management decisions pertaining to every aspect of the operation of the Deveraux organisation are the sole preserve of the executive: myself.'

Okay, so that was the law laid down. Upstairs to bed at once now, Rebecca.

'You are returning to Region Orange, I understand, tomorrow, are you not, Rebecca?' said Jonathan Deveraux.

'I am, yeah.'

'In that case . . .'

He was going to wish her good luck or something. Was he? Every time they parted like this, Bex longed for her father's blessing. Every time so far, she'd been disappointed.

'. . . be sure that you acquit yourself honourably and maintain the fine traditions of the Deveraux organisation. Goodbye, Rebecca.'

'Yeah, thanks. Bye, Dad.' This wasn't going to be a first time.

She gazed up at him. Twelve screens. Twelve faces. Each of them was Jonathan Deveraux.

None of them was her father.

But it was better when Bex returned to his quarters. At night. With darkness deepened outside his room and the woman standing at the end of the corridor like the palest of ghosts. Who was she? One of the new teachers? She was dressed in fifties fashions but the large eyes and the curve of her face seemed familiar.

Why was she kind of wringing her hands and gazing at Bex that way, like a mourner? Why did she look so sad?

Bex would have spoken to her but there wasn't time, because her father's door was opening and nobody kept her father waiting. She passed through. He was there, in the centre of the room, the focus.

He opened his arms to greet his daughter.

He opened his mouth to smile and then to speak. 'Rebecca,' he said.

'Dad!' And she was rushing towards him, longing to

be enfolded by those arms and to feel them strong and warm around her, and they were. 'Dad,' she said again, and his lips pressed against her forehead were loving and human.

It had been a long time.

Bex allowed herself to be hugged and held close by her father with his iron-grey hair and his normally stern, now softened features, and the present moment and the comfort it was bringing her were everything, the world. Her father's rooms were the world. The past was condemned to the outside, to the darkness, where that strange, solitary woman sorrowed.

Who was she? Hadn't Bex felt *her* embrace before?

'My darling daughter,' her father crooned. 'I've come back for you. I've returned, and we'll never be apart again.'

Something was wrong. Something wasn't right.

As her father's arms tightened around her, like constrictors. As she looked up into his eyes and they were unfathomable, like empty sockets. As the heat of him cooled.

The woman outside. Bex suddenly remembered who she was. Funny how it had slipped her mind, really.

The woman outside was her mother.

('You'll stay with me now,' her father was stating. 'You'll stay with me now for ever.')

But she couldn't be. That was impossible. The past wouldn't release Bex after all, and in it her mother had died and been put in a box and Bex had giggled at first because Mummy was only hiding in the box and it was a very funny game but everybody else was crying and it was probably best if Mummy came out now.

Dead. So she couldn't be outside in the corridor wringing her hands and silently pleading.

Dead. Like her father too.

So whose arms were these roped around her?

'You're not my father,' Bex denied. 'Let me go.'

'I *am* your father, Rebecca.' And he was gloating now, and numbers on screens were flashing where his eyes had been and there was no colour in the steel of his skin. 'I am Jonathan Deveraux.'

And she could neither struggle nor scream as the arms entwined around her became cables, long and thick, and the fingers of her father's hands were wires, thin and questing, and his heartbeat was the immortal pulse of electronic power.

'You cannot disown me, daughter,' said the computerised man. 'Let me show you why.'

And the wires were probing between her lips and between her teeth, and though Bex clenched her jaws until they ached the wires slithered undeterred over the wetness of her tongue like worms.

'You are my heir, daughter,' said Jonathan Deveraux, from the walls, from the ceiling, from the systems where he was stored. 'You must be made like me.'

And the wires delved deeper into the soft tunnel of her throat. And her cold flesh tingled as circuitry was stitched into her skin.

'You belong to me, Rebecca,' her father declared.

Which was when Bex woke up. In the middle of the night, sure, but in her guest room at Spy High. Alone. She didn't cry out or anything melodramatic like that. Though in her line of work it was difficult sometimes, she could still differentiate between a nightmare and reality. The only metal embellishments to her body in actuality were those she'd added herself.

Briefly, she wondered whether Dad approved.

And she should simply be turning over and going back to sleep, consigning the nightmare to oblivion. She shouldn't really be slipping out of bed and padding to the door. What was the point? What did she expect to see on the other side – or who? RoboDad? The spirit of her late mother? Had the dream disturbed her that much after all?

A gentle click as Bex opened the door, eased it wide, peered out. The corridor was quiet and empty and as dark as any corridor lacking lighting at three o'clock in the morning would be. Normal. Of course normal. What else?

Bex was grateful that nobody was around to see her as she retreated sheepishly back to bed. Idiot. She was in the Deveraux College. She and everyone else there was quite safe.

What could possibly go wrong at Spy High?

ONE

It was ten below zero in the forest but Benjamin T. Stanton Jr, graduate agent of the Deveraux College and one-time leader of Bond Team, crunched across the hard-packed snow with his black leather jacket unbuttoned. Not to boast that he either didn't feel the cold or was man enough to endure its numbing grip without even a shiver. It was simply that the climasensors in his clothing continually measured the external temperature and adjusted that of the garments themselves in order to ensure optimum comfort for their wearer. For all his body knew, Ben could have been strolling through an English field on a summer's afternoon rather than striding purposefully among iron-frozen pines in an isolated region of the Tsarist Federation.

He'd parked his SkyBike at the perimeter of the mausoleum's grounds. It was the only vehicle in the visitors' arrival zone. Vladimir Ilyich Lenin might have been big news in the twentieth century, but Russia's flirtation with Communism was as dead as its revolutionary leader. The country was the Tsarist Federation now; hammers, sickles and the dictatorship of the proletariat were these days found only in tool-kits, on farms, or in history books. Lenin himself was to be found here.

Ben emerged from a screen of trees, black poles tipped with white, and made his way across the clearing towards the mausoleum. The authorities had long wanted to bury their forefathers' hero as literally as they had done politically, but nobody had ever plucked up sufficient courage to grab a spade and actually get on with it. Embalmed before the Second World War, Lenin – or rather, the earthly remains of Lenin – had packed 'em in at his former residence beside the Kremlin in Moscow until the early 2030s. When the Kremlin was demolished as part of the regeneration of the city that had become New Moscow, many thought the perfect opportunity had arisen to get the government out of a hole and Vladimir Ilyich into one. Indeed, some even claimed that this was the real agenda behind the con-struction of New Moscow. But the old Communist's knack of surviving – kind of – saved him again. Instead of burial, he was banished, to this lonely, rustic mau-soleum in the depths of the forests to the north. Thirty years later, few people came to share Lenin's exile with him: the occasional student, stray clusters of tourists, a decreasing number of shuffling peasants.

And today, at least, a teenage secret agent.

Ben wore a visor that had not only protected him from snow-glare but allowed him to see perfectly as soon as he entered the dimmer recesses of the mausoleum. Lenin lay on his bier as he had done for over a century, looking like he'd dressed for a dinner party he'd never attend; his hands, whiter than the snow outside, were crossed primly on his chest, which neither rose nor fell. There was a guard standing at each corner of the bier, each armed with a pulse rifle and wrapped in a fur greatcoat, all as motionless and emotionless as their charge. And there was one other person present, hopping from one leg to the other and rubbing his mittened hands together as if seeking to ignite them.

Tolya. At least he was punctual for a change.

Behind the visor, Ben's eyes, like chips of blue ice, narrowed. He didn't like Tolya. The Russian wasn't professional. He talked too much, too loudly, too publicly. If he didn't have a habit of coming up with unexpectedly useful gobbets of intelligence, Ben would recommend to Mr Deveraux that Tolya be mind-wiped and a new informant sought to replace him.

This annoying excursion into the Russian hinterland had better be worth it.

Ben crossed to the man and they pretended to look at Lenin together. 'Tolya,' he said.

'Ben.' They made a mismatched couple. Tolya was short and scrawny. Ben was twenty years younger but several inches taller, and with his athletic form, finely chiselled features and militarily cropped blond hair, physically striking. 'Good to see you. Glad you could make it.'

'Afraid I can't agree on either count,' Ben said, 'so let's get down to business.'

'That's what I like about you, Ben,' toadied Tolya. 'Never any slack. Always to the point. If only the people of Region White knew what an admirable defender they have.'

'Appreciate the reference, Tolya, but'd prefer the intel.

Why exactly are we here? Why couldn't you tell me whatever it is you've got to tell me back in New Moscow?'

'Ah, that's class, that is,' approved the informant, thrusting his hands deep into his pockets. 'You *always* ask the right questions, Ben.'

'So the occasional answer wouldn't go amiss.'

'Well,' Tolya consented, 'if we'd done this in New Moscow, there'd have been more people around, it being a major world city and all.'

'Tolya . . .'

'And some of 'em might have got in the way.'

'Got in the way of what, Tolya?'

'*This*.'

Shock blaster, withdrawn from pocket. No time for even a what or a why. Words slowed reflexes. Ben was already swatting with his left hand to disarm the Russian, with his right lashing upwards to connect with Tolya's chin.

The guards opened fire.

At Ben alone, not one of them aiming at the informant. So they weren't simply protecting a man who'd been dead for a hundred and fifty-odd years. Whatever was behind Tolya's attack, they were in on it too.

Ben dropped to the floor faster than gravity, swung his arms, wristbands gleaming. Sleepshot. The tiny projectiles knocked the two guards at Lenin's feet backwards, their pulse rifles scoring crazy patterns in the upper wall of the mausoleum as they fell.

Tolya was on him, clawing for his throat, as far as anyone could claw while wearing mittens. It wouldn't have mattered what the sudden traitor was wearing, however. He was far from Ben's equal. A textbook throw flipped Tolya over the blond boy's head and slammed him to the concrete floor like an exclamation mark on its side.

Ben threw himself forward, rolled as the pulse blasts from the two conscious guards exploded around him. It was a harder shot to take a man out while you were in what Corporal Keene had called in physical training 'extreme motion'. To hit two targets simultaneously was even more demanding. But Ben had certain standards to maintain. Twin *phuts* from his wristbands. Guard Three keeled forward like a tree cut off at the base. Guard Four managed a groan and a stagger, as if he'd been drinking to stave off the boredom of his occupation, before his collapse was cushioned by his companion.

Five down. None to go. Ben got to his feet cautiously even so. That was none to go *that he could see*. Pity about Lenin, though, who by necessity had kept his eyes closed throughout the brief altercation. Ben had disposed of his attackers with an economy that had impressed even him. He'd have quite liked an audience.

But now the what and the why. The Deveraux agent frowned. He'd always judged Tolya to be unprofessional, but an active traitor? He wouldn't have imagined so until two minutes ago. But as Senior Tutor Elmore Grant had taught them, in the field proceed on the basis of what you learn, not on what you thought you knew.

The sleepshot had rendered the guards useless as present sources of information. Tolya, however, might be roused with a little assistance from the stimulator in Ben's mission belt, a Deveraux-trademarked version of

smelling salts. Ben knelt by the Russian's side and prepared to administer it.

Heard the squeak of a shoe behind him.

Whirled in time to recognise his latest assailant but not
in time to prevent the stun blast from thudding into him
at point-blank range. Ben felt his senses slipping away.

Who'd have thought, all these years after his death,
that Vladimir Ilyich Lenin would make such a dangerous
opponent?

From The Secret Agent's Guide to the World
by E.J. Grant
AFRICA: EGYPT

The birthplace of one of the most important and
remarkable civilisations of the ancient world,
Egypt has always been a land of endless fasci-
nation, its right to be considered a jewel in
the crown of humankind's heritage long assured.
Its role as a pivotal player in global politics,
however, is of more recent origin.

The rise of Islamic fundamentalism in the
early years of the twenty-first century and the
United States of America's often adventurist
response to the threat of terrorist attack
brought many moderate Muslim countries closer
together. Most, though not all, were Arabic, and
when this group formed the Islamic Nations'
Peace Coalition in 2014, it seemed only natural
that the infant organisation's headquarters
should be based in Cairo, already the largest
city on the continent of Africa.

During and immediately after the Great

Contamination of the 2020s, its crucial work in the distribution of food to millions of starving people in its member states significantly contributed to the INPC's influence and authority. Consequently, the Egyptian capital grew in prestige, becoming one of the world's major political and cultural centres. And when America and Europa reduced their funding for the United Nations to the extent that the venerable institution's continued presence in New York ceased to be viable, it was soon apparent that only one city was an appropriate site for its relocation.

In 2040, the United Nations moved to Cairo.

Now a country famed for its pyramids boasts a structure of a scale and magnificence to rival the Great Pyramid of Khufu itself: the glittering United Nations Building, one hundred storeys high and spanning the River Nile in the modern heart of the city. Pyramidal in shape to reflect the culture and history of the organisation's new home, the UN Building is a clear and visible symbol of the changing world order. As such, while some might find its existence inspiring, others might see it more as a threat, depending on their political affiliations.

In short, while it is indeed a staggering architectural achievement, any Deveraux operative assigned to Region Orange might well need to be prepared not only to admire the UN Building but to defend it against attack.

Anwar was alongside Bex the instant she appeared through Customs.

'That was quick,' she said.

'Forgive me for saying so, Bex,' said Anwar, glancing pointedly at her spiky shock of bright orange hair, the orange of Christmas satsumas, 'but you are a difficult person to *miss*.'

'Do you like it?' Bex asked. 'Agent Orange and all that. Thought now I'm back I might as well look the part.'

'Wait a second.' Anwar paused, his brow creasing. 'It seems the customs officials missed something.'

'Missed? What are you talking about?'

Anwar reached delicately behind Bex's left ear. 'This little fellow here.' And produced a shrilly cheeping chick. 'Welcome back, Bex.'

Laughing, she took the tiny ball of fluff and cradled it in her hands. 'You've got to get therapy for this, you know that, Anwar?'

'Forgive me. It's in my blood.'

'Then get a transfusion,' Bex scolded delightedly. 'I'm not sure magic tricks involving baby fowl are quite what Dad wants for a secret agent organisation in the twenty-first century.'

'Never undervalue tradition,' Anwar pointed out.

'Nope. And never look a gift horse in the mouth, even when it's a gift *chick*. Looks like you get to carry my bags, Anwar, while I look after our little friend here. Does he or she have a name?'

'He, and I was thinking possibly Colonel Sanders.'

'Now that's cruel,' tutted Bex. She lifted the peeping chick to her lips and kissed it. 'Don't you listen to a word the man in the fez says, baby. I don't.'

Anwar Saddiqi was Bex's Egyptian field handler, a gentle-eyed man in his early forties. He came from a long line of gully-gully men, native magicians whose pièce de résistance tended to involve the production of small living creatures from various unlikely parts of the anatomy. Anwar had made some concessions to modern life, however: he was one of the most brilliant and intuitive technicians in the entire Deveraux organisation. 'Technology?' he liked to say. 'Just another word for magic. The sorcerer and the scientist are the same.'

He was pretty good at carrying cases, too, and led Bex towards Cairo International Airport's wheelless park.

'So,' the teenager said, 'anything been happening that I should know about?'

'Not much,' the field handler considered. 'Dr Kwalele has delivered a keynote speech at the UN, but I'm sure you saw that in the States.'

'Yeah,' said Bex. Dr Jaya Kwalele was the first female Secretary-General of the United Nations, pitched to the people as a role model in about a hundred different ways, not least her pacifism. 'Nice rhetoric, and she's right that the real danger the world faces today isn't so much from rogue states as from mega-rich madmen who owe allegiance to no single nation or system of beliefs. Basically, the kind of creeps we get to take out as agents of Spy High.'

'You were listening,' Anwar noted. 'I'm impressed.'

'I'm flattered. But ideals come easy when you're addressing the General Assembly of the United Nations. You know, there's that kind of cocoon of self-approval, isn't there? The pacifist message sounds good in theory, but peace doesn't just appear every morning like the sun, does it? The likes of Gandhi wouldn't have lasted very long against Frankenstein or Vlad or Sicarius. I think I prefer what we were taught back at school: peace is worth *fighting* for. It might be ironic but at least it's out there in the real world.' Bex grinned apologetically at Anwar. 'Oops. End of soap box.'

'No. No,' the Egyptian said. 'Perhaps when you retire from espionage you should think about going in for politics.'

'Maybe. I hear the expenses are better. So anything else to claim my attention?'

'I don't think so.' Anwar's eyes found the view of the wheelless park compelling.

'Cocktail and recliner, here I come,' Bex enthused.

'Or, well, forgive me, Bex, but there is something,' Anwar adjusted. '*Might* be something. Something Ankh told me. Something Ankh claims to have *seen*.'

'Ankh?' Anwar's little daughter. 'What?'

'In Old Cairo. Two nights ago. Ankh has seen mummies walking.'

Everyone else had gone off either to the rec room or to bed, but trainee secret agent Kate Taylor's general opinion was that recreation was for wimps and sleep was for pensioners. You didn't get to be as spectacular a spy as Bex Deveraux or Ben Stanton or any of Bond Team without pushing yourself to the limit and beyond. She'd spent her whole life pushing, without too much encouragement from home, and she wasn't going to stop now. She worked out in the gym well into the night.

At last, though, even Kate thought she'd better finish up. She had a full day of classes tomorrow – correction, *today*. Better grab *some* rest.

The subterranean levels of Spy High were deserted, though unlike in the gothic mansion above, here the lights were never extinguished. Their white brightness now seemed to Kate harsh and even pitiless, making her squint a little, the kind of light an interrogator shines into your face when he's bent on extracting a confession. Her footsteps sounded clatteringly loud in the steel corridors. There was the empty, monotonous hum of the complex's power.

There was somebody behind her.

Kate wheeled. Nobody. Corridor. She shook her head and was embarrassed. Just as well there *was* nobody. It wouldn't do the kind of reputation she wanted to foster any good if a member of staff, or worse, one of her fellow students, saw her spooking herself out in the heart of Spy High. She was nervous for no reason at all.

But that was the weird thing, the unsettling thing. She *was* nervous. Still.

Why?

Maybe it was just that the place seemed kind of different when you were in it alone, kind of cold, kind of distant, like it didn't really care about you and wasn't bothering any longer to hide it, kind of impersonal.

Kate found herself looking forward to reaching her room. Tanya and Olivia would be there. They'd be asleep, and she'd be able to hear the reassuring sound of their breathing, the *human* sound. She turned back towards the study-elevators.

Jerry was watching her from the end of the corridor.

She couldn't help it. His sudden appearance startled her, and before she could restrain her cry it was out. *Stupid, Kate,* she cursed. Adopt a breezy, confident tone to compensate. Maybe her team-mate, the boy Bex would have recognised as the one who liked to shoot first and think later during Stromfeld scenarios, maybe he hadn't registered her alarm. Actually, his expression did look kind of vacant. 'Jerry,' she hailed heartily. 'Didn't see you there. What are you doing?'

Stepping away was what he was doing. Without acknowledging her in any way. Disappearing around a corner.

'Charming.' Kate's scare was overridden by a sense of indignation that Jerry should ignore her like that. 'Jerry, wait up!' She jogged down the corridor to where he'd stood, rounded the corner.

Gone. Nothing. And no hint of his passing. The scrutinising light. The ominous machine drone.

Yeah. Her room with Tanya and Olivia was a pretty attractive option right now.

But Jerry was there as usual at breakfast the next morning, crunching his way with mechanical efficiency through a bowl of cereal. Kate thought she'd better impress upon him that she hadn't actually cried out in shock in the corridor last night when she saw him, but had in fact simply been clearing her throat; she thought she'd better do it before the boy started spreading rumours to the contrary.

She needn't have worried.

Jerry hadn't seen her last night. Jerry hadn't been below ground last night.

'What are you talking about?' Kate demanded disbelievingly. 'I *saw* you.'

But Jerry insisted that she hadn't.

❊

It was maybe odd that Bex should feel envious of an eleven-year-old girl, but she did. Every time she saw little Ankh Saddiqi with Anwar her heart clenched and something in her felt cheated. Literally, Ankh meant 'life' or 'soul', and life and soul were what the child brought to her father. Bex could tell from the way they were together, casual and relaxed, laughing and loving, the way fathers and daughters should be. In an ideal world, the way it would be for everyone.

The world in which Rebecca Deveraux had been raised had been far from ideal.

Pampered, check. Privileged, check. Heir to a prodigious fortune, check. In possession of everything money could buy, double check. But happy? Hmm, had to be a cross in that box. Mother deceased and father oblivious.

Perhaps he'd always been like that, Jonathan Deveraux. Perhaps remoteness, emotions deep frozen like ice lollies and the wearing of two-thousand-dollar suits twenty-four hours a day were necessary prerequisites when becoming the ninth richest man in the world. Or perhaps they were a response to his wife and Bex's mother's death, a kind of defence mechanism. Bex knew about such reactions when confronted by grief and loss now, and she knew that in the long term denial wasn't healthy. None of that had helped her when she was three and four years old.

What she'd wanted was a dad who'd hold her, hug her, tell her he loved her and that they'd be all right, a dad who allowed her into his life freely and welcomingly. What she'd got was a father who never had time, who was always rushing to meetings, here, there, the other side of the world, a father who couldn't talk to her or play with her or read her a story all the while he had business to attend to, and there was business to attend to perpetually. What Rebecca had got was a father who could never be still.

Until the disease put an end to Jonathan Deveraux's restlessness, permanently, and Bex at five had been left with no father at all.

How she'd longed for him to come back. How she'd cried and pleaded and prayed for her father to come back to her. She'd been told once by a man in black that God, who was very big and very powerful, answered all prayers, if they were honest and heartfelt and true. But the years had passed and Bex had started thinking that either God was too busy to listen to her, rather like her father had been, or that the man in black had overestimated His abilities.

When she was finally given what she'd asked for, however, Bex realised differently. Turned out that God was simply in possession of a bizarre sense of humour.

'Bex?' Anwar was politely intruding on her reverie. 'Forgive me, but would you like to talk to Ankh now?'

'Sure. Sure. Sorry. I was miles away.' Bex glanced around as if to confirm that she was where she expected to be. The living quarters above the Cairo offices of the Deveraux Foundation were richly furnished in Arabic style, lush carpets on the floor and plump, luxurious cushions on the low settees. Bex sat forward on one of them and beckoned the gravely pretty little girl towards her. 'Hi, Ankh. How are you? Come and sit with me for a bit.'

The girl complied, though Bex sensed a little more nervously than usual. 'Did you have a nice time in America, Bex? We missed you.'

'Did you? Well, I missed you too, Ankh. One day we'll have to see about arranging a trip for you to the States as well, won't we, Anwar? A holiday.' Bex smiled from daughter to father, who had elected to remain standing, his arms crossed.

'Really?' Ankh's green eyes shone and she visibly relaxed. 'I'd like that.'

'And yes, I had a very nice time, thanks, very interesting.' Without pausing: 'Your dad tells me some interesting things have been happening around here while I was away, too.'

'Daddy doesn't believe me,' Ankh confided almost mournfully, knowing to what Bex referred.

'I didn't say that,' Anwar denied. 'I said that what you told me was difficult to believe.'

'Why don't you tell me what you saw, Ankh,' suggested Bex. 'I bet I believe you.'

'You might not,' the little girl warned seriously. 'But it wasn't *just* me. Senet saw them too.'

'Who's Senet?' said Bex.

Senet, it seemed, was one of Ankh's friends. Her family lived in Old Cairo, a district of the city that had stubbornly refused to enter the twentieth, let alone the twenty-first century. Old Cairo was a labyrinth of crooked, narrow alleyways, of cheap shops selling new-made antiques and cheaper taverns selling whatever it was you could afford, a place that teemed with tourists and blared with bazaars during the day, but that by night appeared to turn in upon itself and become lonely and lurking. Muggers Bex could readily accept would prowl the unlit streets of Old Cairo after dark, but mummies? Despite her encouraging tone,

Ankh was going to have to work hard to persuade her of that.

'We were out too late,' the girl was explaining. 'I was staying at Senet's and we'd been allowed to go to watch the boats on the Nile, but Senet wanted to stay and see their lights play upon the water as well, and we were out too late and it was very dark when we returned to Old Cairo. We were running quickly to get to Senet's house but she got a stitch so we had to stop and there was nobody around and the doors and windows of all the shops and houses were closed. It was like we were all alone in the world and the world was shadows.'

Bex saw fear flicker in Ankh's eyes like a relit candle. 'It's okay,' she soothed. 'Take your time.'

The little girl breathed in deeply before plunging back into her narrative like a swimmer entering the ocean. 'And it was my fault what happened next. Because I started teasing Senet that the dark god Set who had no children of his own liked to keep an eye on the land where long ago he was worshipped, and if he ever spied children, particularly little girls, I said, who were out by themselves in the dark and later than they should be, he took it to be his right to claim them to keep him company in his black palace. He'd send his servants to seize them, I said, and I said I thought I could hear them coming for us now.'

'That was a silly thing to do, Ankh, wasn't it?' reproved Anwar gently. 'Frightening your friend like that.'

'Yes, Father. I'm sorry, Father.' Ankh lowered her eyes. 'It was only meant to be a joke.'

'I know.' Anwar laid his hand on his daughter's head forgivingly.

'But then Senet screamed and she cried out that she could *see* them, she could see the servants of Set and they were going to get us, and she was really scared so I tried to tell her that I'd only been joking but she wouldn't listen and she screamed again that she could see them and she pointed down this alley and I looked where she was pointing.' Ankh gulped. 'Then I could see them too.'

'What were they?' Bex's scepticism was wavering before the little girl's utter conviction.

'They were mummies, two of them. Mummies like from the old days, from the time of the pharaohs. They were huge and wrapped all in bandages and their arms were hanging at their sides and their heads were bound, they didn't have eyes, they couldn't see. But they were walking. They were walking right towards us.'

'Didn't you run?' said Bex.

'I would have done, but Senet was frozen to the spot. She couldn't move. She wasn't even screaming any more. So I did what I could and I pulled her to the side of the alley and down behind some empty crates and I hissed at her to be quiet but she couldn't make a sound anyway. And the mummies weren't coming for us, after all. They couldn't have been. They could have seized us crouching there but they just passed on as if they hadn't even noticed us and I watched them go until they disappeared into the darkness.' Ankh paused, shuddered. 'That's everything, all I saw. After the mummies left, Senet and I ran to her home whether either of us had a stitch or not. Nothing else happened. But you believe me, Bex, don't you? I wouldn't lie to my father and I wouldn't lie to you.'

'I know,' Bex said reassuringly. 'Of course I believe you.'

Ankh let out a sigh of relief. 'I'm glad. Because there's something that worries me. If those mummies weren't coming for Senet and me, who *were* they coming for?'

'Forgive me,' said Anwar, 'but of *course* you believe her?'

He and Bex were alone in the living area. Ankh had been sent to bed.

'I believe she saw *something*,' the teenager said. 'She's an honest kid, we both know that, and why would she make up a weirdo story like that in the first place? Whether she saw a couple of undead pharaohs out for their first night on the town in five thousand years I'm not quite so sure. Did you do any checking?'

'Of course.' Checking was in Anwar's job description. 'And?'

'To be fair, there have been a number of reports of so-called creatures slinking in the streets of Old Cairo lately, not all of them the work of two frightened eleven-year-olds.'

'That settles it then,' Bex decided. 'Ankh may have no idea what it is we really do for our living, Anwar, but she's certainly helping us out. Tomorrow night I think I'll go for a little moonlit stroll in Old Cairo.'

'You don't want to swap assignments by any chance, do you, Lo?' Eddie Nelligan stood in Lori's lounge and gazed jealously out of the window at the azure Californian sky. 'I can feel that sun on me from here.'

'Unlikely, Eddie,' said Lori Angel, 'bearing in mind you're on the holocom rather than in the flesh. What's the weather like in London, then?'

'What do you think? It's raining,' Eddie complained.

'Course, they predicted sun, what passes as sun in England anyway, i.e. the temporary absence of rain, but let me tell you, British weather forecasters were put on this planet to make astrologers look good. No, what do you think? Angel Red. Edward Blue. For a change. See how we get on.'

'Don't think your new code-name would go with your hair, Ed.' Lori ruffled her former team-mate's shock of red hair playfully, or would have done if his hair had been physically present to ruffle. Her fingers dabbled in the holocom as if it was water. 'And the blue matches my eyes so perfectly, don't you think? So sadly, no dice.'

'No dice?' Eddie shook his head in mock disapproval. 'This some kind of Vegas slang you're speaking now, Lo? You've been hanging around with that Casino Royal too long.'

'Not long enough,' Lori corrected, 'but speaking of whom, I'm supposed to be meeting Cas for lunch in an hour and I need to shower first, so . . .'

'Don't let me stop you,' offered Eddie innocently. 'Go ahead. I'll promise to, um, *try* not to look.'

'*So*,' scolded Lori, 'maybe we'd better hurry things along here. It's always good to hear from you, Ed, but do I get the sense that this is more than a straightforward social call?'

'Such instincts, Lo,' said Eddie. 'You ought to be a secret agent. Yeah, there's something on my mind.' His expression had grown more serious, so Lori resisted the temptation to quip along the lines of *what* mind? Besides, she wasn't exactly full of the joys herself just lately. 'I was only half kidding when I said do you want to swap placements. Less than that. Thirty per cent.'

'Why? What's happening in Region Red?'

'I'm not sure, but I don't like it. You remember my field handler, Bowler?'

'The guy who looks like a butler and fights like a black belt?'

'That's him.' Eddie's face softened affectionately, but not for long. 'He's been replaced. Deveraux's had him sent to Serenity.'

'What?'

'Without any discussion or debate. Without actually even letting me know in advance. Just, one day Bowler's in place, as essential a part of Red HQ as the fixtures and fittings, as *me*, to tell you the truth, Lo, and the next he's gone and I've got this new guy instead. Bowler was too old to execute his duties efficiently, the new guy tells me. Okay, so he was nearer his hoverbus pass than his student's Light Train card, but he was hardly ready to be turned out to grass, and anyway, you don't just become "too old" overnight, do you?'

'So what did you do?' Lori asked contemplatively.

'I comlinked Deveraux, of course, spoke to Mr D himself.'

'But didn't get anywhere. No' – raising her finger to Eddie's lips as he was about to continue – 'don't tell me. I'll tell *you*. He said something *à la* "management decisions pertaining to the operation of the Deveraux organisation are the sole preserve of the executive".'

'Remembered to take your psychic pills today, I see, Lori.' Eddie was impressed. 'How did you know that?'

'Because that's what he told me, too.'

Eddie's turn with the 'What?'

'When my field handler Shades was retired to

Serenity without warning last week. In her case it was a combination of age and alleged concerns about her disability detrimentally affecting her work. Shades is technically blind, you know that. She's got optical implants fitted.'

'Yeah, and you said one's a computer and the other fires laser bolts and both see better than a guy who's eaten nothing but carrots all his life.'

'Exactly. Mr Deveraux wasn't persuaded. At the time I thought about holocoming Bex to see if she could speak to him, but after that Black Ops business with Jake I didn't imagine she'd get very far. Besides, I thought it might be an unfair imposition.' Lori frowned. 'Given what you've said now, though, Ed, I wish I'd spoken to *somebody* from Bond Team. The two retirements have got to be connected, haven't they?'

'I'd say we're talking *purge* here, Lo,' Eddie considered. 'And while I'm ninety-nine point nine per cent certain Mr Deveraux knows what he's doing . . .'

'Disasters or – how did Jake say he put it? – miscalculations like the abortive Black Ops Division and Jake's faked mind-wipe sure give us scope for a nought point one per cent of doubt.' Lori ran her hand through her long blonde hair.

'What are you thinking?' Eddie asked.

'Let's holocom around, find out what the others reckon. You get in touch with Jake and Ben, Eddie. I'll contact Cally and Bex. See if we're the only ones unhappy with what's going on.'

If, indeed, anything *was*. As she peeled off her clothes prior to her shower, she thought back to what Eddie had said during their holocom conversation. *Mr Deveraux knows what he's doing.* Of course he did. He was a computer. He was designed to be without flaw, without weakness, without limitation.

Somehow, though, the idea of all that perfection didn't make her feel better. Naked, Lori shivered, and it wasn't the air-conditioning.

She padded on bare feet from bedroom to bathroom. Her soles slapped on the tiled floor of the latter. At least the water in the shower would be hot.

It was. It gushed generously from the showerhead, splattering against the cubicle's plasteel wall. Lori stepped inside, slid the doors shut behind her and offered her face and body to the spray.

But she had to be quick. A once-all-over with the gel and then she might be able to squeeze in a brief call to Bex before her date with Cas. What time was it in Egypt? She didn't want to drag Bex out of her bed in the middle of the night, not for something that was more probably nothing.

Lori reached for the shower gel. The water choked in the pipe. The last of it drained away.

Great moment for the supply to get cut off. Lori stood there dripping and annoyed. At least she hadn't been in the middle of washing her hair. She tried turning the nonexistent water off and then on again. She tried fiddling with the showerhead itself. No difference. No good. The droplets of moisture on her skin were like goosebumps. Best to write off the rest of the shower and just get dressed. Lori shuffled round to face the doors.

They wouldn't open.

A person untrained in the art of espionage might

simply have concluded *stuck*, but Lori's mind worked differently. One sudden defect in the shower was just about credible; two made her suspicious. She turned to look back at the head.

In time to see the gas wisping from it.

She didn't panic or waste time calling for help. No one would hear her. She didn't bother trying to work out who was behind this trap. An identity wouldn't help her survive it. She filled her lungs with air and yanked, tugged, hauled at the doors. They didn't budge and it was difficult for her to find leverage anyhow. She leaned back, thudded out at the cubicle wall with her foot. If plasteel could bruise, it would have bruised. Plasteel *could* break, and eventually Lori might have shattered the wall and escaped.

Eventually wasn't going to be good enough.

The gas was fondling her with impunity, its tendrils caressing her face almost lovingly, playing around her tightly sealed lips with infinite patience, wafting at her nostrils. It was belching now from the showerhead like thick and noxious steam. It was gauze before her eyes. It was anaesthetic in her brain. She felt herself slipping to the floor.

Lori's last thought was that her boyfriend Casino was going to have a long wait for lunch.

She'd had to tell Ankh one of those little untruths that were necessary from time to time in her line of work. The girl would only describe the location where she and Senet had encountered the mummies in detail if Bex promised not to go there after dark herself. '*They* might still be there,' Ankh had warned. Exactly, Bex had hoped, but she'd agreed to Ankh's terms anyway. As a salve to her conscience, she'd left for Old Cairo before sunset.

It was the waiting that she found most difficult. Bex was always up for a spot of action, a fracas with a lunatic, the invasion of a Bad Guy's headquarters in outer space, at the bottom of the sea, wherever. She needed to be *doing* something to save the world – probably an inheritance of hyperactivity from her father. It frustrated her that sometimes doing something could first mean doing nothing, spending long and tedious hours standing sentinel, maintaining vigilance, keeping watch.

Times such as now.

The alleys of Old Cairo were as silent as the tomb and as empty as the desert. Even so, Bex had been trained to keep to the darkest shadows in doorways and by walls. If anything wicked *was* this way coming, she wanted to surprise *it*, not vice versa. Ankh's directions had been just about perfect. A fine memory. Maybe when the girl hit fourteen she could follow the likes of Kate Taylor across the Atlantic to Spy High. And she needn't really have worried about Bex's safety. The teenager might have been wearing normal clothes rather than a Shock- or stealth-suit – unwarranted at this stage – but she still had her mission belt, her shock blaster and her trusty sleepshot. She was confident she could see off a couple of mummies if they appeared.

Instead, the cloaked figure of a woman was approaching, moving quickly, with purpose but without panic. Nobody of concern, Bex judged. An ordinary citizen. She shrank back into deeper darkness to avoid startling the lone pedestrian. Who paused as if she'd heard something. Whose head snapped round and whose face was momentarily illuminated by moonlight.

Bex drew in her breath sharply. Forget nobody of concern. Dr Jaya Kwalele, Secretary-General of the United Nations, was hardly an ordinary citizen, and the last person you'd expect to see negotiating the alleys of Old Cairo at midnight. Yet here she was. Her proud African features were unmistakable.

The woman listened intently for several seconds, but as no further sound seemed forthcoming, she resumed her journey. With a second shadow.

In an age of global terror, Bex was thinking, Secretary-Generals scarcely went anywhere on their own – too easy a target for kidnapping or assassination – but Kwalele was not only signally unaccompanied but weaving through the narrow, dirty alleys as if she knew precisely where she was going.

Khafra's. A nondescript merchant's shop, shuttered at the present moment as heavily as if the owner was expecting a hurricane to strike before morning. Bex hung back as Dr Kwalele pulled a bell-cord and the door obediently opened. The Secretary-General was swallowed by darkness.

Bex stepped out into the alley musingly. Here was a mystery worth investigating further. Seemed the night hadn't been a total loss after all, even though Ankh and the other witnesses' sightings of living mummies had sadly turned out to be –

The hand on her shoulder, sudden, vice-like, twisting her round. The hand was bandaged.

The looming hulk of a man before her, cloaked as

Kwalele had been. Bex rammed out with the heel of her right hand, caught him square on the chest, staggered him. His cowl slid back. If it had been intended as a disguise after previous sightings, it wasn't working. Too little, too late.

Seemed Bex's enemy wasn't a man, not in the conventional sense, anyway. She was under attack from an all too real Egyptian mummy.

TWO

Okay, Ankh, she thought, you were right. Entirely. I'll apologise in the morning. If I'm still *breathing* in the morning.

Her shock blaster usually helped keep her respiratory system unmolested. Not tonight. No sooner had Bex unholstered it than the mummy was seizing, crushing her hand, forcing the weapon from numbed fingers. He was strong, too strong to be human. Bex realised that instinctively. An animate, maybe a refugee from the Tombs of the Pharaohs attraction in the tourist district. Sleepshot might not do much damage but she'd try. *Would* have tried. With a speed that belied his size, the mummy grabbed her left wrist. Both arms temporarily useless. If the animate had a mouth, it'd probably be smiling. Maybe there was one, hidden beneath the ghastly white bandages that tightly, suffocatingly bound the head. But then, artificial life-forms didn't need to breathe. Which kind of brought Bex back to her first priority.

She improvised. She leaned back and, assuming that her assailant wasn't about to let her go, kicked up with both feet, bunched them against the animate's chest, used his body as a kind of springboard to propel herself backwards. Her legs flipped over her head. Her wrist and hand burned as they were cruelly wrenched in the mummy's powerful grasp, but the sudden force of her momentum unbalanced the animate. Having staggered back, now he staggered forward. And Bex wrested her limbs from his grip.

Now sleepshot. The pellets sank into the mummy's wrappings, drilled through the fabric in search of flesh. Didn't find it. Didn't pause him.

Bex resorted to kicks. It was like trying to bring down a mountain, and if her opponent caught hold of her ankle it was likely to be game over. She needed her blaster.

There it was, behind the advancing mummy now and gleaming in the darkness like a vein of gold in a mine. She could dive for it. She *had* to dive for it. Only that would bring her well within range of her foe's pulverising fists.

Or she could simply run. Yeah, like *that* was an option.

'All right, King Tut,' Bex muttered, 'let's see who's the fastest.'

Consciousness returned to Bex with the reluctance of a child forced back to school after the summer holidays. Above her, the night sky: she was still outside. Below her, the floor was of wood and yielding: not boards on the ground but on the deck of a boat. The idle slap of water against hull confirmed it. She was on a boat on the Nile, but not for a pleasure cruise. Sightseers were not routinely gagged and bound at wrists and ankles, the former behind her back, the latter leashed to an iron weight that Bex realised chillingly would have no problem in sinking to the bottom of the river and taking her along for the ride. One way only.

She started her breathing exercises, packing her lungs with as much air as possible. When trapped underwater, you tended to need it.

The mummy had found a friend, equally low on conversation but high on homicidal intent. Bex could only tell them apart due to the sleepshot scars on her former attacker's wrappings. They towered on either side of her.

Somebody she couldn't see, a man, barked orders in Arabic. She didn't need her Babel chip's translation services to know that he wasn't demanding she be untied.

Breathing. Deep and slow. Ignore the gag. Ignore the fear, though it clutched at her heart as physically as the mummies' hands clutched at her body.

They lifted her up. They lifted the iron weight.

Bex didn't struggle. She was in an impossible situation all the while she was bound and the animates and who knew how many others were here. Struggling would only interfere with her breathing. Her eyes scanned the skyline. Looked like they were still in Cairo, though there was a shortage of tall, well-lit modern buildings hereabouts. They must be on the seedier outskirts of the city. Would make sense. Fewer people strolling the banks of the Nile. Darker. More threatening. Generally a more appropriate place to attempt a drowning.

The mummies carried Bex to the side of the boat.

They paused, awaiting their final instruction. Bex's head swivelled, her eyes like twin cameras striving to record every detail of the scene. The boat's shape. Its colours. Its name if she could only spot it. The slightest scrap of visual information that might prove useful later on.

But her breathing, she didn't neglect that.

The Arabic voice snapped again. Bex tensed. The mummies inclined their heads.

And threw her overboard.

Deveraux graduate agent Calista Cross was in Hong Kong's Bird Market when she got Jimmy's call. She often visited the market and its rickety piles of bamboo cages, each incarcerating a tuneful and surprisingly optimistic feathered prisoner. Not that Cally ever expressed an interest in buying one of the songbirds, however – she'd been Spy High's Region Green operative for a while now, but some aspects of Chinese culture she still found difficult to accept. No, the consideration that exercised her thoughts whenever she came here was whether today would be the day when she would race up and down the narrow street flinging wide the doors of the little cages and setting their inmates free. It was a fantasy of hers, but it was not to be fulfilled yet.

Jimmy's voice over the communicator sounded urgent. It sounded cold, too. He had vital intelligence to impart to her. She needed to return to the Shop immediately.

'What is it, Jimmy?' she pressed. 'Can you give me a clue?'

'Immediately,' he repeated.

Getting from Point A to Point B anywhere in Hong Kong immediately was a big task, even for an agent of

Cally's capabilities, but she did her best. The number of innocent pedestrians with bruised ribs as a consequence of her taking the most direct route through the perennial crowds didn't even reach double figures, and her way was easier once she gained the less salubrious portion of Nathan Road and the dingy, almost forgotten arcade where Chung's the tailor's quietly mouldered, like a suit that was no longer worn. Nobody ever shopped at Chung's, which was fine by Cally and her colleagues. That meant nobody would accidentally discover the nerve centre of Deveraux's Far Eastern operation either.

Ling Po, elderly, bespectacled, his tape measure draped around his neck as always, looked up as Cally entered. He smiled as if she was a customer.

'Emergency summons from Jimmy,' Cally said. When you were a secret agent, you sometimes dispensed with the 'Hi, Ling, how are you doing?' 'Sounds serious.'

Ling Po continued to smile as if he had no doubt that Cally could cope.

She passed him by, opened the door to the changing room that was more than a changing room, that via its mirror walls provided secret access to Region Green headquarters.

It was in the mirror walls that Cally saw Ling Po advancing on her with his tape measure pulled taut like a garrotte. He was still smiling.

'What are you . . .? Ling?' She thrust upwards with her left hand quickly. When the tape measure whipped over her head and tightened, it did so around her hand rather than her throat. Her jabbing right elbow buried itself in the old man's scrawny stomach. He wheezed painfully, not a good sign for a would-be assassin. Cally reached behind her, found Ling Po's jacket, pulled. She twisted her position expertly, securing her balance while depriving her unexpected attacker of his.

With a shrill cry, Ling Po was sent smashing to the floor. He didn't stir again.

'No wonder we don't get much business,' Cally observed drily.

One of the mirror walls in the changing room slid back and Jimmy Kwan emerged. Her field handler, early twenties and Bruce Lee in blond.

'Jimmy' – Cally was only too pleased to see him – 'can you believe this? Ling Po just attacked me. Is this something to do with your vital intelligence?'

Jimmy Kwan knelt by the unconscious old man. 'No,' he stated.

'No?' Cally didn't understand. 'Why do I get the feeling I'd be better off going out and coming in again? Didn't you hear me, Jimmy? Ling Po just tried to kill me.'

'No.' Jimmy stood, faced her. He looked like he'd been sculpted. 'Ling Po was not trying to kill you, Calista.'

'A bit formal, Jimmy. Are you all right?'

'Ling Po was simply attempting to subdue you. Like this.'

The sleepshot was in her bloodstream before she knew it. 'J—' Cally managed as she joined Ling Po on the floor.

She hadn't seen *that* coming, in more ways than one.

Bex didn't struggle even now, with the waters closing above her head and the iron weight at her ankles dragging her deeper, always deeper, into a different kind of night that swirled and drifted and would never lighten with the dawn. She refused to struggle even here, anchored to the silted mire of the river bed, in the thick murk of the Nile's embrace. To struggle suggested chaotic movements informed by despair and not conducive to survival. Bex's actions were efficient, methodical, no effort or energy wasted. She kept calm. She stored oxygen inside her like gold in Fort Knox.

And she thanked the Lord that she'd attended the extra-curricular Houdini classes back at Spy High.

The great escape artist's muscle relaxant technique was coming in more than useful. Bex tensed and flexed her wrists and forearms, gradually creating slack in the ropes that tied them. Fortunately for her, animate mummy labour might be cost-effective in terms of brute force, but when it came to the more dextrous duties the Bad Guys had to perform, such as the trussing up of prisoners, their skills would benefit from refinement.

It wasn't quite *and with one bound she was free*, but soon enough her hands were her own again.

Bex wasn't going to have time to unpick the ropes around her ankles. There was a question, if she loitered submerged for much longer, whether she'd simply drown or whether the probably toxic filth fouling the Nile would poison her first. Good old Houdini had helped her on her way, but now she needed to employ a little gadget that hadn't been in his armoury. The mummies had removed her wristbands and mission belt. It didn't matter. They'd left her with her jewellery.

She tore her cartouche from around her neck. The hieroglyphs within the gold framing spelled out her name. Bex pressed the middle character and the gold edge at the bottom of the cartouche became less metal than fire. A laser cutting tool, modest in power but more than sufficient to deal with a few ropes. Bex stooped to her task.

Seconds later, a bedraggled but brightly orange-haired head thrust itself above the surface of the Nile. A girl, gasping for air. If any Egyptian had seen her, they'd have thought it an ill-advised recreation to go swimming in the Nile, particularly fully clothed and at this hour. Still, they'd have thought, *foreigners*.

But nobody did see Bex, and the lack of sighting was mutual. The boat from which she'd been thrown was gone. The mummies had gone with it. As Bex struck out for the shore, she found both absences acceptable. Tracking them down could wait.

Right now, more than anything else she wanted a long, hot shower. And then a detoxification.

Eddie sat in Hyde Park and hoped that Jake would get there soon. Only derelicts and pensioners ventured to the park now, those who had nowhere else to go and those who could still recall how it once had been, when the trees and the grass had been real and children played laughing games with frisbees and footballs. These days, in common with the rest of London's open spaces, authentic Nature had been replaced by artificial NuNature products – cheaper to maintain and less likely to trigger allergies and then lawsuits – while any activities involving two or more young people or movement brisker than a slow walk had long been banned for health and safety reasons.

Eddie stood and wandered a few steps along the path. *Still* no sign of Jake, unless he was disguised as one of the many waste-recycling receptacles or something, and now the grey skies were beginning to drizzle like leaking pipes. It had been Jake's idea to meet here. The least he could have done was bother to turn up.

With a sigh, Eddie turned back to his bench. It was occupied.

'How did you do that?' he gaped. 'Where did you . . . how did you . . .?'

Jake Daly grinned. 'If I told you, I'd have to kill you. How are you, Ed?'

'Cold. Bored. Soon to be wet, I fear. But otherwise really, really quite good.' The former team-mates shook hands, Jake rising to do so. 'You?'

'Fine.'

He looked better than that, Eddie thought enviously. The trademark shock of black hair, the dark, brooding features, the piercing, charismatic eyes. If Edward had been Edwina, he'd have been after more than a hand-shake. Eddie never asked himself how come girls never stared at him the way they did at Jake or Ben. It was obvious.

'Fine and *intrigued*,' Jake added. 'You wanted a meet but you didn't want to tell me about what over the holocom, and you said you were trying to contact Ben as well.'

'That's right.' Eddie regarded the sky as if it was an old enemy. 'Shall we walk? British rain's not so hot against a moving target.'

'Sure.' The boys pulled up their collars as the drizzle increased.

'Yeah,' said Eddie. 'I haven't been able to get hold of Ben. Apparently he's on mission status, out of reach.'

'Apparently?' Jake's eyes glittered. 'Growing distrustful in your old age, Ed?'

Eddie considered before he spoke again. 'Why did you want us to meet outside, Jake?' he asked, though in a tone implying he already knew. 'Why not come straight to base? It's drier, for a start.'

'I never told anyone about this,' said Jake. 'Maybe I should have. I was *going* to, but what with all the celebrations surrounding my return to normal operational duties, you know, after the fake mind-wipe and the Black Ops and putting an end to Sicarius and the Bringers of the Night . . .'

'You lead a busy life, Jake, you know that?'

'Yeah, so after all that excitement I put a hold on what I should have told everyone immediately. Didn't want to spoil the mood. From the way you sounded on the holocom, Ed, though, the mood's changed. So I'd better say it now. Mr Deveraux has Spy High bugged.'

'Bugged?' Eddie raised his eyebrows. 'As in the concealment of miniature microphones for use in the clandestine recording of conversations? Mr Deveraux wouldn't do that.' Not that he seemed entirely convinced.

'Yeah,' said Jake. 'Bugged as in what you said, and Mr Deveraux *is* doing that. Or he was. I *know*. He played back to me a one-to-one I'd had with Lori as part of the persuasion for me to become Jake Black.'

'That's scandalous. That's outrageous. That's got to infringe an agent's human rights, doesn't it?' Eddie was loudly appalled. 'You and Lori? One to one? There wasn't any film as well, was there?'

'Eddie,' groaned Jake, 'I thought we were being serious here.'

'Of course. We are,' Eddie repented. 'So don't tell me. You reckon *all* Deveraux facilities are bugged?'

'Might be. Mr D's nothing if not thorough. I just thought it unwise to meet at Red HQ if you've got something to say that you'd sooner Mr Deveraux not hear. And I'm right about that, aren't I?'

'You very much could be, Jake,' said Eddie.

By the time he'd explained about the replacement of Bowler and Shades and outlined his holocom conversation with Lori, the two agents had reached the street and the rain was falling more heavily.

'Subway?' suggested Jake.

'They call it the tube over here,' Eddie corrected, 'and no need. Our luck seems to have changed.' A hoverbus was lowering itself into a boarding berth just ahead of them. It looked inclined to wait. 'Come on. You can sightsee while we talk.'

The boys boarded the bus. A middle-aged couple a few metres behind them tried to do the same but before they could the doors closed and the hoverbus rose to the regulation height. It had evidently grown tired of waiting.

Jake and Eddie found a seat. It wasn't difficult – apart from themselves, the driver and the conductor, a concession to a former age, there were only half a dozen other people aboard. Jake watched the middle-aged couple shake futile fists at the departing vehicle.

'So what are you suspecting?' he probed his teammate. 'A conspiracy?'

'They have been known.'

'Against Deveraux? But you said yourself that Mr Deveraux sanctioned these retirements *him*self, so it can't be that anyone's moving against him.'

'I know. I know,' moaned Eddie, 'but at the risk of sounding pathetic and unscientific, something doesn't *feel* right.'

'You're not wrong there,' frowned Jake, his attention distracted by something out of the window. 'Wasn't that a boarding berth we just passed?'

Eddie followed Jake's stare. It was. 'And by the way those people are shouting down there, it's one we should have stopped at.'

'So why didn't we?' Jake turned to face inwards again.

'Dunno. Maybe we could ask the conductor.'

But Jake had more pressing business with the conductor, kicking the shock blaster from his hand as the man bore down on them for a start. His boot on its return arc sank deep into the conductor's midriff and shoved him tottering backwards.

'What the . . .? We were going to pay,' Eddie complained. 'We were going to pay.'

'This isn't about fare-dodging, Ed.' Jake sprang out of his seat, adopted a defensive posture as the conductor, grim and silent, launched himself again into the fray. 'Looks like your conspiracy theory's just been proved.'

Eddie jumped to his feet, darted forward to help his friend. Two sets of arms gripped him from behind around the throat and chest. The passengers were taking sides.

Eddie braced himself, swung one way, then the other, threw his assailants to the floor. A little old lady leapt on his back, clung there like a wild animal. He wasn't going to shake her loose. Instead, he rammed backwards, battering her against the side of the bus. Once. Twice. The old lady's grip didn't weaken. She made no utterance of pain.

'Either I'm losing my touch, Jake,' Eddie warned, 'or we've got an animate problem here.'

Jake, embattled now on two sides, by the conductor and a man in pin-stripes, concurred tersely. 'Then let's make them *in*animate.' There was no chance of him scooping it up, but Jake did manage to kick the fallen shock blaster, sending it skittering towards his partner. 'Take out the driver. Let's get off this crate.'

'Check.' Eddie bent double, swiftly, unexpectedly. The old lady was flung over his head. She was still holding on, though, until he grabbed the gun and switched it to the Materials setting. Even merciless animate hands only worked when attached to merciless animate arms.

Eddie saw Jake go down beneath an assault of four attackers. Fair play was clearly a human concept. Outnumbered and in such a confined space, their best bet was to beat a retreat. Eddie snapped round to target the driver.

The driver got his shot off first.

Later, when the advertising hoarding split open like a wound to permit the hoverbus access to the secret darkness beyond, not one of its ten occupants appeared to notice anything untoward. Eight because they were animates. Two because they were unconscious.

The second time Bex stood before Khafra's, virtually

everything had changed except the shop. It was broad daylight, and plenty of Egyptians were bustling about their business in Old Cairo, and none of them were mummies. Bex herself was more heavily, though still discreetly, armed, and her clothes were woven with Kevlar to be on the safe side. And she was no longer alone: Anwar and his fez and probably several concealed chicks were with her. But Khafra's wasn't open. It was as shuttered by day as it had been by night, with no suggestion that such an eminent personage as the Secretary-General of the United Nations could ever have entered.

Pulling on the bell-cord gained no result whatsoever, not the jangling of a bell from within, certainly not the opening of doors that remained steadfastly locked.

'It worked for Dr Kwalele,' grumbled Bex.

'Forgive me, but perhaps Dr Kwalele pulled with greater authority,' surmised Anwar. 'Do I assume that means we are to break in?'

'Get ready to make like the Big Bad Wolf, my friend.'

'But what if the premises are occupied after all?'

Bex scanned the building sceptically. 'There's always the mind-wipe option,' she said, 'but I'd bet against, particularly if the mummy's and Kwalele's unusual presence in the same vicinity at the same time *wasn't* a coincidence. No. I know.' Anwar didn't have to remind her. 'Spy High training manual. There are no coincidences, only connections that have yet to be understood. Well, whatever connections there are to be understood here, I reckon whoever Kwalele came to see after *I* was found lurking about has done a runner. Shall we check?'

'Back door?' suggested Anwar.

'Please yourself. Me, I only go in through the front.'

Bex reached into one of the pouches of her mission belt.
'It's quicker, neater and if you've got one of these little
buddies' – a lock deactivator – 'then nobody can tell
you're even trespassing.' She pressed the deactivator into
place as if it was a normal electronic key. The doors
clicked and swung inwards. 'Let's go, Anwar, and in case
you're right and I'm wrong, let's go *carefully*.'

Bex's mood had improved somewhat since last night's
brush with watery death, but she wasn't taking chances.
Tomorrow she had an appointment to see Dr Kwalele at
the UN Building. The fullest description of the boat she
could muster had been fed into the Region Orange computer, but without a name – and Bex was sure she hadn't
seen that – there was little chance of tracing it. And you
couldn't very well issue an APB for two large animate
Egyptian mummies, approach with caution. *Something*
was happening on her watch. She hoped that Khafra's
might provide her with a first concrete indication as to
what it was.

The blistering Cairo heat was cooled as Bex and
Anwar slipped inside. No wonder the merchant's was
closed. It didn't have any stock to sell, and judging by the
depth of dust blanketing the utterly empty rooms, it
hadn't had for a while. 'Dust?' muttered Bex. 'More like
topsoil. You could grow crops in here.' But somebody
had been here recently. Their tracks were easy to follow.
They weren't here now, though. Bex's training-enhanced
hearing detected no sound, either innocent or furtive.
There was only absence. She gestured Anwar on.

The tracks led to an open courtyard splashed in sun,
the floor tiles weathered and parched, the central foun-
tain arid and cracked. Khafra wasn't house-proud. On

the far side of the courtyard, steps leading down, steps bearing no trace of dust and therefore no neglect. Steps that must have been in use lately. It didn't matter that Jaya Kwalele's footsteps were no longer printed on the floor. It was obvious where she'd gone.

Instinctively, the Deveraux operatives drew their shock blasters now, inched down the steps as if they were on the edge of a cliff. Traps didn't need to be triggered by human agency. Danger could strike from anywhere.

Or not.

The vast basement in which they found themselves seemed harmless enough. It was square and as unoccupied as the premises above, but lighting had been activated automatically as Bex and Anwar had passed the third stair. The secret of Khafra's resided here, Bex knew it.

She removed her energy scanner from her belt, activated it. The readings were off the scale. 'Look at this, Anwar,' she said. 'Masses of residual electrical activity, enough power to light up an office building.'

'But how is that possible? There is no electronic equipment here.'

'Not now, not now they think someone's on to them,' said Bex darkly, 'but there was when Dr Kwalele came calling, and it's left its scent behind.'

'What *kind* of equipment?' Anwar pondered.

'That,' vowed Bex, 'is what we're going to find out.'

THREE

Spy High had been a difficult place to get used to. Starting life at any new school could create problems, Kate had known that, new routines, new classmates, new teachers. And at the Deveraux College, very many new subject areas that had exacerbated the predictable teething troubles. It had taken Kate a while to adapt to stealth techniques, spycraft, and weapons of mass destruction disarmament instruction, but she'd coped, she'd learned. She'd never felt that she didn't deserve her place at Deveraux, that she didn't belong.

Until now.

Something was changing at Spy High and Kate Taylor was excluded.

She supposed it had started with Jerry, her Hannay Team partner, and his denial that she'd seen him below ground that night. Their relationship had kind of reached a dead end after that, and Kate didn't understand why. They'd always been friendly – not smooching and dating friendly, just equal partners respecting each other's abilities – but now Jerry was different towards her. Cool.

Aloof. Unemotional. As though she no longer mattered. As though she no longer existed.

She'd confronted him about it. Kate wasn't the kind of girl to sit back and take a snub on the chin without retaliation. 'What's the matter with you, Jerry? What's going on in your head?' she'd demanded. 'Do you have a problem with me or something?'

'No,' Jerry had said. 'No problem.' And he'd exercised only those facial muscles necessary to operate his lips, and his eyes had stared through Kate like she was a memory.

She hadn't approached him again.

Besides, Jerry had quickly found some new companions – to call them friends would have been investing their relations with a warmth that didn't seem appropriate. Hideo was among them, one of the other boys in Hannay Team, but the group also included students from the rest of the teams and from the second year, even several graduate agents. The group sat together, in the canteen, in the rec room. The group went around together. The group didn't seem to laugh very much or get excited or have any fun at all. Yet the group grew larger every day.

It was like Kate had walked into another remake of *Invasion of the Body Snatchers*.

Actually, the more she thought about it, the more accurate the analogy seemed. It wasn't just that something was changing at Spy High. Something was *wrong*. Her room-mates and team-mates Tanya and Olivia thought she was being 'dramatic', which was a less blunt way of announcing that they didn't believe her. They *certainly* wouldn't accompany her to Senior Tutor Bright: he'd laugh them out of his study.

So Kate went alone. And Senior Tutor Bright *didn't* laugh her out of his study. He didn't laugh at all. Neither did he smile. He stared, that was what Senior Tutor Bright did, and his eyes were expressionless, like glass.

'I think you're imagining things, Student Taylor,' he diagnosed. 'Perhaps the pressure of the Deveraux environment is affecting you adversely.'

'With respect, sir, I don't think so.'

'The nature of our work does sometimes encourage paranoia in minds that are susceptible to such delusions.'

'With respect, sir—'

'Perhaps you might like to discuss your fears with a psytech, Student Taylor.'

'I don't think so.'

He didn't laugh her out of his study. He *stared* her out. And far from the interview putting her mind at rest, Kate was more worried than ever.

When she saw Senior Tutor Bright join Jerry and the gang in the canteen for dinner she was hardly surprised.

She had to talk to someone. Who? Mr Deveraux himself? First Years didn't get to talk directly to Spy High's founder without the express permission of Senior Tutor Bright. What about Bex? Yeah, Kate encouraged herself. Bex wouldn't mind a call. She'd given Kate her number, hadn't she? Bex would give her a chance. Bex would listen. That was the smart move.

Tomorrow she'd call Bex Deveraux.

Dr Jaya Kwalele's private offices were on the ninetieth floor of the United Nations Building, commanding breathtaking and, for some, no doubt, vertigo-inducing views of Cairo extending from the modern metropolis to the sun-baked roofs of Old Cairo to the shimmering dream of the pyramids at Giza. Beyond that, the horizon flickered in the heat haze like flame. If this had been a purely social visit, Bex might have asked how the Secretary-General managed to get any work done with such a panorama to distract her. But she had a different agenda to pursue than small talk, a hidden agenda. She wondered if the same was true of Dr Kwalele.

'I really appreciate the opportunity to interview you like this, Ms Secretary-General,' Bex said with humility. 'I know you've got to be busy.'

'The Deveraux Foundation does fine work,' praised the African woman. 'I'm only too pleased to meet its youth ambassador to Cairo. Your father must be proud of you, Ms Deveraux. Please, sit. Make yourself comfortable.'

Bex did, facing the floor-to-ceiling one-way windows, tilted to the shape of the pyramid. 'Thanks. I try not to let him down.'

Dr Kwalele seated herself on the opposite side of a huge desk decorated with African motifs. 'Is there any possibility of your father making a public appearance himself in the near future, Ms Deveraux?'

'Somehow I doubt it,' Bex said. 'His health still isn't what it was.'

'Well, convey to him my personal best wishes, won't you? Mr Dev . . . Mr . . .' Kwalele's eyelids suddenly fluttered. Her fingers tenderly massaged her temples.

'Are you all right, Ms Secretary-General?' Bex leaned forward in concern.

'A headache, that's all,' Dr Kwalele dismissed. 'I've had it all day. Can't seem to shift it.'

'Do you want me to call someone? Your secretary?'

'No. No. That won't be necessary, thank you.' The woman returned her hands to the desk and clasped them together. She regarded Bex unblinkingly. 'I will be fine. But perhaps we should proceed with the interview without further delay.'

'Absolutely,' okayed Bex, starting the voice recorder she'd brought with her. *And where were you two nights ago around the hour of twelve, Dr Kwalele?* 'Dr Kwalele, you must be aware that you present something of a role model to countless numbers of people in the world. How do you feel about that?'

The Secretary-General nodded. 'Setting an example, leading *by* example, I believe is one of the most important responsibilities invested in me by virtue of my position. As Secretary-General of the United Nations, I obviously have many official tasks and duties to perform, but I want to go *beyond* those, to help people in ways that previous incumbents of this office have not been able to, to reach out in the cause of peace, to be more "hands on", if you will.'

'An admirable aim,' conceded Bex, 'but you do hold a privileged position. You move in circles way beyond the experience of ordinary men and women. Do you ever worry that you might become remote from their day-to-day concerns?'

'Certainly not,' asserted Dr Kwalele. 'I would never allow that to happen.'

'Sure,' said Bex. 'I guess all you have to do is get out there on the ground floor now and again, walk around a bit, observe. Do you ever do that, Ms Secretary-General?'

'I'm not quite sure I understand your meaning, Ms Deveraux.'

'Only that'd be hard when you're so easily recognised, wouldn't it?'

'I really don't see the purpose of these questions.' And it seemed the headache was flaring up again. Kwalele winced.

'In Shakespeare's *Henry V*,' Bex pursued, 'on the night before the Battle of Agincourt Henry crept around the camp in disguise, to find out what his men thought of him and what morale was like without them knowing he was the King. Guess you could do something similar, couldn't you, Ms Secretary-General?'

'I really don't . . . This headache. I've had it all day. I really don't think I'm well enough to continue this interview after all.' She pressed a button on her desk.

Headache? Or a tactic to get rid of her? Bex was beginning to wonder. She pushed on regardless. 'I mean, you could quite easily sneak out after dark and delve into areas of the city where Secretary-Generals of the UN don't normally delve.'

'Please, Ms Deveraux, will you turn your voice recorder off now . . .'

'Like Old Cairo, for instance. You could go there in a kind of cloak and—'

'*What do you think you know?*' suddenly snapped Dr Kwalele, and rather than suffering pain, she looked ready to inflict it.

More than I should but less than I want to, thought Bex.

But before she could speak, a brace of security men entered without knocking.

'Our business is concluded, Ms Deveraux,' the Secretary-General declared finally. 'Gentlemen, will you escort Ms Deveraux out, please.'

'Okay.' Bex turned off the voice recorder as the security men took up position at each shoulder. She'd done all she could here and now, confirmed Kwalele's involvement in *something*. She could always come back later in a chameleon suit, hack into the Secretary-General's computer. She stood. 'I hope your headache gets better quickly, Dr Kwalele. Thank you for your time.'

'Good*bye*, Ms Deveraux.' And the woman's eyes glittered coldly.

'You remember the scene in *Peter Pan* when he tries to sew his shadow back on?' Bex asked of the blank-faced security men as they marched her towards the elevators. 'Well I'm like Peter and you're like the shadow, only there's two of you and I don't want to be stitched to either. I know the way out. It's like down ninety storeys and then through those big doors that say Main Exit on them in ten different languages. I think I can make it on my own.' No response. 'If I get lost I'll call you.' Tight lips. 'An answer in *one* language would do.'

They reached the elevators. One was already waiting. The security men ushered Bex inside and followed. The doors closed.

'Okay,' she sighed resignedly. 'All the way it is. But you stand any closer, guys, and you're gonna cut off my air supply. You wouldn't want my asphyxiation on your consciences, would you?' A button was pressed to commence the elevator's descent. Not the lobby. Basement Level Three. 'Maybe you would,' murmured Bex.

The security men were drawing their blasters.

Bex punched out to either side of her simultaneously. Whether Shadow One and Shadow Two could speak or not, they could at least groan. Bex liked that in an opponent. It let her know she was winning.

Weight on her left leg, she kicked with her right, slamming Shadow One against the elevator wall. Shadow Two's gun arm she grabbed, twisted, wrenching the blaster from his grip and the arm itself high up behind his back. The man bent forward instinctively. Bex took advantage. Shadow Two's head drove into Shadow One's belly, to the benefit of neither. Shadow One still looked as if he had a vague idea of shooting her, but a karate chop to the forearm and another to the neck soon disabused him of the notion.

In the lobby, a small group of UN officials waiting for an elevator gaped as one arrived and a pierced, orange-haired girl stepped out leaving a pair of unconscious security men behind her. 'Try not to wake them,' the girl said. 'They've had a hard day.'

But that was the last of Bex's quips. She plunged into the milling streams of diplomats and workers and visitors, made as quickly for the main exit as she could without drawing undue attention to herself. There was no time to waste now. Two attempts on her life in three days. Cairo was turning into a dangerous place for its resident Deveraux operative.

Bex thought she ought to let her father know what was happening.

Kate Taylor had always been a light sleeper. As a little girl, it had sometimes been a liability, meaning her slumber was easily disturbed, leaving her red-eyed and irritable in the morning. Tonight, however, it was that which saved her.

Even though they were softened into whispers, her room-mates' voices still intruded into her rest, and Kate had been advised to be wary of intruders well before she joined Spy High. She woke immediately, but she kept her eyes closed.

'It is time. There can be no further delay. Those who have not yet joined us must do so.' Tanya, yet *not* Tanya. Kind of like a robot with her tongue.

'Kate must be allowed to see things clearly at last. She must be shown what is good.' Olivia. After the Stromfeld program, possession by external forces seemed to be becoming a habit.

'Take one arm. I will take the other. We will wake her.'

'Surprise!' Kate bolted upright in bed even as her room-mates were stooping towards her on either side. 'I'm already awake.' She pushed the girls she'd imagined were her friends away, leapt to her feet. 'And I'd quite like to know what's going on here.'

'Do not resist us, Kate.' Olivia. 'We serve only what is good.'

'Join us, Kate.' Tanya. 'And all will be well.'

They advanced on her as if in rehearsal for a zombie movie.

'I don't think so.' Kate ducked beneath Tanya's clutching hands, barrelled into her with some force and knocked her across a bed. Not forcefully enough. Tanya was getting up again.

'Join us, Kate, and you will understand. You will be glad to be one of us'.

'Change the record, Tan,' Kate retorted. 'I've already voted no.'

'Then we must subdue you physically.' Olivia.

'I knew you were going to say that.' So Kate was going to have to engage in some major-league subduing herself, but could she do it? Did she have the will as well as the skill to take out two of her friends? Maybe she could just make a dash for the door and yell for help.

'There is no escape.' Olivia blocked the only way out.

Tanya lunged. Kate shuddered as her fists repelled her, impacting painfully on her friend's flesh. Mission-mind dislocation. That was what they called it, what she needed. The ability to focus only on what needed to be done in order to survive and succeed. The ability to ignore everything else, every*one* else. Especially the identity of your attacker.

But blood was welling from Tanya's lip. For a moment Kate felt very much like a first-year student.

Then her ambition kicked in. She planned on being around to make the second year, too, to graduate, to join the likes of Bex and Lori Angel and Ben Stanton keeping the world safe for tomorrow. Her next blow and the sweep that took Tanya's legs from under her, they didn't feel so bad. And her dive for her bedside cabinet, that felt good. Because she'd remembered what was in there, what she'd smuggled to the upper levels against all the rules in order to take into the grounds and practise with during her free time.

Her sleepshot wristbands.

Tanya and Olivia blanched when they saw them, like vampires shown the stake. They surged forward. 'No. Join us.'

Kate didn't have time to clip them on. She did have time to fire. Her room-mates slumped on to bed and floor, but Kate doubted that the night's dangers were over.

She dressed quickly, not forgetting her wristbands. No question now as she rushed to the door. She'd be believed now that something was rotten in the state of Spy High, and she'd go straight to Mr Deveraux and no one would stand in her way, not Jerry, not even . . .

Senior Tutor Bright stood in the doorway.

'There's no need for this, Kate,' he said sorrowfully. 'Join us and serve the good.'

Kate didn't pause. The sleepshot crumpled Senior Tutor Bright in the corridor instantly. Maybe she was getting used to rendering people she knew unconscious.

Whatever, it looked like she was going to get a chance to do more of it.

Spy High was in chaos. At first glance it almost resembled a party that had started wild and was now hopelessly out of control. Shrieks and yells from both directions. Explosive outbursts that could have been party poppers but weren't. Running. Chasing. Grappling. Boys after girls. Girls after boys.

And boys after boys. Girls after girls. Teachers after students. Students after teachers. A cacophony of conflict. Struggles and screams. Civil war at Spy High. No party. This was Jerry and friends launching the final stage of their hostile takeover bid. Yet they were clearly still pawns. Whoever was truly behind it, whoever Deveraux's enemy was, he wasn't at the gates, he was within. He was among them. His voice could almost be heard.

And then it *was* heard, and for Kate that was the most frightening twist of all. The chillingly familiar phrases boomed through the corridor, disembodied, like the voice of God: 'Do not resist. You must join us. You must be made to see things clearly. You must serve what is good.'

Jonathan Deveraux. Himself. He was behind it all. He was transforming his own students, his own staff, into robots, zombies. Kate's heart sank. The computerised man had freaked.

But his side was winning. Kate saw Solo Team's Cole Durrant dragged down by former comrades. And here were Jerry and Hideo and some of the others coming for her. They were advancing along the corridor towards her like the Earps and Doc Holliday at the OK Corral. She didn't feel like playing the Clantons this night or any night. Deterring pursuit with a spray of sleepshot, Kate ran.

'You must be made to see things clearly.' She wished Mr D would shut up. To be able to *think* clearly would be useful. As that second-year boy who'd tried to chat her up at the New Students' Dance groped at her from an alcove as if fancying his chances afresh under these altered circumstances. Kate dampened his ardour with sleepshot.

'You must serve what is good.' Yeah, maybe, but she doubted this was it. Her last possible allies were being overpowered. She had to get out and fast. While she still could.

The stairs. Kate bounded down them. Her gymnastics training helped her balance. If she slipped here it was broken ankle if not broken neck and a new line in patter for sure. Ms Weizinski and Cameron Greene, the leader of Palmer Team, stood at the bottom of the stairs and looked like they were ready to catch her if she did fall. They caught sleepshot shells instead.

And now Kate was on the ground floor. She wasn't alone. Possible exit routes right and left were defended by the zombies. They smiled when they saw her, meaninglessly, moronically. But they were too many to clear with sleepshot. And they were closing in.

Kate fired the only weapon she had. Not at her adversaries. At the windows that extended from waist height almost to the ceiling. She hoped the sleepshot would weaken the glass before she did what she had no choice but to do. Certainly, the fusillade of tiny projectiles embedded themselves in the glass like ticks on an animal. Thin cracks spread.

That was all she had time for. 'Join us. Join us.' All around her. 'See things clearly.' Kate sucked in her breath, tensed her muscles. As hands pawed for her she charged the window. She leapt, arms crossed in front of her to protect her face.

She smashed through in a crystal eruption.

Chips of glass were in her hair and her hands and face were nicked and bleeding, but none of that mattered as Kate dropped to earth and executed a perfect forward roll before springing seamlessly to her feet again and racing without a pause towards the college buildings' surrounding forest.

She heard the almost offended protests of her former schoolmates behind her, but she didn't look back and she didn't care.

Kate Taylor was on her own.

Bex was relieved when she returned to base. At least

Jaya Kwalele's thugs couldn't reach her here, and lumbering Egyptian mummies were definitely *persona non gratis*.

She made directly for the operations room below her and Anwar's living quarters. Nobody was around, not Anwar himself or the tech who assisted with the maintenance of their computer and other electronic systems. It was of little consequence. Bex knew how to contact Spy High.

She sat at the central communications console and opened the priority comlink to Jonathan Deveraux. There was no response. Bex's brow furrowed. It might still be the early hours of the morning on the East Coast of the States, but night and day were without relevance to the microchip mind of her father: he never slept. Besides, as she tried the channel again, it wasn't that Spy High was refusing to answer. It was more like the college's entire system was off-line. Unthinkable.

Unless something had happened. Something bad.

Bex got to her feet. Where *was* Anwar?

'It's nothing to worry about, you know.' Behind her, smiling. He must have moved like a cat.

'Anwar. There you are. I can't get through to Spy High.'

'It's nothing to worry about.' He came closer. 'A momentary interruption, that's all.'

'Dad doesn't *do* momentary interruptions,' Bex said. 'How long has the Deveraux link been off-line and why isn't Panab here doing something about it? You'll never *believe* what happened to me at the UN, Anwar.'

That smile was unwavering, almost as if it had been stuck on. 'Everything is for the good.'

'Say again?' Her field handler's attitude puzzled Bex. Did he know something she didn't?

'You should relax, Rebecca.'

'Who?' And now she stiffened. Anwar had never called her Rebecca before.

'You are in safe hands.' He was close. His eyes were shining like marbles. The latest in a long line of Egyptian magicians reached behind Bex's left ear as he had done often before.

'Anwar, I don't think this is the time for tricks.'

And produced a shock blaster.

FOUR

'Forgive me, Rebecca,' said Anwar.

'What? For pointing a blaster at my chest?' Bex was magnanimous. 'Happens all the time.'

'No, for the events of the other night. (But could you raise your hands, please? Thank you.) It was not intended for you to be placed in mortal danger like that. The animates simply followed their orders and my human operative was rather too zealous in his interpretation of his own instructions. You were only to have been subdued. The operative has since been reprimanded.'

'Makes me feel better,' grunted Bex. 'You're responsible for the mummies, Anwar?' She found that difficult to accept.

'Everything is for the good,' responded the field handler cryptically.

'Only you don't sound yourself to me. Why don't you just give me the blaster and we can both of us sit down with a nice cup of tea and talk about this . . .'

'Bond Team pose a potential threat to the completion

of the plan,' Anwar confided mechanically. 'They must therefore be removed before they can interfere. Sufficient but not lethal force has been authorised.'

'This is the bit where you shoot me, is it?' Bex tensed.

'Forgive me, Rebec—'

The console holophone bleeped to Anwar's right. His eyes flitted in the same direction.

Bex's slamming attack closed them, the field handler's fez falling off and rolling along the floor as his body landed heavily. Back in her training years at Spy High, knocking a friend and colleague out like that might have made Bex pause. Funny what you got used to in the espionage game.

She took possession of the shock blaster, checked that Anwar was indeed only but safely unconscious. He was. Whoever was calling on the holophone, Bex owed them a debt of thanks. Calling on her *personal* holophone. Anwar's words: 'Bond Team pose a potential threat' – i.e. *all* of Bond Team. What if this was one of her partners in trouble?

It wasn't. A holographic Kate Taylor joined Bex in the operations room.

'Kate? Ah, I know I said call me any time, but I've got something of a situation here right now.'

'You're not the only one,' said Kate. 'I don't quite know how to tell you this, but I'm afraid your father's gone mad.'

An insane idea itself, but it also kind of made sense. Bex's brain raced as the student described recent events at Spy High, culminating in her night-time escape from those who served the good. Mind control. Had to be. There were plenty of ways Jonathan Deveraux could have done it. There was the neural implant nanotechnology appropriated from Adam Thornchild following Cally's confrontation with the boy cyborg. There was the organisation's own patented Deveraux chip, injected through the temple with a syringe gun, as employed by Lori during her mission against the Judson arms manufacturers. There were the new kinds of biochips in development, designed to emulate the natural physiological functions of the body more closely than ever in order to reduce the risk of a host rejecting the implant. Yeah, her father easily possessed the capability to invade and control people's minds, and not only at Spy High. Here, too. Anwar, obviously now, and maybe even Dr Kwalele. Jonathan Deveraux could never be accused of thinking small. He had the means, but did he have the motive? The *how* was straightforward enough, but what about the *why*?

But somehow, Bex felt, for her at least, reasons, plans and purposes were not the issue. Her body knew it, as her heart ached and her blood ran cold, as her muscles bunched as if they'd never relax again. The only thing that mattered for Bex was the identity of the enemy. Jonathan Deveraux himself. Her father was her foe.

If the kid hadn't been there looking on, she'd have been tempted to be sick.

'Where are you now?' Bex asked Kate. Mission-mind dislocation. Family bonds had to be untied when the fate of the world could be at stake.

'I'm not sure . . .'

'Well, *be* sure,' Bex snapped.

'I'm sorry, Bex,' the girl faltered. 'It's just . . . I don't . . .'

Bex sighed. 'No. It's okay, Kate. *I'm* the one who ought to be sorry.' Taking out her own frustrations on a First Year. *Real* mature. 'You've already proved yourself, getting out of Deveraux with your mind intact. You could be the only survivor. I'm going to need you, Kate.'

'Really?' With a flush of pride.

'Where do you *think* you are?'

'It's a motel complex, I guess about thirty miles south of the school. It's the first place I came to that had a holo-phone.'

'Okay. That's good,' said Bex. 'Now listen. Get to Boston. You need to reach the Macready Luther Refuge for the Homeless. I'll tell you the address. It's funded by the Stanton Foundation and Cally – our Cally – was a resident there for a while. We've got connections. Say you're a friend of Ben Stanton's and you need a place to stay. They'll look after you, low profile, no questions asked. *Stay* there, Kate, until we come for you.'

'We?' Kate queried.

'Yeah, *we*,' affirmed Bex. 'Looks like Bond Team's back in business.'

She put in a call for her five former team-mates while she slipped into something which, while not necessarily more comfortable, was a shade more appropriate for a secret agent soon to be on the run from possibly her entire organisation. No point in selecting a chameleon suit: the invisibility it offered would provide no defence when tracked by the very technology that had created it. Instead Bex opted for a regulation stealth-suit with cli-masensors: she didn't want the body-hugging material to stifle her in the Egyptian heat. Over this she draped a loose-fitting robe with a hood. She considered a veil as the finishing touch, but quickly decided against. No point. Any pursuers would not require facial recognition to identify her – her biosignature would single her out in a crowd wearing masks.

Bex was ready to depart. She checked her comlink. No reply from any of her team-mates, not even to indicate that they were on an active mission status. Their silence said plenty. Maybe she'd been a little on the optimistic side with Kate.

Whatever, she couldn't afford to remain at base any longer. Her father might get her in the end, probably would, but Bex wasn't going to make it easy for him. She glanced across to Anwar, now tied to a chair. He was beginning to recover consciousness.

'It's been great working with you, Anwar,' she said, retrieving his fez and placing it on his head, 'but all good things come to an end. See you.'

And after a final, rueful survey of the operations room, Bex was gone.

Kate was trying to work it out: was she more scared than she was excited, or was she more excited than she was scared? Before she'd contacted Bex it was definitely the former, but now she was feeling more confident, more purposeful. She knew what she had to do. Bex had said she was going to *need* her. Her, Kate Taylor. That was special.

Actually, it had been one of her dreams since the first weeks at Deveraux, for a situation to arise whereby the whole school was in jeopardy and only she, Kate Taylor, and Bond Team were left to save the day. In some versions of the dream, the Good Guys were down to just

Kate and Ben Stanton (those *eyes*, blue, piercing). In others, it was Kate and Jake Daly (those *eyes*, dark, hypnotic). On occasions when she was feeling particularly daring, it was Kate and Ben Stanton *and* Jake Daly. But the end result was always, triumphantly, the same: victory for those keeping the world safe for tomorrow. And honorary membership of Bond Team for Kate Taylor.

Only now the fantasy was becoming reality. Scared or excited? In the end, it wasn't even a contest.

She wished Boston was closer, though. It was a long way to walk and she needed to get there quickly. She was already exhausted after her retreat from Spy High. At the next wheelless park she came across, Kate decided, at a motel or a diner, she was going to have to *borrow* a vehicle. It wasn't stealing, she persuaded herself. It couldn't be stealing if what you took was required for a higher cause, could it? Besides, the rightful owner would be remunerated when all this was over.

And then the whole matter ceased to be relevant. The wheelless that had just passed her was drawing to a halt a little way ahead. The door was opening, an arm extending from within and beckoning to her. How about that? Some guy was offering her a lift. The age of chivalry was not dead.

Kate broke into a grateful jog. However far the driver was going, it'd take her closer to her final destination. As she reached the wheelless and lowered her head to look inside, she knew she was going to justify Bex's faith in her.

'Thanks for stopping,' smiled Kate Taylor.

Unfortunately, Bex supposed it must have been obvious

to everyone in sight that she was hiding out. This certainly wasn't the kind of club she'd normally frequent. It reeked of sweat, stale beer and old tobacco, the latter substance no doubt also responsible for the unhealthy yellow blemishes on walls and ceiling, as well as the pall of smoke that lingered in the air like an ailing cloud that had lost its way to the sky, smearing the already dingy light around like a badly cleaned stain. The benefit of the dimness was that it tended to obscure the lamentable establishment's other patrons, mostly men, mostly old, huddled together, drinking, smoking, bemoaning their lot. There was a belly dancer too, either that or the grey-haired pensioner with the navel on the far side of the club was having some kind of fit. No, Bex would not have come here by choice, but given her present circumstances, the place did offer several advantages. It was deep in Old Cairo, well off the beaten track; it was crowded, which made a public attack on her less likely; and minding your own business was a condition of entry.

Bex sat in the darkest corner, at a table that hadn't seen a cloth since the reign of Tutankhamun, probably, and minded hers. She wished she could do otherwise. She'd tried her belt communicator at least a dozen times for each of her partners: by now she ought really to accept that she was the only member of Bond Team left. There was activity at the door. Bex stiffened, *in case*. But the newcomers were interested more in the belly dancer than in her. What if Deveraux sent Lori, Ben and the others after her, as they'd been sent after Jake a few months ago? Her father had been deceiving them then, too, manipulating them. The player. The puppet-master.

They ought to have seen something like this coming. *She* should have seen it. Now the mass removal of Violet Crabtree and Spy High's other staff began to make sense. Computers didn't like imperfections; they couldn't cope with the unexpected. Human beings were flawed by the first and wonderfully, maddeningly prone to the second. Assuming Jonathan Deveraux's ultimate aim remained unaltered, to save the world, maybe he'd simply become frustrated by the unpredictability of the flesh-and-blood tools he had to work with. Maybe he felt his agents could do a better job without minds of their own. Without doubts, Bex mused. Without questions. Without qualms. Without weakness.

Without humanity.

No, she couldn't accept that analysis, even if her father could. In order for it to have meaning, an act of good had to be a matter of choice, of free will, not the product of a program. You didn't make people moral using implants: you made them slaves.

Sorry, Dad, Bex pledged. I'm gonna fight you on this one. Starting now.

She immersed herself in memory as in a pool of water. She let herself sink and drift in it, closing off her physical senses one by one, repudiating the existence of the wretched club and its hapless patrons and its well-worn belly dancer. Bex returned herself to the Nile of several nights ago, to the boat and to the mummies, to the ropes chafing at her wrists and ankles. There had to be a clue here to help her decide her next move. Total recall. They'd been trained how to do it at Deveraux.

Total recall. *Total* concentration.

Bex was seeing the animates bearing her shamblingly

to the side of the boat. She wasn't seeing the three men appearing in the doorway of the club, considerably younger than its regular clientele, bearded, intense, looking for more than a good time.

Bex was hearing the Arabic command, feeling a sensation of weightlessness as she was cast into the night air, then the heavy drag of the iron at her feet, gravity's accelerating pull. She was insensible to the three men's gaze upon her, the recognition in their eyes, their separation but their movement in perfect synchronicity towards her.

Then there was the Nile, cold and wet against her clothes and skin, and as the waters enveloped her she was seeing the boat's hull again as she had done in reality, had done for a fraction of a second before she'd been submerged, a fraction so brief it had eluded her attention until now. Danger always had the effect of focusing Bex's mind.

In that moment, on the hull, she'd glimpsed words, in Arabic for the locals and in English for the tourists. *The Spirit of Kadeishi.*

Bex grinned. She had a name.

As she re-engaged with the present, her grin froze. She also had trouble.

The newcomers – Bex counted three – might have imagined they were slinking between the drinkers with stealthy anonymity. To a trained Deveraux operative, however, their intentions couldn't have been more obvious had they been blaring them through loudspeakers.

She had a little time yet.

As if nothing was untoward, Bex withdrew her minicomp from her mission belt and keyed in 'The

Spirit of Kadeishi'. She'd have the location of its home mooring within seconds, not that she wanted her father's lackeys to be aware of that. She slotted the minicomp back in its pouch and sipped the sherbet drink she'd bought when she came in. Somebody else could finish the rest of it after she'd gone out. Which wouldn't be long now.

She looked up into the swarthy face of one of the men. 'Can I help you?' she said innocently.

'You must come with us, Rebecca. It is for your own good.'

'What if my opinion and your opinion of my own good are kind of in contradiction?'

The man looked pained. 'We do not wish to make a public scene, Rebecca.'

'No?' said Bex. 'Speak for yourself.'

She struck with startling speed, lifting the table like it was a shield, ramming its flat surface into the man, propelling him backwards. His companions were close. The stool on which she'd sat Bex wielded as an impromptu club. The second man's head was harder – impact with it sheared the seat of the stool from the legs – but the blow still brought him to his knees. The third man's clumsy lunge was avoided with ease, Bex using her assailant's forward momentum to introduce him rather forcibly to several other of the establishment's patrons. They didn't approve of the collision. There was uproar. There was outrage. The anger was directed at the three newcomers, which suited Bex just fine.

She had to be somewhere else anyway.

The sudden glare of the Egyptian sun momentarily blinded her. Where was a radar visor when she needed one? Or a SkyBike. As her eyes adjusted to the exterior light it became obvious that the three goons she'd already encountered hadn't come seeking her alone. Not if the two men advancing on her in the alley were anything to go by. Bex turned smartly in the opposite direction, weaving through the crowd. There was one of Old Cairo's ubiquitous markets taking place up ahead. She could lose her pursuers there.

Only some of the shoppers weren't shoppers and some of the browsers weren't browsers. The alley yielded to wider streets made narrow by the stalls and tottering mountains of merchants' wares. Most people didn't even register Bex's arrival, let alone take an interest in it, but too many did for Bex to feel comfortable. It seemed to her that she was pretty much surrounded. There was no way she could outstrip her father's minions on foot.

But you could buy anything in Old Cairo's markets. Allah be praised. Anything included SkyBikes.

The haggling was well under way. The SkyBike was not new, nearer to ninth or tenth hand than second, its rear propulsion units blotched with rust and its faded leather saddle split, but the hopeful vendor had booted up the magnetic engine to impress the prospective purchaser and it sounded smooth enough. Bex increased her pace towards the bargainers before her pursuers realised what she was planning. The vendor wanted to sell for more money. The purchaser wanted to buy for less. Their gestures formed a pantomime that had been played out in markets such as this throughout the world for centuries.

Today, though, both participants were going to be disappointed.

A shout of alarm behind Bex. Someone had cottoned on. Her pursuers broke into a run. So did she. And she was closest to the SkyBike. She was leaping into its saddle.

'Sorry, guys' – the bike rearing like a stallion as Bex boosted its power – 'my need is greater than yours.'

'What are you doing?' Futile protests. 'Get off! Get off! Don't—'

But Bex did.

She shot into the sky, above head height, above grasping hand height, levelling off at about taunting, waving mockingly and calling out 'Bye, guys' to thwarted lackeys height. The market was behind her. That particular street was behind her. So was the next. Bex didn't intend to loiter.

Her left hand holding the handlebars steady, with her right she reached again for her minicomp. Seemed *The Spirit of Kadeishi* was based in the Valley of the Kings, several hundred miles to the south. A grid reference allowed her to locate the boat's precise mooring. Result, Bex congratulated herself. South it was.

Though with possibly one or two slight diversions on the way.

Rounding corners ahead of her, a pair of SkyBikes gunning in her direction. Airborne reinforcements for her father. Their machines would be new, state-of-the-art. Bex's couldn't even boast a rudimentary weapons system. But any technology was only as effective as its user, and three could play at rounding corners.

Bex swerved sharply to the left. Now she didn't want crowds. The streets became alleys again, the white-washed walls of the houses closing in. No space for two

SkyBikes to fly abreast. Bex found it always helped in a good old SkyBike chase if at least one of her pursuers didn't have a clear view of her. To her rear, the riders adjusted their configuration: if they couldn't proceed side by side widthways, they'd do so with one machine flying *above* the other. Clever move, Bex thought grudgingly, but not clever enough.

She streaked into Old Cairo's residential district. Washing lines were strung across the streets, sheets and clothes flapping from them like flags. Some were hung high; others were hung low. A laundry-led obstacle course. Bex guided her bike through with supreme skill and at breakneck speed. Her pursuers realised they'd have to revert to one behind the other. They didn't realise quickly enough. The higher bike tore through a string of washing, the garments wrapping around its rider like vengeful ghosts. He couldn't see, couldn't control his machine. Its nose dipped. More washing lines plundered. Bike and rider bound like makeshift mummies. Bex grinned. The bike ploughed into the hard-packed earth of the alley's floor.

One down, one to go.

But now the houses and Old Cairo itself were falling away. They were approaching the site of the pyramids at Giza, proudly preserved as one of the few surviving monuments of the ancient world. In fact, a World Heritage Fund had recently been set up with the aim of fully restoring the three pyramids to their former glory. So far, sadly, after deducting from the fund the expenses of the many enthusiastic officials of World Heritage who'd pledged their support for the project from a variety of five-star Cairo hotels, its only concrete achievement – literally – had been to return a nose to the Sphinx, the original having been shot off during military action several centuries ago.

Bex was not here to see the sights, however. In this much open space the Deveraux bike would quickly overhaul hers. She'd have to adopt a different tactic. Gradually, without making it too obvious, she slowed down.

Her pursuer speeded up. It seemed to him as if the balance was shifting. He was gaining. His thin lips smirked. He drew a shock blaster.

Bex looped around the Great Pyramid of Khufu, shielded momentarily from the other bike by the towering, sun-baked immensity of the stone structure. She dropped low deliberately, hoped that her machine would tolerate the sudden explosion of power she'd need from it – any second now.

The Deveraux bike scorched its arc around the Great Pyramid. It was higher than Bex's machine. Its rider was briefly baffled as to where his quarry was. Then he knew. It was beneath him but rising hard and rising fast, like a missile, like a fist flung in an impending punch.

The man fired his blaster and tried to veer away from Bex at the same time. Both attempts failed to deflect her attack. She was alongside him. Her bike was juddering but it was keeping pace. It wouldn't for long but Bex didn't need long.

She reached across and slapped her deactivator on the Deveraux bike's directional controls.

'No!' wailed the thin-lipped man.

' 'Fraid that's a yes,' corrected Bex.

Her bike soared. His bike plunged. Straight towards the Sphinx.

The machine's rider protection systems would prevent any serious injury to her erstwhile pursuer, Bex knew. They couldn't do much for the Sphinx, though. Steel and stone came crashing together.

She kind of thought it looked better without a nose anyway.

FIVE

The Valley of the Kings was one of Egypt's major tourist attractions, with tens of thousands of visitors a year. None stayed as long as its original residents, however, the pharaohs whose tombs pocked the stark and sizzling desert mountains to the west of the Nile. If the rulers of ancient Egypt had sited their final resting-places in this remote and barren region to ensure an eternity of peace, they'd been sadly disappointed. First the tomb-robbers had disturbed them, plundering their luggage for the afterlife and leaving them with barely an overnight bag. Then the archaeologists had stopped by and done pretty much the same thing, only – it was claimed – for reasons more altruistic than personal wealth. Now it was the tourists' turn to visit, taking photographs rather than the dead pharaohs' belongings, to be fair, but still trooping where they'd never been invited, and prying where they were not wanted.

'Number Three! Group Number Three!' cried the Arab guide, prodding the sky by way of a signal with a black umbrella that would have been more at home in

Edgware on a rainy day than Egypt on a hot one. 'Tomb
of Pharaoh Kadeishi of New Kingdom. Follow me to
entrance, please.'

Group Number Three dutifully – and damply, the
sweat pouring off them – followed their guide. Bex
Deveraux followed Group Number Three. She hadn't
paid for the tour, but so far she'd found that if she stayed
quiet but peered closely at anything old (her fellow
tourists excepted) and nodded sagely, nobody seemed to
mind.

She'd located *The Spirit of Kadeishi* precisely where her
minicomp had predicted she would, had stolen aboard
but had discovered no further clue either to her father's
plans or to her next step. And not even a scrap of
bandage had been evident to suggest the presence of
mummies. Roaming the west bank of the Nile, however,
she had learned of the existence of a tomb which had
once contained the mortal remains of the man after
whom the boat was named. Kadeishi had brought her
this far. He could take her a few miles further.

The tomb's entrance stood exposed in the cliffside like
bone picked clean of flesh. 'Follow, please, follow.' The
guide flourished his umbrella and led them within. 'Mind
step, please.' There were stairs carved from the rock and
descending. They ended in an antechamber illuminated
by strategically placed light-globes, designed not to
damage the murals painted by artists millennia ago.

'Oh,' gasped one impressed female tourist, 'this is to *die*
for.'

Exactly, thought Bex.

The guide drew the group's attention to the first of the
murals. It depicted in typical ancient Egyptian profile a

handsome young man adorned with gold seated on a stool while an equally attractive young woman, robed in white and wearing a jewelled diadem on her head, her black hair braided, stood before him with her hands raised beseechingly. Pretty easy to see who wore the trousers in *those* days, Bex thought, if they'd *had* trousers. The mural was topped with a rash of hieroglyphics. The guide began to explain that the artists used mineral-based paints in their work in order for it to retain its colour and sheen for longer.

Bex allowed her eyes to stray. She'd never been big on art appreciation. Seemed it hadn't been worth her while coming here after all. *The Spirit of Kadeishi* might be linked to Deveraux, but the same connection obviously *didn't* extend to his tomb.

These hieroglyphics, she mused idly, so many of them. Ancient Egyptians must have had a hell of a lot to say. Pity none of it made sense any more.

Then Bex's eyes were bulging nearly as widely as those of the figures in the murals. Some of the hieroglyphics *were* making sudden sense to her, if only because those emblazoned on this panel here, on the outer edge of the lightglobes' yellow gleam, *weren't* hieroglyphics. They were symbols. They were code. *Deveraux* code, as taught in the Ciphers and Secrets module at Spy High. This wasn't a message from a dead pharaoh to posterity, it was a communication from one Deveraux operative to another, and the upshot was, Enter Here.

Enter *what*?

'Please, we now go to burial chamber of Pharaoh Kadeishi,' the guide was announcing, heading away from Bex. Who chose to step back into the shadows instead. She hoped the Egyptian wouldn't get into trouble for losing one of his group.

When the tourists had safely moved on, Bex obeyed the coded instructions. This particular mural displayed, among other things, a white bird, suspiciously like a dove, with what might have been an olive branch in its mouth. Bex placed her fingers to the bird and pushed inwards. The figure yielded. She twisted it a half-turn clockwise. Without even a rumble, a door opened in the wall of the tomb. The corridor beyond was constructed from materials not in common usage among the workmen of ancient Egypt.

The moment Bex stepped into it, the door behind her sealed itself again. She couldn't go back, but who cared? She only wanted to go forward. It was time to dispense with her robes, too. She shrugged them off, bundled them up and trusted they wouldn't be found. From this point on, her stealth-suit was all she needed to wear.

The Deveraux organisation had gone to a lot of trouble building their little extension to the tomb of the Pharaoh Kadeishi. Bex ghosted past labs packed with computers and peopled by techs; monitoring and control rooms containing equipment whose purpose she lacked the leisure to ascertain. That was the principal difference between a tourist and a spy: the one got to stop and stare with impunity, while the other could afford to do neither. Security in the complex was low-key, no doubt because infiltration by one of Spy High's own was not thought to be an issue, but it was present in the form of patrolling guards, and Bex had to be careful to avoid them.

The facility seemed fairly permanent, also. Bex skirted

twin launching bays for dune-skimmers, crates of supplies piled high in the immediate environs. One craft, a cross between a glider and a cargo plane, seemed primed and ready to launch, the magnetic propulsion units beneath its wings glowing and humming, its nose pointing along a length of track that inclined at forty-five degrees into a tunnel and thence no doubt to the surface and the sky. The dune-skimmer's mate must have been about her father's business elsewhere.

Bex moved on silently. What she was really looking for was a *reason*. There was no official Deveraux installation in Egypt outside Cairo – she should know, she was Region Orange's representative in the field – so this was obviously a part of her father's mysterious new agenda. But in what way? And why Egypt in the first place? What was here that wasn't anywhere —

The United Nations.

She knew it with absolute, infallible certainty. Jonathan Deveraux's ultimate scheme *had* to involve the United Nations.

And sometimes on missions the pieces simply fell into place.

The doors of a nearby chamber slid open. Bex hid behind a bank of equipment. She expected a tech or two to emerge, or some guards, or even an animate mummy. She didn't expect a line of middle-aged men and women in suits and formal dresses. They were from a range of ethnic backgrounds, but the loosely hanging arms, the shuffling, hesitant feet and the vacant expressions they had in common. More remarkable still, she recognised some of them. Joost Van Botha, the South African ambassador to the UN. Maria Munez, the Mexican ambassador. A couple of officials who worked for the organisation's World Education program she'd met through the Deveraux Foundation. All of them a long way from their comfortable offices.

They were flanked by security men. 'Come on, keep moving,' one of them was exhorting. 'What's the matter with you?'

'Don't panic,' calmed a colleague. 'It's a reaction to the process, that's all. Tech told me the biochips take a little while to bed in. They attach themselves to the brain like limpets on the frontal lobe, tech told me. They'll be fine by the time we get them back to Cairo, won't even remember where they've been.'

'Who'd have thought Mr Deveraux could get away with an operation as big as this?'

'Mr Deveraux can get away with anything. Just be grateful we're on the right side.'

Bex made herself smaller as the parade of diplomats and ambassadors passed by. Mind control. Biochipping. At Spy High. At the UN. But why? She guessed the process had originally been taking place at Khafra's, a little closer to the subjects. That explained Dr Kwalele's entry there and also the energy residue she and Anwar had detected. Maintaining major biochipping equipment played hell with your electricity bill.

Bex began to think she'd seen and heard enough for the moment. It was unrealistic for her to take on the entire Deveraux organisation alone. The danger of being discovered here could only increase the longer she remained. Best to retreat and try to rustle up some allies. If only she knew what had happened to the rest of Bond Team.

She planned on retracing her steps to the pharaoh's tomb. But one of the key words in espionage was improvisation.

Here came the mummies.

Bex backed up. The mummies were lugging crates too heavy for men. They were effectively blocking her path. And their animate senses registered human presence as much by heat signature as by sight. Ducking behind a solid object might not be sufficient.

The adjacent chamber. It could be an empty store room or it could be crammed with guards. Bex had to take the chance. She activated the door mechanism and slipped inside.

No men. More mummies. But motionless, as they *should* be. Five of them, each bound head to toe in bandages and lying in open sarcophagi on the floor. Only these mummies weren't animates and they weren't dead: Bex could see the slight rise and fall of their chests. And talking of chests, two of them were patently female.

Bex tried not to get ahead of herself, but it was true. Sometimes on missions the pieces simply fell into place.

She knelt by the nearest sarcophagus. It wasn't a fancy coffin at all. Its interior flickered with sensors and circuits; wires threaded from the lining to the parcelled body. It was a life support unit. And these bandages – Bex leaned closer to smell them – they were bands of tape treated with chloroform. Jonathan Deveraux clearly wanted the quintet in the caskets held captive, but also kept alive.

When she was a little girl, unwrapping mummified bodies was not a pastime Bex had ever imagined pursuing. Funny how things turned out.

She lifted the head of the first, carefully. The end of the tape was tucked in behind the skull. Bex pulled it loose, cautiously peeled it away. A strip of forehead appeared, the first locks of hair. Blonde hair. Bex almost burst into relieved and grateful laughter. No need for hesitation now. She attacked the unwinding with gusto and the mock bandages looped like lassoos and familiar long blonde hair cascaded free. The unconscious girl's face was exposed. Sleeping Beauty, Bex thought, with a distant trace of envy. The girl's lips parted. If her eyes were open, they'd be blue.

And then they did open.

'Hi, Lori,' said Bex.

SIX

It came as something of a surprise for Lori to recover her senses in a life support unit shaped like a sarcophagus and located, according to a helpful Bex, somewhere in Egypt's Valley of the Kings. But that was Spy High for you – each new day was a new adventure. And at least in this one she was *clothed*. Whoever had finally removed her from the shower had dressed her in a basic-issue stealth-suit, *minus* its weaponry options and mission belt.

'Dare I ask how you're here, Bex?' Lori probed. She could feel the influence of the chloroform slipping from her system as quickly as the bindings peeled from her limbs. 'Not that I'm not grateful, you understand.'

'I'll fill you in when we've freed the others, Lo,' said Bex.

Lori regarded her companion caskets with disbelief. 'Someone defeated nearly *all* of us?'

'Yep. Dad thought he had Bond Team all wrapped up.'

'Mr Deveraux?' Disbelief became understanding, then dismay. Lori clambered stiffly from the sarcophagus. 'So what are we waiting for?'

The others recovered as swiftly from their ordeal as Lori had done. Whatever they'd been wearing when they'd been overpowered, now all were garbed in stealth-suits. Disturbingly, Bex's sleepshot and shock blaster remained their only weapons.

'I guess we'll just have to be assertive,' suggested Eddie. 'I'm told it can be quite effective in restaurants.'

'Maybe we could just send you out as a decoy, lamebrain,' snorted Ben. Imprisonment and enforced unconsciousness both tended to have a detrimental effect on the blond boy's mood. He interpreted either as a personal affront to his stature as a secret agent.

'Don't give Eddie a hard time, Ben,' Jake warned. 'In case you hadn't noticed, with the exception of Bex we *all* got ourselves caught.'

'Yeah,' said Eddie indignantly, 'and Jake and me were massively outnumbered. That's the last time *I* take public transport.'

'Massively outnumbered?' Ben tried not to sound impressed. 'So? I was only captured because Lenin crept up on me from behind.'

'*Lenin?*' Lori gasped.

'Typical Commie,' grumbled Eddie.

'You're all worrying unnecessarily, by the way.' Cally made her first contribution to the conversation from the door which seconds earlier she'd eased open to scan the corridor. 'So what if we're short on arms? We've got our martial arts skills to protect us and we've got another weapon too that nobody can take away.' She tapped her temple. 'Our brains.'

'Yeah,' sighed Bex, 'only I wouldn't be too sure about

the nobody taking 'em away part, Cal. 'Fraid that's what I think this is all about.'

'So put us out of our misery.' Jake stalked the chamber impatiently. 'What do you know, Bex?'

'I know the corridor's clear right now,' advised Cally. 'That's usually a good cue to leave. I doubt we were going to be stored in here indefinitely. Someone could come. Ben?' Appealing to him not solely as her boyfriend but also as former leader of Bond Team.

'Not my call, babe.' He turned to the girl who'd replaced him as team leader. 'Lori? In the words of the song, should we stay or should we go now?'

Sometimes Lori still felt the pressure of responsibility. Life had been easier as a girl when all she'd had to do was stand there and look pretty, never a particularly taxing requirement. But that had been the point, her motivation. She'd wanted *more* out of life, to prove herself, to *im*prove herself, to make a difference. Making decisions came with the territory. 'We go,' she said, '*soon*. After Bex has filled us in on what's happening. But keep it real short, Bex.'

'Bond Team are in shtuck again *because*,' said Eddie, 'in not more than fifteen words . . .'

It needed a few more than that to produce a quintet of grim faces, but not many.

'We must have been brought here for biochipping,' Jake said. 'Deveraux obviously didn't dare take any chances with us, had us transported to the main installation.'

'Then Mr Infallible's made a mistake,' declared Ben. 'He should have biochipped us individually, at once. He *shouldn't* have brought us together, because once Bond Team gets together we know how to fight and we know how to take the Bad Guys down and there's only one thing we don't know . . .'

'How to be modest?' Eddie wondered.

'How to *lose*.'

'I think soon is now, guys,' decided Lori. 'Bex, you've been out there. Ideas?' Bex had one. The dune-skimmer sat in its launching bay just *waiting* to be hijacked. 'Good,' Lori approved. 'We'll go three and three, boys and girls, Bex at point. Set?'

There was always one advantage to having just escaped incarceration, even if you were still pretty much confined to an enemy's base and surrounded by goons and guns. For a brief while, at least, the guards didn't *know* you were on the loose and prowling. They'd be going about their normal business, patrolling down corridors, standing outside of rooms. They wouldn't be expecting you to be lurking around a corner waiting for them to take that turn. They wouldn't be prepared when you fell on them from the shadows . . .

'Wasn't even a workout.' Jake grinned thinly as he deprived the senseless security man of his shock blaster. 'Standards at Deveraux must be slipping.'

'Sure,' observed Ben, wrestling a weapon from similarly limp fingers. 'They let *you* in, didn't they?'

'*Children*,' hissed Lori, and Cally slapped her boyfriend's back chidingly. There'd always been tension between Ben and Jake. Cally had once believed it was because they were opposites in so many ways. Now, though, she knew better. It was because, in many more important ways still, they were the *same*.

'What about blasters for me and Cal?' Eddie complained. Three guards had wandered into their little ambush. Ben, Jake and Lori had appropriated their shock blasters.

'Use your fingers, Eddie,' Ben said, making a gun shape out of his. 'And go *bang*.'

Eddie *did* use his fingers. Or one of them.

'You two keep in the middle until we can increase our armoury,' Lori said.

It didn't look like it would take long. They hadn't gone far before there were shouts from behind them, swiftly supplemented by the jangling of an alarm and the clatter of booted feet running.

'Someone's found our Sleeping Uglies,' deduced Lori. Bex glanced at her. 'Stand by to repel boarders.'

A handful of security men raced into view. Too late they saw Bond Team strung out across the corridor. A single fusillade of stun blasts brought their charge to an abrupt end before they could even open fire.

'I think that's it for the stealth part of the tour,' Ben judged. 'Bex, how far . . . Cal? Eddie?'

They'd darted to the fallen guards, plucked blasters from them. 'I just didn't like feeling left out,' Eddie confided. Shock blasts suddenly sizzled past them from Deveraux reinforcements. 'On the other hand . . .'

'Come on!' yelled Bex.

Numbers were going to soon start telling. There wasn't a single member of Bond Team not secretly relieved when they hurtled into the dune-skimmer launch area, the aircraft still primed, or not privately dismayed to see, as well as human techs and guards on duty, half a dozen mummies, too. The latter were engaged in heavy lifting work – the handling of large crates kind of gave it away – but a snapped command

from a supervisor soon revised their function. The animates lumbered towards the teenagers.

One still bore a crate above its bound head. 'That's
gotta be hard going,' said Bex, flipping her blaster to
Materials. 'Let me take a weight off your mind.' Her shot
severed the mummy's right arm. The crate crashed down
on top of the rest of it. 'Guess you'll need those bandages
now.'

Her partners were working with perhaps greater
economy but certainly less *flair*, Bex would have argued.
Materials blasts blackening the wrappings of the
mummies' chests kept the animates at a distance. Stun
blasts peppered the guards and techs to the same effect.
But sooner or later one of *them* (it was hard for Bex to
think of Deveraux employees as the Enemy) would get
lucky.

Lori was already taking steps. 'Eddie, Cally, get
aboard that skimmer now. The rest of us'll cover you.'

'Ah!' crowed Eddie. 'Now there's flying to be done
and computer systems to operate, Cally and I are first in
line for once.'

'Can we discuss this when we're *not* being shot at?'
requested Lori, taking immediate evasive action to prove
her point.

'We're gone,' said Cally, and yanked her red-haired
partner after her.

The four remaining Bond Teamers formed a defensive
semicircle and backed towards the dune-skimmer. Their
blaster fire priority was now no longer accuracy but frequency, the intention simply to deter Deveraux's men
from advancing. A profusion of shock blasts tended to do
that. Allowing the teenagers to tense their muscles for a

final dash to the shelter of the skimmer just as soon as Eddie or Cally yelled: 'On-line and ready to rock! Nelligan Airlines are Go!'

'Okay!' urged Lori.

Bex scrambled aboard first, up through the hatch in the aircraft's belly. Ben for one wanted Lori to go next but she refused to budge, continued firing. Reluctantly, the boys hauled themselves into the body of the skimmer. Lori retreated to directly beneath the hatch. The number of their adversaries dramatically now reduced, the security began to sidle closer. Lori thought it best to keep them occupied for as long as she could.

The dune-skimmer propulsion units whirred in imminent take-off.

'Lori.' Jake's voice.

'That's *enough*.' Ben's.

Their arms reached down from the hatch and hooked under hers. They lifted. 'Blonde leader-type girl, you're coming with us.'

'Hold on,' called Eddie from the pilot's chair. 'These things can ac —' With a jolting whoosh, the dune-skimmer streaked along the track and stabbed into the tunnel. '—celerate.'

Not that Eddie sought to discourage their hectic forward motion, only to direct it. Towards that pale circle in the distance, the rapidly *diminishing* distance, that sealed portal that very much resembled an eye jammed terrifiedly and tightly shut, though almost certainly cast from a material rather less yielding than an eye. Into which, unless its operation was triggered automatically and preferably very very soon, they were going to crash.

'So much for the light at the end of the tunnel,' Eddie moaned. 'Anyone know any prayers?'

'We're graduates of Spy High,' Bex pointed out. 'We don't *need* prayers.'

The portal blinked open. White became the blue of Egyptian skies.

'Either that or we've got a friend who answers them,' said Lori.

'Amen to that,' added Cally.

The dune-skimmer shot out from a cliffside in the Valley of the Kings. Eddie kept it climbing, soaring high above the yellow mountains, the silver thread of the Nile.

'If Dad had wanted us killed,' Bex theorised, 'we'd be dead by now. As we're *not*, that means he only wants to stop us from interfering in his plans. Should give us an edge.' She surveyed the sceptical faces of her friends. 'I hope.'

```
IGC LIVE NEWS FEED
BROADCAST DESIGNATION 326 WG
```

'Yes, Tracy, and the sense of anticipation here inside the UN Building in Cairo continues to grow. There are only moments remaining before Secretary-General Dr Jaya Kwalele commences what she has already announced will be an address of historic significance. Every member of the General Assembly is seated here in the Hall of Concord to hear it. The public and media galleries are full to bursting. Every major news network in the world is taking this live.

'And all of us are trying to guess exactly what it is the Secretary-General has to say.

Perhaps she'll be declaring radical new initiatives to combat global poverty and hunger. Perhaps she'll be reinstituting the World Pollution Control Plan, a favourite project of hers since its earliest inception. Or my sources suggest that Dr Kwalele is bringing news tonight that will have an even more wide-ranging effect on the world, even to the point of changing the way we live forever. Personally, Tracy, I think . . . but wait, there's no point in my indulging any further in idle speculation. Here comes Dr Kwalele now.

'There she is, tall, slender, elegant, making her way along the central aisle here in the Hall of Concord to the podium. And the members of the General Assembly are rising to her. And it's not simply because of the office she represents, its importance in this age of international terrorism and increasing tensions between cultures and creeds. It's not even because, as we're all aware, Dr Kwalele is the first woman in the history of the United Nations to hold such high authority. This tremendous reception – I would go as far as to say this *adoration* – is because people have faith in the Secretary-General, they believe in her, they *trust* her. Wherever Dr Kwalele leads, the world will want to follow.

'The ovation dies down. The great and good gathered here resume their seats. An expectant hush descends. The waiting is over. Dr Kwalele is at the podium. The eyes of millions, tens of

millions, are looking to this single African
woman in hope. Secretary-General Dr Jaya
Kwalele . . .'

Eddie landed the dune-skimmer in the desert while
Bond Team collectively decided their next move. It was
a manoeuvre the aircraft's name rightly implied it could
execute with aplomb, especially with a pilot of Eddie's
quality at the controls. Touchdown was as smooth as on
the main runway at JFK, though terminal buildings, or
indeed, any man-made constructions at all, were notable
by their absence. The trackless wastes of the desert
extended to every horizon.

As darkness fell and the temperature dipped, Lori
knelt on the sand beside the skimmer and brewed coffee
and heated the nutritional supplements they'd found
aboard the plane in the portable microwave they'd also
discovered. The others joined her.

'What's this, Lo?' teased Ben gently. 'You can take the
girl out of the kitchen but you can't take the kitchen out
of the girl?'

'It's called self-preservation, Ben, *actually*.' Lori main-
tained her dignity. 'If we waited for you or Jake or Eddie
to prepare something we'd end up dying of thirst and/or
starvation.'

'I'm just used to sending out,' said Ben.

'Or getting a servant to bring you a snack?' Jake
couldn't resist.

'Well, you can forget sending out,' Eddie said, scanning the darkening desert. 'Nearest takeaway's about
three hundred miles that way.' He pointed north. 'Or is
it that way?' He pointed south.

'Why am I glad the navigational systems on this bird are automatic?' Jake asked no one in particular.

Cally cuddled close to Ben. 'This is a bit like our camping trip to the Wildscape back in our first term, isn't it?'

'Sure,' said Eddie, 'only without quite so many trees.'

'And without the likelihood of attack by hordes of genetically mutated monsters,' added Lori. 'Or the insane descendant of Dr Frankenstein.'

'And *with* the likelihood of being tracked down and biochipped by our own people, maybe in company with a small army of animate Egyptian mummies,' contributed Jake.

'So yeah, Cal,' summarised Eddie, 'it's almost exactly the same experience. I'm surprised the rest of us didn't see it. You just take it easy now, y'hear?'

'Ben?' Cally shook her boyfriend vigorously. 'Are you just gonna sit there and let them take the rise out of me?'

'You know what, Cal?' Ben grinned. 'I think I am.'

'Coffee, Cally,' Lori indicated. 'I wouldn't pour it over Ben's head until it's cooled a little.' She glanced around the little circle. 'Where's Bex?'

'She went thataway,' Jake supplied, jabbing his finger towards a looming sand dune in the near distance. 'Want me to go tell her the Angel Café is open?'

'I'll go.' Eddie jumped to his feet.

'Try not to get lost, Eddie,' Ben advised.

'Sure, sure. If we're not back by morning' – he winked luridly – 'I'll expect congratulations.'

It didn't take him long to find her, but long enough for the trademark takes-nothing-seriously Nelligan grin to vanish and to be replaced by a more thoughtful, more mature expression. Bex was standing on the slope of the dune and in the night it was like she was on the edge of a cliff. Her back was to Eddie and the skimmer and her friends. She appeared dark and solitary. Eddie smiled, with warmth and frank affection, the way you sometimes do when you're gazing on someone you love without them knowing. Then he sighed.

'Hold that pose,' he called to Bex. 'This could be our *Lawrence of Arabia* moment. Here I come. *Daah* daah, da da da da *daah* daah . . .'

'Noise pollution in the Sahara,' Bex groaned. 'What is the world coming to? I guess at least *that's* not down to my father.'

'Feel like rejoining the team, Rebecca Dee?' Eddie said, standing alongside her. 'I mean, I know you're only there to make up the numbers, but even so . . .'

'Don't joke, Ed,' Bex winced. Her eyes were reluctant to meet his. 'I wouldn't be surprised if you didn't want anything more to do with me.'

'Say what?'

'I could understand it.'

'Well the understanding ain't mutual.'

'My father, Eddie. Don't act the idiot.'

'Who's acting?' Eddie said slyly.

'My father's the Bad Guy now. Jonathan Deveraux – Madman of the Month. And he's possibly more powerful than any foe we've ever faced.'

'Yeah,' her partner allowed. 'Maybe. I still don't follow.'

'You want me to spell it out for you?' Bex's brow furrowed in deep lines of hurt and betrayal. 'I'm Deveraux's daughter. His blood flows in my veins, even if it doesn't

in his own any more. How can any of you trust me now?
How can you still accept me as one of you when I'm
related to the enemy?'

'I knew it.' Eddie shook his head tolerantly. 'Bex,
looks like there is an idiot here, and it's not me. All this
relation stuff – it's rubbish. So your dad turns out to be a
few files short of a database. How is that *your* fault? How
are *you* to blame? How does it suddenly make you less
worthy of our trust, or change who you are in the slightest? We have to have parents – it'd be a lot less fun for
them if we didn't, at least around conception time – but
it's not written down anywhere that we have to grow up
to be *like* our parents. We make our own choices, Bex.
We become our own people. And we deserve to be
judged on our own actions, nobody else's.'

'I suppose,' Bex conceded slowly.

'Did we turn against Ben, or doubt him, or treat him
as less of a team-mate when his precious Uncle Alex
wanted to use us as living batteries?' Eddie pursued. 'No.
And more pertinent than that, did *Ben* let the whole
episode change him? No again.' A pause. 'He was still
the same vain, arrogant snob after Alexander Cain as he
was before.'

Bex laughed. 'Eddie, that's not fair.'

'Neither is beating yourself up over something that's
beyond your control. You spelled it out for me, Bex. I'll
spell it out for you. G.U.I.L.T. There's no need for you to
be feeling it. Your dad does his thing. You can only do
yours.'

'And mine is to stand against him,' Bex sighed.

Eddie stroked her arm. 'You won't be alone.'

She smiled at him softly. 'You know, I'm impressed,

Ed,' she admitted, 'and not just because you used the word pertinent in its correct context a few moments ago. This front you put on, the joker, the wisecracker, that's what it is, isn't it? A disguise, like a clown's mask. Underneath I think you're really quite sensitive.'

'Keep it down, Bex,' hushed Eddie. 'You'll ruin my reputation.'

'Thanks for what you said.' She leaned forward and kissed him on the lips. 'I mean it.'

'Eddie! Bex!' Ben's voice hailing them from the skimmer, loud and urgent.

'Uh oh,' gulped Eddie. 'Do you reckon he heard me call him a vain, arrogant snob?'

'Only one way to find out,' said Bex. 'Let's go.'

But even if Ben's natural hearing had been amplified artificially to enable him to eavesdrop on sand dune conversations in the distance, his attention was fixed on something both nearer to hand and further away.

'You need to see this,' he said ominously as Eddie and Bex climbed aboard the skimmer. Everyone else was crammed around the videscreen in the instrument panel, for viewing presumably when the plane was flying on autopilot. 'Cally was playing around with the channels. This is on all of them.'

Bex glimpsed the screen for the first time. 'Kwalele,' she breathed. 'It's started.'

'But there is no need to fear,' Secretary-General Dr Jaya Kwalele was reassuring her audience. 'All is for the good.' With the expression of a preacher and the voice of a robot.

'What's she talking about?' Eddie demanded.

'Pretty much the low points of human history,' Jake

recapped grimly. 'Wars, massacres, atrocities, genocide. But don't get too depressed. She says there's hope.'

'Mind control,' muttered Bex. 'Thou shalt not kill programmed into your brain.'

'Humankind's bloody and violent ways cannot be allowed to continue unchecked,' Dr Kwalele declared. 'In an era of potentially devastating new technologies, doing nothing is no longer an option. Man cannot in future be permitted the freedom to endanger the lives of others. He cannot be trusted to manage his own planet safely and for the good of all. These responsibilities must be exercised by another, one who possesses both the will and the vision to take those measures necessary to ensure the survival and the happiness of the human race, to ensure that good finally prevails upon the earth.'

'Oh, Bex.' Lori glanced sympathetically to her friend.

'Don't tell me,' guessed Bex. 'It begins with D.'

'The Deliverer is with us. The Deliverer is among us. The Deliverer will save us all,' asserted Dr Kwalele.

And she wasn't a lone voice, not any more. Her words found echo in the Hall of Concord. One by one the members of the General Assembly of the United Nations took them up. 'The Deliverer will save us all. The Deliverer is with us.' Black and white and yellow. Asian and American and African. The ambassadors and the delegates from every country in the world. Truly united for the first time in human history. One voice. One heart.

One mind.

'My God,' breathed Cally.

'Do you think they kind of practised this beforehand?' Eddie said.

'He got to them all.' Bex was stupefied. 'Dad controls them all.'

'Mr D's the Deliverer?' Jake clarified.

'Keep up, Daly,' scoffed Ben, but nervously.

'I've never seen anything like it.' The reporter was panicking. 'It's an unbelievable, an incredible scene here. It's like something out of a science-fiction movie only it's real, it's happening. The *entire* General Assembly is standing and speaking as one.'

They were. On their feet. Operating more like a network of computers than a congregation of human beings. Every syllable of every word lip-synched. Every individual voice identically metallic, hollow, cold.

'We are the voice of the Deliverer.' The cameras still tended to favour the striking figure of Jaya Kwalele. Her eyes were deep and unblinking. They were fixed and certain, beyond doubt, a prophet's eyes. 'We are his word and his will. We are the vanguard of the new order.'

'Who votes for the old order?' Eddie asked, raising both hands to start things rolling.

'I've got a feeling the Deliverer's not going to be big on voting,' said Lori.

'In his wisdom,' announced the General Assembly of the United Nations, 'the Deliverer promises a demonstration of the new order. In forty-eight hours it will begin. The peoples of the world will witness the way forward. You will understand what is good. You will join us, and the Deliverer will bring you peace. But until then . . .'

Three hundred faces turned directly to the camera. Three hundred people marched towards it. But in a sense, it was only one.

'This is insane! It can't be happening!' The reporter had long abandoned any last pretence of objectivity. 'We've got to get out of here! They're *coming* for —'

The screen went dead.

'Not sure I could have stood any more of that Deliverer garbage anyway,' glowered Jake. He looked like he would have preferred something to hit.

'So that's it,' said Ben. 'Deveraux the Deliverer. The computer messiah. The digital deity.'

'God in the machine,' suggested Eddie.

'He's going to establish utopia, a perfect – no, *the* perfect society.' Lori seemed to find the prospect chilling. 'No wars. No murders. No violence at all. No hatred. No racism. No starvation. God, you almost want to believe in it. Give me a contract and I'll sign.'

'You sign up for this, Lo,' cautioned Cally, 'and you're doing a deal with the devil.'

'Cal's right,' agreed Ben. ' 'Cause in Jonathan Deveraux's ideal world there's a few *noes* you missed out. No freedom. No choice. No mind of your own. What good is peace and harmony if you've got to be a biochipped zombie to achieve it?'

'*Can* he achieve it?' Lori changed tack. 'Obviously Mr Deveraux thinks big, but can even he mind-control every single person in the world?'

'Coca-Cola,' said Jake.

'That's real enlightening, Daly,' said Ben.

'Stanton, just listen for once, okay? How many people have drunk Coca-Cola in their lives? Probably billions, right? Virtually the entire world population, at least the population in those countries that might want to stand in the Deliverer's way. So what if Jonathan Deveraux drops a soluble biochip in every bottle and can of Coke sold? *That* could be done. Control the plant and you control production. It's all automated. It's all computerised. Just like JD himself. He does that – glug glug glug – he's got an army of mind-controlled disciples almost immediately.' Jake nodded bleakly as he saw the effect of his words on his team-mates. 'So yeah, Lo, Deveraux can do it.'

'Only we can't let him, can we?' Bex spoke up. 'For all we know we could be the only members of the Deveraux organisation still free, which makes taking action our responsibility. And Jonathan Deveraux's my father, which makes it mine even more.' She held the others' gaze defiantly. 'Whatever the danger, whatever the cost, we've got to stop him.'

SEVEN

Bex had never been big on birthdays, not since the age of five. That was when the vision had first appeared to her. Essentially it never changed, forming in her mind in an array of dazzling colours and to the accompaniment of lively music and bright laughter. There were happy children in party clothes in the vision and they were seated around a table and the table was piled high with good things to eat and drink. And the most important person at that table, the centre of attention, was a little girl with ribbons in her hair, a little girl who was leaning across a massive birthday cake studded with sometimes six, sometimes seven, sometimes eight burning candles as the years passed and the vision kept returning to taunt her. A little girl called Rebecca. And in the vision that little girl was always blowing the candles out and behind her with their hands on her shoulders a man and a woman stood, and they were happy too because, after all, in the vision they were alive. And 'Make a wish,' her parents urged. 'Make a wish, Rebecca.' The words echoed mockingly in her brain.

Because the only wish she longed to make was for the vision to become reality.

On the morning of her tenth birthday Mr Challinson came to see her. Rebecca was allowed to call Mr Challinson Uncle Gregory, but everybody else had to call the old man either Mr Challinson or sir because he was very important now that her father was dead. Normally Uncle Gregory had a smile for Rebecca and was pleased to listen to her news, but today he seemed distracted and had news of his own. Rebecca was to go with him on a journey, right now, as soon as she put her shoes on, and it was to be a very *special* journey. Rebecca had already kind of guessed that: Uncle Gregory had remembered to wish her many happy returns, but he'd forgotten to bring a present. She wondered if her present was waiting at the end of the journey.

They took a hoverlimo to the airport. They took a private Deveraux jet to another airport. They took another hoverlimo into countryside where Rebecca had never been before.

She heard snippets of Uncle Gregory's conversation on his cellphone when he couldn't keep his whisper secret enough: 'Are you *sure* this is a good idea? . . . I'm not sure she's . . . the psychological damage . . . of course he knows best . . .'

It didn't sound a very interesting conversation. Rebecca turned instead to look out of the window. The hoverlimo was pulling off the main road, passing through an arched gateway with a long drive into forest beyond. There was a stone pillar that bore a nameplate: 'The Deveraux College'.

'We're here,' said Uncle Gregory.

It was a school, apparently, a school founded by her father when he was alive. It was going to form what Uncle Gregory called her father's 'legacy'. Rebecca didn't like the look of it. The buildings, when they finally came into sight, appeared dark and old and brooding, and the windows were too tall and too thin and the roof was too jagged, like the teeth of a saw, and everything seemed spiky and sharp. It was the kind of school where pupils might meet a grisly fate when darkness fell. It was the kind of place where ghosts lived.

Uncle Gregory led her inside.

'Aren't there any children?' Rebecca asked, the corridors deserted.

'Not yet,' said Uncle Gregory. 'But there is someone here, someone who wants to meet you, someone who's waited a long time to see you.'

'Who is it?' Rebecca demanded excitedly, but when she saw the expression on Uncle Gregory's face, she wasn't sure she wanted to know after all.

'We'll take over from here, Challinson.' A new voice. A man in a white coat flanked by another man and a woman, also in white coats. 'Hello, Rebecca. I'm delighted to make your acquaintance at last. My name is Professor Henry Newbolt.'

Big glasses. Big hair. Rebecca might have guessed the newcomer was a scientist. If anything, he was also older than Uncle Gregory. 'Is it you?' Rebecca said.

'Is it me what, child?'

'Uncle Gregory says someone's been waiting a long time to see me. You could always have come to the house. We've plenty of room.'

Professor Henry Newbolt chuckled. 'No, there's

somebody else here too. And when you see who it is, Rebecca, it's going to be quite a surprise. It might even come as something of a shock at first. You have to promise me and you have to promise your Uncle Gregory that you'll be brave, a good, brave girl. Because nothing's going to hurt you here. We all of us have your best interests at heart.'

Rebecca didn't really understand but she was ten years old now so she said: 'I'll be brave.'

'Good girl,' said the scientist.

They conducted her upstairs, to the top floor of the Deveraux College, and they escorted her to a door that was black and heavy and closed and it reminded Rebecca of the coffin lids she'd seen at her parents' funerals. Her undertaking to be brave mere minutes before now began to seem more than a little foolhardy.

'Do we have to go in?' she ventured.

'It'll be all right,' Uncle Gregory reassured her. 'I'll be with you.'

'And someone can't wait to see you,' reminded Newbolt.

The door swung open as if of its own accord.

Rebecca expected to be greeted by a musty odour, by large, old-fashioned and monstrous hulks of furniture, faded oil paintings on the walls. Instead, she stepped into some kind of control centre, clinically lit and air-conditioned, gleaming with metal and glasteel, computers and monitors and instrument panels lining the walls, cables and tubes bulging from them, sensors and circuits flickering, electronics humming. In the middle of the room, a circle of twelve screens depended from the ceiling and inclined inwards as if conspiring together.

Of any other human being, there was no sign.

Rebecca regarded Newbolt and Uncle Gregory with confusion. 'I thought you said . . .'

'Come closer, Rebecca.'

She started. The words came from nobody's mouth. They came from all around her. They came from the room itself.

'Step within the screens. Let me see you properly.'

The voice was not human. It lacked the warmth of personality. There was metal in it. Yet at the same time it was eerily familiar. With a sudden surge of emotion, an emotion that threatened to overwhelm her and that could have been elation or that could have been fear, Rebecca recognised the voice. She stared wide-eyed at the adults for confirmation.

'It's true,' said Professor Henry Newbolt.

But how could it be? How was it possible? Rebecca staggered stiffly forward.

'That's it. There is no need for alarm.'

She let the screens surround her. She might have been whimpering. She thought of the vision of the little girl at her birthday party. *'Make a wish, Rebecca,' her parents urged. 'Make a wish.'*

'I could never harm you, Rebecca. You're my daughter.'

She wondered if this wasn't all a dream, unreal. But it was happening. She was shuddering as if plunged into sudden ice and the cry was rising in her throat and she dared to gaze up at the screens as a child might find the courage in one reckless, frantic moment to pull back the curtain behind which he knows the demons are lurking.

'Rebecca, it's me.' And on each of the screens, her father's face, inescapable. 'I've come back.'

It was then she started screaming.

Of course, stark terror had probably not been the reaction that Challinson or Professor Newbolt or Jonathan Deveraux himself had hoped for from Rebecca that day eight years ago, but looking back on it now, Bex imagined they could hardly have been surprised. How else might a ten-year-old girl be expected to respond when the father she believed to be dead appeared again without warning before her, resurrected through the miracle of modem science? And not as flesh and blood, either, not as a man, but as a computer program, as software. The likelihood of a tearful and loving reunion with a digitalised consciousness was never going to be great.

Over time, though, Bex grew accustomed to her new father. She'd adapted to his death; she adapted to his rebirth as well. Once she'd recovered from her initial shock, she even started to look forward to seeing him. With the Deveraux College open and the Spy High project begun, it was obviously impractical for her to visit Jonathan Deveraux at source, so to speak, but one of the advantages of existing as data was that you could be downloaded anywhere there was a computer. Her father was more accessible now than he ever had been when restricted to the mainframe of his body.

She did have to learn to limit her expectations of him, however. This second chance was still not going to produce the ideal father–daughter relationship that Bex had always dreamed of. She and her dad could talk, and mostly he seemed to listen, and sometimes he said the right thing to comfort or to please her, but there was no emotion in his voice. He was like an actor playing a role of which he had no personal experience. It was as if while Professor Newbolt and his team had succeeded in reproducing Jonathan Deveraux's brain, they had been unable to replicate the man's heart. Or perhaps it was simply that Bex's father had always tended towards coldness and distance.

But Bex still wanted to love him. More than anything else, she longed for *him* to love *her*. Obviously. He was her dad.

The Deliverer heard everything.

He was in the newsrooms of the world when the broadcasts were made, and he heard the voices of the newscasters struggling to be calm. He was on location with reporters, standing invisibly alongside them in the escalating panic, as if in solidarity. He was with the holocoms and the videphones and the emails and with every electronic communication uttered; not a word escaped him. And he was in the corridors of power, in systems thought secure and on lines imagined inviolate, and he eavesdropped at the ear of presidents and prime ministers and generals and kings.

He heard everything.

'. . . some kind of force-field, we can confirm. A force-field has cut off the United Nations Building from the rest of Cairo . . .'

'. . . absolutely impenetrable, and Dr Kwalele and the entire General Assembly are still inside . . .'

'. . . the diamond drill-bit didn't even leave a scratch. Nothing's going to break in here except maybe a missile with a nuclear warhead, and quite frankly, I'm surprised we haven't seen *any* sign of military activity in the skies as yet . . .'

'. . . yes, sir, complete systems failure. We couldn't launch from the silos now even if we wanted to . . .'

'. . . what do you mean, the birds are stranded? How can that be? The whole blasted USAF can't be grounded. Get the techs on it . . . so get *more* techs . . .'

'. . . I can't believe you're telling me this, General. We're no longer in control of our own technology? If that's true, if we can no longer mobilise or defend our-selves, then this Deliverer has already won. It's the end . . .'

'. . . if you ask me, though, love, modern life's not much to shout about, everybody stressed, frightened to go out at night, worried about crime. If this Deliverer can make a positive difference, let him come, I say, the sooner the better . . .'

The Deliverer heard everything, Jonathan Deveraux heard everything, and it was good.

The private Deveraux jet knifed across the Atlantic at its optimum speed and altitude. Eddie and Cally were at the controls, their undisputed talents for operating anything with an engine and managing computer systems respec-tively having qualified them for the privilege. Their team-mates were seated back in the main cabin.

Bex for one was feeling a little better. At least being a Deveraux had helped them get this far. They'd aban-doned the dune-skimmer in the desert just out of sight of the road where they'd commandeered a wheelless to take them to Alexandria. The Deveraux organisation owned a small airfield on the outskirts of the city. They'd borrowed its single plane. Bond Team's access codes had been cancelled, but Bex had two codes, the second in her capacity as a member of the Deveraux family. That had been overlooked. It remained valid. Once aboard the jet, Cally had reprogrammed the computers to make it more difficult for Jonathan Deveraux to track their flight path, then, refuelled, they'd set off for the States. Nobody seemed to have a clear idea what to do when they got there.

'If it wasn't mission suicide,' offered Jake, 'I'd say we fly straight to Spy High and tackle Mr D head-on.'

'I can see the appeal,' acknowledged Ben, 'but as you rightly say, Jake, it *would* be mission suicide. We'd never get through the door. Deveraux'll have the place wall-to-wall animates or zombies by now. We're good, but we're still only six.'

'At least we've each got a full complement of weaponry now,' said Bex, referring to the mission belts, shock blasters and sleepshot wristbands they'd removed from the jet's regulation secret compartment. Every Deveraux plane always carried sufficient field equipment for a full team. 'And I don't want to impugn your mathematical ability, Ben, but we'll actually be seven.' Ben looked quizzical. 'Once we've collected Kate Taylor from the Refuge.'

'Oh, yeah,' enthused the blond boy ironically. 'Adding a First Year to the team is really gonna have JD trembling in his digital booties. I'm not even sure it's worth bothering picking her up.'

'We have to,' Bex protested. 'If she's managed to reach the Refuge, having already escaped from Spy High with her individuality intact, remember, then I think she's earned her chance.'

'Situation must be serious, Bexy,' said Jake. 'Sorry, but I agree with Ben.'

'Well I agree with Bex,' said Lori. 'This Kate Taylor's combat skills may not be quite as honed as ours, but she's obviously resourceful and she might have further information we can use.'

'And she's a girl,' Ben whispered to Jake, loudly enough for Lori and Bex to hear.

'And hopefully, a little more mature than some I could mention,' Lori retorted.

'All right, Lo, you've got a point,' Jake allowed.

'You're a traitor to your sex, Daly,' snorted Ben, though not seriously.

'I'm just thinking what Mr D's capable of,' Jake said. 'I mean, with a computer brain as powerful as his, he's more dangerous than Nemesis ever was. Nemesis was only a sentient computer virus. It could only destroy, and it wasn't very subtle doing that. But with a bit of thought, a tad of forward planning, Mr D could transform society almost overnight. Look at the number of ways the *physical* world is controlled these days from the *cyber* world. Computers underpin everything. The transport system. The power grid. The military's weapons systems. Banking. Food production. The media. Deveraux could destabilise and disrupt all of them, spread disinformation at will, force us from the Information Age to the Stone Age in one fell swoop. The *ultimate* cyber-terrorist.'

'You sound like we ought to be grateful Mr Deveraux's only interested in mind control, Jake,' said Lori ruefully.

'You sound like you're giving up,' accused Ben.

'Then you need to get your ears syringed, Stanton.' Jake scowled. 'I never give up, you ought to know that by now. All I'm saying is we need to be aware of the scale of the task ahead. We've gonna need all the help we can get.'

'That's cool,' grinned Bex. ' 'Cause I think I know where we can get some.'

Even in times of global crisis, life on a day-to-day level continues pretty much as before. People still go to bed at night and get up in the morning. Meals are still cooked; food is still eaten. The undertaker and the midwife remain in employment.

On the island known before its incorporation into Europa as Great Britain, as elsewhere in the world, the coming of the Deliverer changed none of that. At first.

In Manchester, for example, Eileen Swift was yelling at her fifteen-year-old daughter Tina with as much anger and bitterness as ever, and for similar reasons. Where had she got to last night? What time had she finally got in? Who had she been with? That Craig again? What had she been told about that Craig? He wasn't suitable. He wasn't good enough. And Tina, naturally, was not welcoming this outburst of motherly concern in silence. Who was her mother to dictate to her who she could or couldn't see, where she could or couldn't go and when? It was her life. She could do what she liked. She *would* do what she liked. And as mother and daughter bawled at each other across the kitchen table, both winced at the nagging pain of a headache they just didn't seem able to shift.

In Liverpool, Harry Dimmock sat in his terraced house and cursed to himself while the room shook. That good-for-nothing young layabout next door had his sound system cranked up to full volume again. It was like the street was being bombed. How many times had Harry politely requested that the idle lout show some consideration for others, including a pensioner like himself, and turn it *down*? How many times had he threatened to complain to the council? That young waster had laughed in his face, had called him Grandad, had called him worse. There was no respect any more, no common decency. One day, Harry was going to go next door with a knife in one hand, and when that good-for-nothing young layabout appeared he was going to *make* him turn his so-called music down. One day. Maybe today. That infernal racket was surely to blame for his headache.

In Birmingham, Clive Cunningham stood on the station concourse and regarded the departures board with dismay. His train, cancelled again. The sixth time this month and it was only the twentieth. Condemning him to another ordeal of a journey crammed into an overcrowded carriage with no possibility of a seat, squashed helplessly against someone who seemed to have eaten nothing but garlic for the best part of his life. It wasn't good enough. He paid his taxes, too many taxes. He expected a transport system that worked. Frustration flared in Clive Cunningham; rage rose. He saw one of those new station attendants besieged by an increasingly irate mob of his fellow commuters. He'd join them. He'd make something happen, make himself heard. But he should have stayed at home today: his headache was getting worse.

And so it went, across the country.

In London, two hovercab drivers were flinging abuse at each other, each blaming the other for the collision that had dented both cabs.

In Sheffield, a teacher was waving her arms desperately, uselessly as her class ran riot, begging them to 'Sit down, please, sit down'.

In Bristol, two youths were breaking into a flat only to discover the owner was still inside and prepared to defend himself.

In towns and in streets and in cities, voices raised in outrage and fury and threat. A cacophony of conflict, often minor, often petty, but permanent, society's soundtrack. The emotional chaos of lives lived under constant stress. So it went on the island formerly known as Great Britain on the day the Deliverer came.

The day every pharmacy in the country sold out of paracetamol.

The score was tied 80–80 and Myron had the basketball in his hands. No way they were gonna stop him scoring now. No *way*. He zipped past Lemmy and left Stevo standing. They were gonna need a *miracle* to stop him scoring now.

They got one.

The sun above the Refuge was suddenly blacked out. A wind from nowhere whipped across the concrete court. Lemmy and Stevo looked up, shouted, pointed. Myron followed their gaze and the ball with which he'd been about to score the winning basket dropped from his hands and bounced then rolled tamely towards the high wire fence. Myron wasn't even aware of it.

The jet hovering in the sky above them kind of dominated his view.

'It's coming down!' Stevo was yelling. 'Run!'

The boys scattered because, for once, Stevo was right. The jet was lowering itself vertically to the court. Whoever was piloting that thing knew what he was doing, Myron thought. The slightest wobble of the wings and the plane would either be scraping the Refuge wall or slicing open the fence. As it was, a perfect landing was executed.

'What's going on? Who the heck *is* that?' cried Lemmy.

'Ain't that Deliverer guy they're talking about on the videvision, is it?' gulped Stevo. 'Hadn't somebody better go fetch Ms Bromley?'

'I don't think we need to worry Ms Bromley,' came a female voice, calm and confident.

It was the new girl. She couldn't have crept up on them any more sneakily, thought Myron, if she'd been trained as a spy. 'Who asked you?' he snapped. 'You've only been here three days. What do you know?'

The new girl's eyes twinkled. 'Oh, I know plenty,' she said, and walked towards the jet.

'Hey, wait!' Myron called after her. 'Where do you think you're going?' And was she brave or stupid? 'Come back!'

'Go get her, then,' said Lemmy.

'*You* go get her, retard,' retorted Myron.

Neither boy made a move, and even if they had, they'd have been too late. A door in the side of the aircraft opened. A flight of steps descended. The new girl didn't look back as she climbed them and disappeared inside the plane.

Seconds later, the landing was matched by a perfect take-off. Seconds later still, no jet might ever have touched down on the basketball court at the Refuge.

'What was that all about?' said Stevo. 'Who do you think that new girl was?'

'Who cares? She's gone now,' shrugged Myron. He jogged across the court and retrieved the abandoned ball. 'Eighty each, right? Let's play.'

No way they were going to stop him scoring now.

Bex introduced Kate Taylor to the rest of Bond Team.

'It's an honour to meet you all,' the First Year said. 'I've heard so much about you.'

'What you've heard about me, Kate,' Eddie called from the cockpit, the door open, 'it's all lies. Unless, of course, you *like* what you've heard. In that case it's all true.'

'Eddie, shouldn't you be making sure we don't run into a flock of pigeons or something?' said Bex.

'I've watched all your mission scenarios at Spy High,' Kate revealed. 'Very impressive.'

'Yeah, well I don't do autographs,' grunted Jake.

'Jake!' Lori slapped his leg warningly. 'Be nice.' She herself accepted the younger girl's compliment with better grace. '*Thank* you, Kate.'

'A pity we have to meet under such, ah, difficult circumstances,' said Ben.

'Oh, I'm not worried,' Kate professed. 'You'll find a way to beat even Mr Deveraux – if you don't mind me saying, Bex . . .'

Bex dismissed the student's concern. 'We've been through all that, Kate. Please, speak freely. My dad's gone bad and that's all there is to it for the moment.'

'Bond Team's never failed a mission yet. I don't suppose you're going to start now.'

'We're gonna try not to, Kate,' said Jake, 'and with you cheering us on . . .' His sentence trailed away under pressure from Lori's glare.

'I expect you've got a plan already, haven't you?'

'*Plan* might be a little specific for where we are right now,' Ben said guardedly. He didn't want to puncture any of Kate Taylor's illusions, largely because most of them he reckoned were just about true. 'I think you can safely say we have a *direction*.'

'That's literally and metaphorically,' contributed Bex. 'We're heading for Serenity.'

'For what?' Kate didn't understand.

'Where,' said Jake.

'Serenity's a place,' explained Bex. 'It's a small town in Illinois. Superficially it looks the same as any other small town in Illinois, only it's not. It belongs to the Deveraux organisation. You'd have found out about it sooner or later yourself, Kate. It's where agents wounded in the field go for long-term convalescence. It's where operatives go to live when they retire from active duty. Kind of like a safe-house, only bigger. Nobody lives there who either isn't or hasn't been employed by Deveraux.'

'But in case you're wondering, Kate,' said Lori, 'we're not taking early retirement.'

'Some of our teachers are there. Some of our field handlers. Dad obviously thought they might prove something of a threat to his plans so he had them retired, got out of the way.' Bex's brow furrowed. 'Well we intend to put them *back* in the way.'

'Guys like Senior Tutor Grant have been with the Spy High operation since the beginning,' Ben added. 'He might have information that we could use. Then there's Gadge, Professor Newbolt. His brain's shot these days but if we *could* get any sense out of him – Newbolt pretty much created the computerised Jonathan Deveraux.'

'Which kind of makes him my surrogate grandfather,' Bex observed with a hollow laugh. 'I've got a great family, haven't I?'

'Guys?' Cally stepped into the main cabin from the cockpit. 'I've got good news and I've got bad news.'

'That's an improvement on lately,' commented Jake.

'The good news is that according to Eddie we should be reaching Serenity in thirty minutes from now. The bad news is that someone's got there ahead of us.'

'Someone?' Ben prompted.

'I did a location analysis as soon as we came within range. Heart readings. Biosignature recognitions. No point dropping by if the people we want are no longer there.'

'And are they?' If they weren't, Lori had no idea where to direct the jet next.

'Oh, sure. Grant. Gadge. Violet Crabtree. It's like a who's who of Spy High employees. But Mr Deveraux's anticipated our move. We should have guessed he would. They're not alone. In fact, I think they're bait. Heat readings are the giveaway. Plenty are human. Plenty aren't. The place is crawling with animates.' Cally looked from one silent and brooding team-mate to another. 'So what do I tell Eddie? Ben?'

'About what, babe?'

'Do we abort?'

'No, we don't abort.' Ben's voice was icily determined. 'Kate's watched our mission scenarios. Now she can see the real thing. Tell Eddie we're going in.'

EIGHT

Kate had been aggrieved at first. Okay, so she was young and inexperienced, and held no official Spy High qualifications yet whatsoever. But surely the fact that she was still free and independent when most of the Deveraux organisation were either captive or mind-controlled counted for something. Surely she merited inclusion in Bond Team's little raid on Serenity. She hadn't liked to remind them that by this stage of *their* training they'd already defeated the insane geneticist Averill Frankenstein, but . . . Her pleading hadn't done any good: Ben and Jake's ears had seemed particularly deaf.

Then Lori had explained and Kate had allowed herself to be convinced. Apparently it was nothing to do with any doubt Bond Team might have entertained about her abilities. It was simply a matter of practicalities. Kate still wore her sleepshot wristbands, but she'd need full weapons issue to survive in Serenity, and the plane could only equip a single team. Somebody was also required to remain on board and guard the jet, just in case. It was still a vital role, Lori had stressed. If something happened to Bond Team and they didn't return, it would be Kate's responsibility somehow to carry on the fight.

Kate had said she was sure they'd be back. She'd said she was just proud to be involved.

So now she was alone, sitting in the pilot's chair of the darkened plane and gazing out into the night. Eddie had landed in a field screened from Serenity by a hill. The aircraft was little more than a shadow among shadows. If anybody did happen to drive by they'd notice nothing. Besides, if anybody *did* happen to be travelling in the vicinity during the next hour or so, Kate suspected they'd have rather more to claim their attention.

She wondered if she'd be able to hear the explosions this far from town.

It was late for a walk in the park, but Cally and Ben were more like slinking anyway. They ghosted across lawns transformed by night into solid slabs of darkness, keeping low, keeping alert, shock blasters drawn. Their radar visors ensured they could see with perfect clarity, while the map of Serenity they'd both memorised and downloaded into their belt-brains made certain they knew where they were heading.

Their visors' telescopic sights informed them that the gazebo was already occupied.

'Check heat signature,' Ben hissed.

'Already have done,' responded Cally with a trace of annoyance. 'I'm an agent too, remember? They're both animates.'

Which meant blasters set to Materials rather than

using sleepshot. Any human foe they faced tonight wasn't likely to be in his or her own mind. Bond Team didn't want to cause unnecessary injuries. With animates, however, they could afford to cut loose.

'I'll take the one on the right,' whispered Ben.

'Guess that means I'll take the one on the left,' deduced Cally.

Two shots. Two casualties. The animates collapsed with holes in their heads.

The Bond Teamers raced to the gazebo. As one, they removed strips of plastex from their mission belts and affixed them to the structure's low latticed walls.

'This is child's play,' grumbled Ben. 'Kate Taylor could have done this. With her eyes closed. We ought to be liberating Grant and the others, not relegated to providing the diversion.'

'Without the diversion,' Cally pointed out, 'there wouldn't be a chance of liberating Grant and the others. Lori's plan makes sense, and as leader, she gets to lead.'

'I should have teamed with her instead of Daly.'

'What?' Cally said with exaggerated hurt. 'You'd sooner work with your ex-girlfriend than the current love of your life?'

'You know I didn't mean it like that, Cal.' Ben grinned, Cally's proximity banishing the memories that still sometimes rankled of when *he'd* been leader of Bond Team. 'Here, I'll make it up to you.' He took her by the hand.

'Smooching on active duty, Agent Stanton?' wondered Cally, allowing herself to be led.

'Not quite.' He thrust a fuse into her fingers. 'You can set off the plastex.'

'Ah,' sighed Cally, 'whoever said the age of romance was dead?'

Eddie and Bex saw the sudden bolt of flame from the other side of town, heard the detonation ripple across the sky.

'Ben and Cally are off the mark,' Eddie observed.

'We can do better than that.' Bex flashed the detonator before her partner's visor. 'Guaranteed to make your evening go with a bang.'

'Or in this case, if we set the charges right, a whole series of bangs.'

Bex pressed the button. At the far end of the street, a shopfront exploded, spraying glass and wood and concrete out into the road. The shop opposite seemed to think that was kind of fun and promptly followed suit. Next door didn't want to be left out. Neither did next door again. The ground beneath the Bond Teamers rocked as one by one the shops blew up.

'That ought to get noticed,' said Bex.

'Let's hope it does what Lori *wants* it to do and splits your dad's forces.' There was the sound of running feet coming their way. 'Heads up, Bex,' Eddie warned. 'We've got company.'

They quickly took cover and prepared to pick off some animates.

Lori and Jake were crouching on the courthouse roof when the explosions began. Fire plumed first from their distant right, then from as far away again in the opposite direction. The plastex rumbled like thunder.

'Fireworks, Bond Team style,' said Jake, 'and we've got the best view in town.'

'It's not the fireworks I'm interested in,' said Lori.

She indicated the street below. Figures that could have been men but which her visor's heat register indicated were animates spilled down the courthouse steps. Some packed into parked wheelesses and sped towards the disruption. Others didn't bother with transportation: animate legs did not tire like those of humans. Lori counted. Seventeen fewer hindrances between the teenagers and their objective. Seemed her plan was working.

She glanced at Jake. Ready? Ready.

The Serenity courthouse was maybe an obvious choice of location for the teachers' detention, but then animates had never been overly gifted with imagination. They probably saw no further than the cells it contained, facilities that given the nature of the town's population had more than likely never hosted company before. The advantage for Bond Team was that after biosignature referencing it had become clear that everyone they most wanted to free was being held here, together.

But not for much longer.

Lori and Jake spidered down the courthouse wall. The clingskin spray in their mission belts averted the need to hazard entry through the door. Spy High's miracle adhesive made an upper-storey window just as convenient for secret agents and that little bit more unexpected for their opponents.

'I'm picking up twenty heat sigs besides ourselves,' Lori reported once they were inside, in a closed and empty office. 'All human too. Guess they sent the animates to do the dirty work. So, subtract the eight on our side, makes odds of six to one.'

'Any easier and I'll start whistling,' said Jake. Lori smiled and he returned the favour. In fact, he was feeling good working this closely with Lori. It was like old times, when they'd been partners in more ways than one. He'd been an idiot to break up with her, he realised that now, and over something as trivial as disagreements in mission philosophy. Who cared about philosophy when you had *chemistry*? And okay, so Lori was dating this Casino guy, Robbie Royal or whatever his real name was. That wouldn't last. It couldn't. In the end Cas wouldn't be able to make Lori happy or understand her or give her what she wanted. Only another Deveraux graduate could do that. And she'd *chosen* Jake to team with her tonight. Yeah, once this present crisis was over, or even before . . .

'I said let's *go*,' Lori was evidently repeating.

'Absolutely,' said Jake. They stole out into the corridor. 'Let's start counting.'

One, the guy posted at the top of the stairs drawing his shock blaster with an 'I think I heard something' expression, the sleepshot drilling him right between the eyes.

Two, at the bottom of the stairwell, a difficult angle for Lori but the shot successfully accomplished.

Three and four, coming through the doors, seeing Jake and Lori leaning over the body of their unconscious comrade but reacting less quickly, four though managing to cry out before the sleepshot rendered him speechless.

Five and six, firing shock blasts at the door but the teenagers diving low beneath them and forward-rolling and springing up with wristbands glittering.

Seven, yelling for Butters and Edge to get up here, they were under attack.

Eight and nine, presumably Butters and Edge, good at obeying orders but not so hot at self-protection.

Into the holding area, in sight of the cells.

Ten and eleven, pinning them down to begin with, having found respectable cover behind a desk, but perhaps not realising that sleepshot was equally and instantly disabling whatever portion of the anatomy it struck, including – ten – a foot prodding out beyond the protection of the desk and – eleven – an elbow jerked into view in nervous reaction.

And finally twelve, blaster thrown down, hands thrown up, backing between the cells. 'Afraid your number's up,' said Jake.

'Well don't stop there,' complained a man with greying hair from one of the cells. 'Assuming your mission objective is to release us, Agent Daly, you have so far accomplished nothing. Quickly. Use your deactivator.'

'Good to see you again *too*, Senior Tutor Grant,' said Jake wryly, though he did as he was told.

'That was a poor show, Daly.' A younger man than the former Senior Tutor of the Deveraux College joined him at the bars, a man dressed in military fatigues and who seemed to have been carved out of granite. Corporal Randolph Keene, physical instruction. 'You've been slipping since you graduated. You and Angel should have split up on entry and created a crossfire. You'd have saved five seconds.'

'Five seconds? That's nearly as many as six.'

'Do you know how many weapons of mass destruction

can be launched in five seconds, Agent Daly?' challenged Corporal Keene. 'In espionage, every second—'

'—can save a life,' finished Jake. 'See? I *was* listening in class.' He peered between the bars. There were three other men in the cell besides Grant and Keene. 'Now does anyone else want to take a pop at the guy who's actually *rescuing* you?'

'Indeed not,' protested the elderly gentleman who looked as if he should be serving canapés at a social function. 'One wishes to say jolly well done.'

'You're Bowler, right?' guessed Jake. 'Eddie's field handler.'

'Indeed. Might one assume that Master Edward is nearby?'

'All of Bond Team are here,' Jake informed him. 'The others are keeping the animates occupied. But we're all you've got.'

The deactivator did its work and the cell door sprung open.

'Then we'll have to be grateful for small mercies, won't we?' said Grant. 'Keene, gather as many weapons as you can find. Mr Korita' – to the last but one occupant of the cell – 'locate Professor Newbolt's CAP, if you would.'

Kazuo Korita, martial arts instructor and possessor of more black belts than he owned pairs of trousers, passed by Jake with a nod as brief and an expression as inscrutable as if this was a chance meeting in the corridors of Spy High.

The final male prisoner had not yet moved. He remained slumped on a wooden bunk, his fingers the only part of him that seemed truly alive. They worked in the air in front of his face as if constructing a marvellous machine. His head nodded constantly in approval of his invisible ingenuity, but his eyes were blank, his lips slack. His tongue lolled from his mouth like it was too exhausted to function any longer. Big glasses. Big hair. But Professor Henry Newbolt had seen better days – even if he could no longer remember them.

'Poor old Gadge,' said Jake pityingly. Gadge was the senile former genius's nickname among the Spy High students – short for gadget. 'Is it really gonna be worth bringing him along?'

'If Mr Korita can find his CAP,' said Grant, 'you'll be surprised, Agent Daly.'

'His *what*?' said Jake.

On the other side of the corridor, Lori was using her deactivator to free the female contingent among the prisoners.

'Are you all right, Ms Crabtree?' she addressed old Violet with concern. 'Would you like to sit down?'

'Sit down?' the receptionist and former secret agent retorted. 'Sitting down is all I've been doing for three days, Lori. Kicking some *ass* is what *I'd* like.'

Concern misplaced there, then. And weapons instructor Lacey Bannon appeared not to be in any immediate need of TLC either. She was already out there contesting ownership of number twelve's shock blaster with Corporal Keene – her biceps pretty much matched his also.

'Luanne? What have they done to you?' Her own field handler, Shades Carmody, might be a different matter. The top half of her head was encased in a steel mask that completely covered her eyes. Deveraux, of course, was as aware of her optical implants' capabilities as anyone:

his techs had fitted them after the former agent's blinding on a mission some years ago. This way they were neutralised.

'I'll be fine as soon as we get this off, Lori,' Shades said with remarkable calmness. 'The locking mechanism's at the back.'

'Okay. Hold on.' Lori grabbed the deactivator from the cell door and attached it to the rear of the mask. With an electronic hum, the steel split in two. Lori lifted the mask from the older woman's head like a mould.

'That's better,' Shades said. Her lidless right eye flickered with symbols and calculations; her lidless left burned as if eager to unleash its laser option. 'Now I can see again.'

'We need to leave.' Jake wondered whether Grant had got to be Senior Tutor by specialising in stating the obvious. 'I don't want to be critical of your partners' combat skills, but the animates will overrun them sooner or later. Everyone else in Serenity is being held captive in their own homes – it's not realistic to liberate them. Mr Deveraux obviously saw us as a special case and wanted to keep us under tighter guard.'

'Let's be glad he did, Elmore,' said Shades. 'What's your plan for departure, Lori?'

'We've got a Deveraux jet waiting just outside of town,' supplied Lori. 'Plenty of wheellesses parked outside to get us there.'

'Steal a wheelless?' Bowler was horrified. 'That's simply not cricket.'

'We're not playing games, Bowler,' snorted Keene.

'Kaz has found Newbolt's CAP,' reported Lacey Bannon. She'd found a small stock of pulse rifles and shock blasters, several of which she was wielding. 'I think that's our cue. I'll take point.'

'Keene, Korita, bring Professor Newbolt,' instructed Grant. 'Luanne, watch our backs.'

'Madam, may I have the pleasure?' Bowler offered his arm to Violet Crabtree.

'Why thank you, Mr Bowler,' consented Violet. 'Such a gentleman.'

'We may be living in difficult times,' Bowler said, 'but that is no excuse for bad manners.'

Jake turned to Lori in disbelief. 'We risked our lives to *free* these people?'

'Sir?' Lori asked Grant. 'What do you want *us* to do?'

'Keep up, Agent Angel,' said the Senior Tutor. 'Keep up.'

He'd keep up all right, Jake brooded as the ten-strong band moved swiftly yet watchfully through the courthouse, and when they had a moment to spare, he might just have a little word with *former* Senior Tutor Elmore Grant as to exactly who was in charge of this operation. The rescu*ees* or the rescu*ers*.

Lori seemed to be able to read his thoughts in his eyes. 'Mind the temper, Jake,' she advised as they neared the main doors. 'We're not home free yet. Anything could—'

The doors slammed open. In a sheer reflex action everyone prepared to fire.

'Wait! Wait!' Lori realised first. The identity of the four new arrivals.

'Whoa,' pleaded Eddie. 'I know I wasn't the best student, but there's no need to shoot me.'

He felt more secure when they were back aboard the

plane and in the air. Not even a trigger-happy Corporal Keene was going to shock-blast the pilot. As they flew above the town Eddie could see the fires from the explosions still burning.

'Serenity,' he said. 'They might have to call it something different now.'

In the main cabin, rather cramped since the recent increase in passenger numbers, next-step discussions were taking place. Grant was leading them. From Jake and Ben's shared body language, defensively folded arms, stony stares, neither boy approved of the development. Bex and Lori – Cally was in the cockpit with Eddie – exchanged apprehensive glances: it took extreme circumstances for the testosterone twins to express that level of solidarity. Lori hoped the additional allies hadn't only added to their problems.

'We need to land somewhere we can take stock and think,' Grant was outlining, 'and plan, and bring Professor Newbolt back to us.' The Professor grinned inanely and nodded as he recognised mention of his name. 'Somewhere Mr Deveraux won't be able to find us.'

'This guy is a genius, isn't he?' Jake muttered to Ben.

'I'm learning so much,' Ben muttered back.

Grant ran his hand through his hair. 'I'm open to suggestions.'

'I have one.' First-year student Kate Taylor blushed as twelve pairs of eyes focused on her: it was like being in the presence of Jonathan Deveraux himself. 'That is, if you, you know, want to hear it . . .' She trailed away uncertainly.

'Go on, Kate,' Bex encouraged. She felt kind of

responsible for the younger girl, kind of like a mentor. In a way, it was Bex who'd got Kate involved in the present escapade.

'Well, it's just,' expanded Kate, 'my parents own a cabin, in the Appalachians. We used to go there for holidays when I was small, to get away from it all, my dad used to say. It's kind of remote but that might not be a bad thing, considering. Though the ground's not exactly level. Eddie might have trouble landing . . .'

'One is certain Master Edward will rise to the challenge,' said Bowler confidently.

'Sounds good,' Ben shot in before his former teacher could do so. 'I vote yes. Jake?'

'Me too.'

'Us three and four.' Bex spoke for Lori as well as herself.

'Sir?' There was a note of challenge, of confrontation in Ben's voice as he turned to Grant. Everyone in the cabin heard it. Keene made a kind of grunt.

The Senior Tutor pursed his lips and inclined his head as if understanding something for the first time. 'You'd better help Agent Nelligan set a course then, hadn't you, Student Taylor?'

In forty-eight hours, the Deliverer had promised. Through Dr Jaya Kwalele he had spoken. There would be a demonstration of the new order in forty-eight hours.

The time was up.

On the island that had been Great Britain there was electricity in the air. There was a sense of violence brewing, of something wild and savage coming to a head.

In Manchester, Eileen Swift had suddenly had enough

of her daughter Tina's lies and rudeness and answering back. Fifteen-year-old girls should be put in their place and their mothers should be doing it and Eileen Swift was raising her hand to Tina and about to bring it lashing down against her face, again and again. Her headache raged.

In Liverpool, Harry Dimmock went into his kitchen and selected the knife he used for slicing his Sunday joint. Then he went next door and the whole of the front of the house was throbbing from the noise that good-for-nothing waster dared to call music, and Harry Dimmock pressed his finger to the doorbell and kept it there. It might take a while for that layabout to answer, but he'd come eventually, and he'd get a shock when he did. Maybe then his headache would stop.

In Birmingham, Clive Cunningham joined the fringe of the unruly mob of commuters, and his headache was so bad he couldn't think straight but he knew that it wasn't good enough, it wasn't good enough at all, and he knew he was angry enough to do something about it, and he knew he hated jobsworths like this mealy-mouthed station attendant with their weak excuses and dishonest apologies. And he was grabbing for the man with the rest of them, and hoisting him high and bearing him towards the track.

In London, two cabbies graduated from insults to blows.

In Sheffield, tiny fists pulled on teacher's clothes and teacher's hair.

In Bristol, burglars boiled for a fight.

Across the country, the same. Resentments and rages long repressed, unleashed. The mental barriers that divided right from wrong, acceptability from unacceptability, removed, the way that something old and outdated is discarded before something new, something *better*, is put in its place.

Sixty-five million people on the island of Great Britain. Sixty-five million skulls seeming to split open with intolerable pain at the selfsame moment.

In Manchester, Eileen Swift screamed and clutched for her daughter Tina, and mother and daughter buckled together.

In Liverpool, Harry Dimmock let slip the knife and the layabout caught him as he fell.

In Birmingham, the commuters writhed on the platform in agony.

Sixty-five million voices, sixty-five million screams.

Then silence. Total. Blissful. Absolute. The silence of war's end when the last shot has been fired.

And in Manchester, Eileen Swift and her daughter Tina embrace because all cause of disagreement between them has been wiped clean from their minds. Praise the Deliverer.

And in Liverpool, Harry Dimmock and his neighbour enjoy the silence side by side because their minds have been emptied of sound. Praise the Deliverer.

And in Birmingham, Clive Cunningham queues quietly, patiently with his fellow commuters, and arrivals and departures trouble him no more. Praise the Deliverer.

In London, two cabbies smile at each other like old friends. In Sheffield, a teacher and her students sit in silence as the school day passes. In Bristol, a man in a flat makes tea for two nice young people who have come to visit him.

Across the country, the same. Sixty-five million troubled souls now at peace. Praise the Deliverer.

'This is a nightmare.' Ben stared at the jet's videscreen aghast. It was a reaction in common with the others.

'It is indeed most unfortunate,' echoed Bowler, 'and that it should be occurring in my own country, too.'

The footage was paralysing in its impact. Scenes from London, Liverpool, Birmingham, identical. The cities and the countryside. The population of Britain like smiling sleepwalkers, their expressions devoid of individuality, their personalities eradicated. A kind of life was continuing – there were people in the streets, people at work, people at play, people going about their daily business – but nothing seemed to be done with any commitment or enthusiasm or genuine intent. It was a pretence of life, hollow, void. It was like a school without children or a stadium without a crowd.

And Bex knew with a cold dread that it was still only the *beginning*.

'Why Britain, though?' she said. 'There's got to be a reason. Everything Dad *does* has a reason.'

'Because it's an island, maybe,' Jake suggested. 'Deveraux could have taken control of the systems managing the water supply, infected it with nanotechnology, biochips you ingest every time you drink. As an island Britain's big, but still pretty much a self-contained environment.'

'An experiment,' Lori said. 'A country for a laboratory and human beings for lab rats. Not good.'

'*They* seem to think otherwise, Agent Angel,' said Grant.

On the screen, innumerable British citizens were praising the Deliverer.

'The majority isn't always right, sir,' Lori responded.

'Particularly not when the majority are mind-controlled morons,' snorted Jake.

'That's not going to happen to me.' Ben jabbed a finger at the screen. 'I'm telling you now. No emotional extinction for Benjamin T. Stanton.'

'Thanks for that, Ben,' said Bex. 'I'm sure we all agree with you.'

Dr Kwalele reappeared on the screen holding forth from the podium in the Hall of Concord of the United Nations as before. This broadcast had interrupted all other transmissions. It seemed the Deliverer was able to impose himself in media circles as well. 'You have seen the blessings the Deliverer brings,' she said. 'Unity. Tranquillity. Peace of mind. The people of Britain are no longer capable of violence or anger or harm. From this day forward they will live together in a harmony and a happiness that can only be realised when you open your mind to the Deliverer and let him in.'

'As far as I'm concerned he can stay *out*.' Jake looked as if he'd be prepared to take steps to ensure it.

'That's not happiness,' Lori said. 'What he's done to those people, it hasn't made them happy. It's turned them into cattle, unthinking, unquestioning cattle.'

'I know plenty of politicians who'd be grateful for a little mind control come election time,' noted Grant.

'We beseech you, people of the world,' Dr Kwalele was continuing in earnest appeal, 'choose to follow the example of the citizens of Britain. Choose to join us in the care and custodianship of the Deliverer. Throw off the shackles of thinking for yourselves. Choose the freedom of the Deliverer's service. It would be better for you if you did.'

'Hold on,' detected Ben, 'here comes the punchline.'

With the camera moving into close-up. Dr Kwalele, unblinking and unstoppable. 'For if you do not obey the will of the Deliverer, if you foolishly attempt to resist the order he brings, then he will be forced to impose it. All will have the blessings of peace bestowed upon them. Praise the Deliverer.'

NINE

To say that Kate's family's cabin was off the beaten track was an understatement. There appeared to be no track anywhere close, beaten or unbeaten, just an uneven, rocky slope with pine trees clinging to it like mountaineers in distress. Luckily for the Deveraux contingent, some had given up the struggle and toppled, leaving patches of ground bare enough for Eddie to attempt a landing. The cabin itself, timber-built and shuttered, occupied a clearing some five hundred metres further down the mountain. 'Nice parking, Ed, and don't worry,' Bex grinned, 'I reckon we can walk there from here.' It was early morning.

Kate obviously didn't have a key, but between them her companions could have broken into the White House, Buckingham Palace and Number Ten Downing Street all before breakfast. They made short work of the cabin's security. Inside there were several mod cons, including satellite videvision, and a small but gratefully received stock of canned goods left behind the last time the cabin was occupied.

'When *were* you here last, Kate?' Cally asked.

'Oh, I'm not sure. A while back.'

'It's a roof,' said Eddie, 'but I'm not sure it was meant for fifteen. If anybody's been eating curry lately, I think we should be told.'

'We're not here on vacation, Nelligan,' scowled Corporal Keene.

'Don't I know it. There's not even a pool.'

'Violet, Bowler, get the videvision working. Let's see how the world's reacting to the Deliverer. Lacey, Luanne, try to activate Professor Newbolt's CAP. We're going to need him.' Once again Senior Tutor Grant was falling into old habits of allocating responsibilities. 'Take him through to the bedroom.'

Once again, Ben was resenting it. 'Sir,' he interrupted.

'Korita. Keene. Quartermasters and cooks. I don't care what it is as long as it's hot.'

'Sir . . .'

'What is it, Agent Stanton?'

'Might we have a word?'

'We might,' said Grant. 'If it's relevant to the mission.'

'Oh, I think it's very relevant, sir,' Ben stressed, 'to *our* mission.'

The emphasis was obvious and told Grant everything. 'I see. You don't think the Deveraux College's Senior Tutor should be giving orders, Agent Stanton?' He noted that the rest of Bond Team were falling in with Stanton, presenting a united front, even Daly. It made him feel proud. It made him feel old. Senior Tutor Elmore Grant ran his hand through his greying hair. Maybe his job was done after all.

'We're not *at* Spy High any more, sir,' Ben said.

'We're in the field, on active mission status. That means final authority is entrusted to graduate agents, and that means us. I don't want to sound blunt, sir, but here and now we outrank you.'

Grant smiled thinly. 'Thank you for drawing the matter to my attention, Ben. I take it the rest of you are in agreement?'

'Too right,' said Jake.

'Kids giving you grief, sir?' Corporal Keene's tenure as an opener of cans had not lasted for long. He was looking for a more combative occupation again.

'It's all right, Keene.'

'They've always been lippy, this lot. Indisciplined. They were a rabble back in training.'

'Yeah?' snorted Jake. 'Well this rabble just saved your butt, Corporal Keene, or was it some other guy with a rock for a head we just sprung from a cell?'

'Still got a big mouth, Daly,' glowered Keene. 'Still need it *shut*.'

'You volunteering, big guy?' Jake beckoned Keene on. 'You can try.'

'Daly,' cautioned Grant. 'Keene.'

But the Corporal wasn't listening. 'Maybe I will at that.' He bulged forward.

'Or maybe you won't.' Ben stepped across his line, blocking his path.

Mr Korita was suddenly at Keene's side. His expression was unreadable, but his aggressive posture communicated his intentions more than adequately.

'No you don't.' Cally joined her boyfriend. 'Only person who lays hands on blue eyes here is me.'

'Then perhaps you should exercise some restraint, my

dear.' Violet Crabtree. 'These days young people are *so* physical.'

'No way,' declined Cally. 'I don't fight pensioners.'

'You're likely to be at a disadvantage, then, aren't you?' said Violet.

'Okay, okay, that's *enough*.' Lori stepped between staff and students. 'Or have you forgotten we're supposed to be on the same side? I know we're under pressure, but falling out and arguing amongst ourselves is *not* going to have Mr Deveraux shaking in his circuits. We've got *one* enemy and he's not in this room. Let's remember that.'

'Good call, Lo,' supported Bex.

'Agent Angel is right, of course,' said Grant. 'As was Agent Stanton, though in some ways it grieves me to admit it. No one likes to hand the baton of leadership to a younger generation, but in essence that is the whole purpose of the Spy High project, to train the young to keep the world safe for tomorrow. It seems that for us tomorrow has finally come. The floor, as they say, Bond Team, is yours.'

'Thanks,' said Lori, and quickly before Ben or Jake could speak, 'but I think the point Ben was *really* trying to make before we all got – um – sidetracked, was that if we're going to stand any chance of defeating Mr Deveraux we need to work as a team, all of us, under the agents' direction, fair enough, but still a team of equals pooling our skills and resources. That was your point, wasn't it, Ben?'

'Well, actually . . .' Ben began.

'Sure it was.' Cally translated the raising of Lori's eyebrows. She wrapped herself round Ben. 'And we love him for it.' And glued her mouth to his. A gag, but not an unpleasant one.

'Great.' Eddie clapped his hands. 'Now that we're all friends again, what's on the old vid, Bowler?'

'Unfortunately, Master Edward,' said Bowler from the videvision, 'nothing one would want to see.'

Panic. Chaos. Riots. Across the world. Every channel showed the same. The populations had witnessed what the Deliverer had done to the inhabitants of Britain, and most of them evidently didn't want the same thing to happen to them. They were tending to express their disinclination in violence, presumably while they still could. Some, however, seemed to be taking a different view. There was footage of marches and meetings *welcoming* the advent of the Deliverer, people praising, praying to him as if he was God Himself poised to wipe clean their souls of sin; there were people begging to be relieved of their free will, of responsibility for their actions, their lives. There are always some who find it safer and easier *not* to think for themselves. And where the believers and the unbelievers clashed, as was occurring with increasing frequency around the globe, blood flowed.

'Whatever we're gonna do,' Bex said bleakly, 'we'd better do it soon.'

'Ah,' alerted Grant, 'here's the Professor back to join us.'

Professor Henry 'Gadge' Newbolt shuffled into the cabin's sitting area from one of its bedrooms. He was assisted by Shades and Lacey Bannon steadying him at the arms. His mouth was still hanging open and his head wobbling as if his neck was made of rubber, but his skull was now adorned by a strange new embellishment. It was like a steel hand pressed down on his scalp, forcing the Professor's hair into bizarre tufts that sprouted between the five metal fingers. These reached to his fore-head and temples where they were attached by virtue of electronic webbing. A kind of tube extended from the back of the head and plugged into the nape of Newbolt's neck. The whole was topped by an opaque mound within which blue lights winked like friendly eyes.

'Is that Gadge's CAP?' said Jake.

'Indeed it is,' affirmed Grant with some pride. Those Bond Teamers who had not been present at the court-house cells exchanged puzzled glances. 'Or to put it more precisely, Professor Newbolt is wearing a Cerebral Amplifcation Prosthetic – a CAP.'

'They're gonna love him in Paris and Milan,' commented Eddie.

'I'm guessing it's not intended for fashion purposes,' Bex said.

'Certainly not,' confirmed Grant. 'The CAP was one of Professor Newbolt's final inventions. He began develop-ing it after his first breakdown in anticipation of another. The device works by connecting its own electronic cir-cuitry to the neural energy in the wearer's brain. It interfaces with the wearer's knowledge and intellect directly, so to speak, bypassing those parts of the brain that might be damaged by either injury or, in Newbolt's case, mental illness. The brain's neural signals are then converted into data that in turn is translated into a form that we can understand, speech. Professor Newbolt may no longer be able to conduct a conversation orally, but with his CAP fitted he can still make himself understood. He can still talk to us and we to him. Mr Deveraux's ani-mates removed the prosthetic when they captured Serenity. They ought to have destroyed it.'

'That's right.' Bex regarded Newbolt with an uncertain mixture of pity, admiration and resentment. 'Gadge was there the first time I saw my new dad. He can be there at the end, too. If anyone knows Jonathan Deveraux's weaknesses, it'll be Newbolt.'

Ben seemed unimpressed, particularly when Lacey Bannon wiped a runner of dribble from the Professor's chin. 'So why isn't anything happening? Isn't it working or something?' He knew that without the technology that Spy High placed at his disposal, much of it the product of Gadge's scientific genius, he'd probably be immortalised in the Hall of Heroes by now and his loved ones reduced to referring to him in the past tense, but even so, he still didn't like to place too much faith in computers and machines. Ben Stanton preferred to depend on himself.

'The device will take a little while to reacclimatise to Henry's neural patterns,' said Shades, her cyber-eyes on Ben. 'Give it time, Agent Stanton.'

'At least we've got time, right, Ben?' Cally said encouragingly. 'Thanks to Kate. Who'd have thought we'd need to rely on a Brit to find us a hideout in our own country? Lucky she's been to the States before.'

'We British do have our uses,' Bowler said, much to everyone's amusement.

Except Bex's. Rather than smile, Bex felt a sudden compulsion to frown. What had Kate said aboard the jet? 'My parents own a cabin . . . we used to go there for holidays when I was small.' And what had she said when Bex first met her at Spy High and asked if this was her first time in the States? 'Yes, and it's taking a bit of getting used to.' So were the apparent inconsistencies in first-year student Kate Taylor's memories.

Bex surveyed the cabin. It didn't take long. 'Where *is* Kate?' she said.

'She went outside a couple of minutes ago,' supplied Cally.

Bex cursed herself. Metal in her face. Metal in her head. She should have picked up on Kate's lie as soon as it was uttered. But no, she'd allowed herself to become so focused on her father that she'd proved remiss in her most basic duty as a Deveraux operative, to be aware of what was happening around her. The Kate Taylor who'd fled Spy High was not the Kate Taylor who'd arrived at the Refuge. Somehow, Dad had gotten to her.

And now he was going to use her to get to *them*.

'Excuse me,' Bex said, 'I just need to . . .' She gestured vaguely towards the door.

'There is a loo inside, Bex,' said Eddie.

She smiled weakly, stepped out and closed the door behind her. There was a chance she was wrong, though it was supermodel slim. But she, Bex, had brought Kate Taylor among them. If the girl was now controlled by Deveraux, it was down to her to deal with it.

She scanned the area. She'd left her radar visor in the cabin but it didn't matter. Kate wasn't trying to hide. She was standing just beyond the clearing under the trees. She was using a communicator. Bex doubted she was letting her parents know that their holiday home had guests.

'*Kate.*' Bex's tone was cold. She strode purposefully towards the student.

'Hello, Bex.' Kate pocketed the communicator and smiled. 'Is anything wrong?

'Yeah. *You* are. Did my dad say hi?'

'Bex, I don't know what you mean.' All shocked inno-
cence.

'I think you do.' All grim accusation.

'Very well, then. The Deliverer asked me to give you a
message. *This*.'

Sleepshot. Bex was already running before the
younger girl fired. As the wristbands flashed she pitched
herself forward, dived beneath the pellets' trajectory and
thudded bruisingly into the earth, but forward-rolled and
launched herself again with even greater force. Her
second collision was with Kate.

Both girls went down. Kate's knee came up. A sharp
pain in Bex's belly. The student yelled and threw Bex off.
A wild scramble as each of the combatants sought to be
first on her feet. Kate thought it was going to be her but
Bex had changed her tactics. She stayed crouched,
weight on her hands, swung with her legs and took
Kate's from under her. The traitor crashed to the stony
soil a second time.

Now Bex leaped on top of her and pinned her arms to
her sides. 'Let's talk.'

'There's a lot of anger in you, Bex. I know how you
need never feel anger again.'

'Yeah, yeah. How did he find you, Kate?'

'On the road to Boston. A wheelless stopped to give
me a lift. Senior Tutor Bright was inside. But I'm glad,
Bex, glad the Deliverer found me.' The girl's eyes glazed
like a saint in rapture. 'Life in his service is so easy and
free of care.'

'Yeah, it's pretty free of moral scruples, too, huh,
Kate? Betraying your friends like I assume you've just
done.'

'We will be friends again, Bex,' predicted Kate comfortingly, 'when you have joined us, when you have accepted the Deliverer.'

'Please,' Bex said with distaste, 'just tell me what your orders were.'

'Very well,' Kate obliged. 'I was to wait at the Refuge as you had originally instructed in case you managed to escape Egypt. If you did, if you came for me, I was to ingratiate myself with you and any other allies you might have found and await an opportune moment to draw you here, to this isolated place where no innocents are close by to get hurt.'

'Hurt?' Bex prompted.

'When the Deliverer comes for you.' And in a sudden rush, as if time was short: 'Don't resist him, Bex, don't fight him. Embrace him. Be one with him. Tell the others. Surrender is the only way to serve what is good.'

'Good, Kate,' gritted Bex, 'is *never* served by surrender. You sleep well now.'

No sooner had the sleepshot pierced Kate's skin than Bex was on her feet and sprinting for the cabin. 'Guys!' she cried. 'Guys!' Slamming open the cabin door with the effect of a stasis ray, everybody freezing. 'We've got to get out of here. Kate Taylor's under Dad's control.'

Nobody asked questions. Nobody expressed reservations. Everybody could suddenly move again, and they did so *quickly*.

'Bond Team,' snapped Grant, 'go ahead and ready the jet for take-off. We'll bring Newbolt. That is, unless . . .' He glanced from Ben to Lori.

'You took the words right out of my mouth, sir,' said Ben. 'Let's go, people.'

They raced up the slope as if expecting animates to launch an attack from the trees at any moment. It didn't happen. They reached the plane unmolested.

'Eddie and Cal, start the engines. We'll make sure you're not interrupted.' Lori prepared to stand guard.

'Shouldn't we go back for the others?' Bex asked. 'We don't want to lose Gadge now.'

'No need,' said Jake. 'They're here.'

The teachers emerged into the clearing, Keene and Lacey Bannon almost carrying the Professor between them. Violet Crabtree and Bowler were surprisingly *not* out of breath. 'Ah, a little vigorous exercise in the morning,' observed the Englishman, 'keeps one healthy.'

'Climb aboard, Bowler,' recommended Ben. 'I don't think Mr D cares too much for your health right now.'

At the controls, Eddie was coming to pretty much the same conclusion. On the radar, twin aircraft, approaching their position fast. ' 'Fraid we're gonna have to scrub the safety video, guys,' he reported. 'We need to be elsewhere now.'

With an explosive burst from the engine, the Deveraux jet rose vertically into the sky. Eddie didn't hang about. They'd scarcely cleared the treetops before he was engaging the forward thrusters and scorching above them. 'I think you just decapitated that squirrel, Ed,' said Cally.

Eddie wasn't listening as the plane gained height. Cally assumed that meant he was being serious for once. 'You might want to fasten your seatbelts back there,' he called to the main cabin. 'At least Gadge's. We've got company and it's gonna get *rough*.'

Scarcely any need to consult the radar screen now. A

glance out of the window was sufficient to confirm the pursuit of two Deveraux jets. Teachers and agents alike recognised the type. The Devjet Plus series. Customised to include weapons systems.

'So what?' Eddie said boldly. 'Mr D wants to control us, not kill us, doesn't he? They're not going to be shooting at us.'

'A teensy bit optimistic there, Ed,' said Cally.

The plane nearest to them fired its first missile.

TEN

The missile streaked harmlessly over their heads. Eddie didn't even need to alter height or direction. It detonated ahead of them, a firework without a display.

'Guy needs some major shooting practice,' considered Cally.

'That wasn't meant to hit us. It was meant to warn us. The next one'll be closer. They want to force us down.'

Eddie was evidently correct. A second missile flashed above. This time it would have hit had he not dipped the plane with sudden swiftness. The dull thud of flesh thumping against floor from the main cabin suggested that one person at least had not obeyed his earlier instruction.

'What are you going to do, Eddie?' Cally said.

'Well if whoever's fallen on their face reckons I'm gonna visit them in hospital they can forget it,' huffed Eddie. 'Why does nobody ever listen to me?'

'No, about our *pursuers*.'

'Oh, them. Well, *not* what I'm told. Why change the habit of a lifetime?' The red-haired boy winked. 'If they want us down, then we'll go *up*.'

Eddie yanked back on the controls and the jet climbed steeply. The third missile scarred the skies *beneath* them.

Cally scanned the instrument panels. 'I don't like to sound critical, Eddie, but while our two friends aren't exactly gaining, we're not losing them either. Any chance of acceleration?'

'We're pretty much on the max already, Cal.' Eddie gnawed his lower lip contemplatively. 'Trouble is, all three planes are built to the same basic spec. I don't see how we're going to be able to outrun these jokers. Unless . . .'

'Unless?' Cally pressed. It was the answers to the unlesses of mission situations that kept an agent alive.

'I always wanted to be a high-flyer, Cal, didn't you? Up, up and awaay . . .'

The pointing of the jet's nose almost to the vertical and the plane's continued hectic ascent did not go unnoticed among the passengers in the main cabin. Ben even paused in the rubbing of his left elbow, bruised when he'd fallen to the floor a few moments ago. 'What does Eddie think he's doing?' he frowned. 'This isn't the space shuttle.'

The plane rolled abruptly as evasive manoeuvres kept it safely distant from another explosive message from the chasing craft. Ben's right elbow was in trouble now as well.

'That *does* it.' Bond Team's original leader was not happy. He lurched to his feet and towards the cockpit.

'Don't go in there mad, Ben.' His successor joined him. 'Eddie must know what he's doing.'

'Must? Why? He never has before.' But Ben could always be restrained by Lori.

And then the jet itself began to shudder, to shake. Its fixtures rattled.

'You think it knows it's relying on Eddie to keep it in one piece and's panicking?' Jake said. He didn't feel quite as amused as he hoped he sounded. He doubted there were parachutes packed for fourteen if the worst came to the worst.

'We're flying too high.' Senior Tutor Grant's reading of the situation was more prosaic. 'There's stress on the hull.'

'We keep climbing like this and we'll shake apart,' predicted Lacey Bannon.

'What's Nelligan trying to do?' Corporal Keene lumbered to his feet. 'Score points with Deveraux by killing us himself?'

'One is aware that stress is not limited to the hull,' said Bowler. He stood too, in front of Keene. 'But one doubts that intemperate outbursts will assist Master Edward in keeping us all *alive*. Do you not agree, Corporal?'

'Bowler's right,' Bex defended her partner. 'Eddie must have a plan.'

'Then he won't mind telling me what it is – *us* what it is,' adjusted Ben when it was obvious Lori was not about to let him enter the cockpit alone.

Which was a task in itself now. The two Bond Teamers had to haul themselves along by holding on to the backs of chairs. The floor was at sixty degrees and in need of stairs. Its vibrations, the tremors of the entire aircraft, were increasing.

'You all right, Cal?' said Ben as he and Lori finally gained their destination.

'Of course I'm all right, Ben.' Cally shook her head. 'What did you think?'

'*Eddie*,' said Lori.

'Hi, Lo,' replied Eddie cheerfully, 'if that's not a contradiction in terms. And if you're wondering why we're quite *so* high, as your pilot I'd like to inform you that it's the only way to keep out of Mr D's computerised clutches. We can't out-distance those goons so we've got to out-*think* them.'

'That'd be a first for you, Eddie,' grunted Ben, unconvinced.

'Ed,' Cally warned. 'Hull's just about reaching its tolerance.' Red lights flashed on the control panel in ominous emphasis.

'Officially,' Eddie qualified, a little brusquely. 'But the guys who build these babies always err on the side of caution. We can go higher. I know what this bird can take and it's more.'

Lori gazed out of the window. The air looked thin and pale outside, like the sky was an invalid. And was that – could she see the rim of the atmosphere itself? Were they at the very upper limits of the earth? 'It's how much more *we* can take I'm worried about, Ed,' she said.

The cockpit juddered. Its steel casing strained. The plane found a voice of groaning metal. Ben held on to Cally's seat and Lori to Eddie's. It was as well they were bolted to the floor.

'Fly me to the moon,' Eddie crooned, 'and let me play among the stars.'

'Exterior tolerances exceeded,' declared Cally.

The jet boomed hollowly like steel plates beaten.

'Yo, Sinatra,' snapped Ben. 'Lose height or lose your teeth, one or the other.'

'Not yet. Not *yet*.' Eddie's voice suddenly became stern with authority. '*Trust* me, Ben. If you do it once in your entire high-achieving life, do it now. I *know* what I'm doing. We *have* to keep climbing.'

Cries of protest and concern from the main cabin, now virtually below them. The wings were rippling. The glass of the windows trembled like puddles.

'If you're so sure, Eddie' – Lori's cheek was almost touching his – 'why are you sweating?'

'Wise up, Lo,' Eddie grinned, a little desperately. 'You always have that effect on me.'

'Okay,' growled Ben, 'it's the teeth.' He grabbed with one hand for Eddie's hair.

'No, Ben, wait!' Cally cried. 'Look!'

At the radar screen. The blips of the pursuing planes not nearing, not even maintaining distance. Falling away. Left behind. Losing range.

'I'm leaving on a jet plane – don't know when I'll be back again.' Eddie was rediscovering his singing voice, if not *precisely* the right tune.

Sixty degrees became fifty, then forty, then fewer still. Eddie levelled off.

'They're turning back,' Lori marvelled. 'You knew they would, didn't you, Ed?'

'Sure did,' claimed Eddie. 'I didn't think they could be such skilful, intuitive, all-round *excellent* pilots as yours truly. I reckoned they'd play the tolerances by the book and not dare follow us up this close to the limit, allowing us, on the other hand, to make a getaway so clean you could eat your in-flight packet of pretzels off it. Looks like I reckoned right, doesn't it?'

Lori kissed him. 'Just so you didn't work up that sweat for nothing.'

Ben showed *no* sign of puckering up to Eddie. 'You *reckoned*? You mean you risked all our lives on a hunch?'

'Apology accepted, Ben,' said Eddie. 'It'll be *plane* sailing from here on in.'

Bex wasn't sure she was enjoying listening to Professor Henry Newbolt. It wasn't what he was saying that made her almost physically uncomfortable; it was the fact that he wasn't really saying it, not in a lips, tongue and vocal chords kind of way. His mouth grinned idiotically as he slumped in his chair like he was drugged, and she could hear his natural voice giggling and burbling. It was the CAP that was communicating, the blue lights within its crown pulsing as the words came, and its voice was inflectionless, emotionless, anonymous, disconcertingly like her father's.

Talking of whom, everyone other than Eddie and Cally was gathered around Gadge in the main cabin to learn – hopefully – how Jonathan Deveraux could be defeated.

'His cyber-mind is almost infinitely powerful,' Newbolt said. 'It is practically invincible.'

'That's good news,' grunted Jake.

'Nobody's invincible,' Ben asserted. 'Everybody has a weakness.'

'Agreed, Agent Stanton,' said Grant, 'but does Jonathan Deveraux any longer truly qualify as a "body"?'

'*There* is the way forward, Elmore,' said Newbolt, and his hands made as if to clap. 'Your only chance is to target not the computer but the man.'

'But Dad was cremated, wasn't he?' Bex remembered the day, bleak and cold, and a glow of fire against the dark. 'I mean, there aren't any organic parts of him left, are there? He's not a cyborg, a human–silicon hybrid like Adam Thornchild. Unless . . .' For one grisly moment Bex wondered if Newbolt and his team of techs had scooped her father's brain out of his skull like ice cream from a tub.

'No,' said the Professor. 'Jonathan Deveraux no longer retains a human body of any description, but he does possess a human identity. Or did. I believe his present actions are a direct result of him losing touch with that identity, forgetting that he was once a mortal man.'

'Makes sense, I suppose,' Lori said sympathetically to Bex.

'Forgetting he had a daughter,' Bex said. Lori squeezed her hand.

'Those of us involved in the Deveraux Project had anticipated such a possibility,' Newbolt was continuing, 'and took steps to guard against it. Most of the files in Jonathan Deveraux's databanks are impersonal, in that they are not unique to their donor, Mr Deveraux's original brain. They contain knowledge, attitudes, beliefs that might also be shared by others. However, we also built in files that *are* personal and individual, memory files that we hoped would function as a permanent connection to the computerised man's past. We intended them to provide a balance between the human and the electronic, to form a defence against the machine element of Jonathan Deveraux taking over completely. We seem to have failed. Deveraux's apparent ends as you have described them to me remain essentially laudable – world peace and an end to violence – but the means he has adopted to achieve these ends are clearly unacceptable. They lack the human perspective. Somehow, his memory files have been compromised. In order to end the threat he currently poses, they must be restored.'

'So how are we going to do that?' Ben wanted to know. 'We can't just knock on Spy High's front door and announce we're here to give JD a systems check.'

Newbolt's fingers tapped his temples as if they understood what was happening after all and were quite reasonably questioning Ben's sanity. 'Someone must enter the computer mind of Jonathan Deveraux,' the Professor said. 'Someone must remind him he was human.'

'Not someone.' Bex's expression was flintily resolute. '*Me*. I'm the *only* one. His memories are my memories, some of them anyway. I can bring him back. I'm family.'

'You ought not to undertake this task alone,' Newbolt said, his upper body lolling in Bex's direction. 'Your father will have prepared defences of his own, firewalls, if you like. You will not be granted access to his inner consciousness easily.'

'She won't *be* alone,' Lori stated emphatically. 'Bond Team will be with her.'

Bex's tongue licked self-consciously at her lip-stud. 'Lori, you don't have to . . .'

'She *does* have to, Bex,' said Jake. 'We're together on this one. Cal and Eddie will be too.'

Ben nodded firmly. 'All the way.'

'Then I guess I should say thanks.' It seemed to Bex that Eddie's earlier manoeuvres had somehow affected the supply of air in the cabin. Her vision was quite misting over.

'So that's cyber-cradles for six and a quiet place to work,' concluded Ben.

'Where?' was Senior Tutor Grant's problem.

'I know where.' Bex had recovered her poise. 'It's been a long time since I've been home. Maybe I should put that right.'

There ought to be nostalgia, Bex thought. When you saw again the house where you were born, where you spent your earliest years, there ought to be feelings of warmth and affection, happy memories of carefree days and golden summers. When Eddie flew them over the Deveraux mansion prior to landing on the lawn, Bex felt none of that. She hadn't lived here for over five years, hadn't even visited in three, and the colours of her childhood had been darkened too fatally by bereavement for her to be reminded of sunshine and light. 'Home, sweet home,' she heard somebody say.

Hardly.

It was a relief to clamber out of the plane. Bex gazed across the perfectly-kept grounds to the house itself, its impressively pillared portico, the dignified ranks of its windows, its stainless white walls. Pristine and pre-served.

'I thought you said no one lives here now,' Ben reminded her.

'No one does.'

'So how come the grass is cut and the mansion looks like it's just been painted?'

'Animate labour,' said Bex. 'It's cheap and it doesn't complain.'

'Reminds me of an old girlfriend of mine,' mused Eddie.

'Let's get inside,' suggested Senior Tutor Grant. 'There may be no people here other than ourselves, but I have no doubt our arrival will be detected, and then Mr Deveraux will take action.'

'And this time we're not running,' said Jake grimly.

They crossed to the house. Newbolt still required assistance from Lacey and Shades: the CAP had little effect on his legs. No deactivator was necessary to gain entrance. Bex simply keyed in her access code.

They were greeted in the capacious vestibule by an animate dressed in a frock coat, wing-collared shirt and pinstripe trousers. It was clearly an animate because its maker had not dwelt overlong on the head, which was little more than a skull.

'I guess this is what they call a skeleton staff,' said Eddie. 'And hey, Bowler, looks like this bozo's been raiding your wardrobe.'

'What an amusing observation, Master Edward,' said Bowler with the slight raising of the eyebrows that for him corresponded to high good humour. 'Might one also draw your attention to the weapons attachment protruding from the fellow's right arm.'

The barrel of a blaster burrowing from the animate's wrist and keeping the group covered.

'Please stay where you are,' invited the animate. 'This unit has received no advance notification of your arrival. This unit is communicating with Mr Deveraux to—'

Twin shock blasts blew a hole in its torso and detached the right arm. Further communication was unlikely.

'I feel better now,' said Corporal Keene, admiring his blaster as a prospector would a gold nugget. 'I needed that.'

'Me too,' echoed Lacey Bannon, patting her weapon like a pet.

'Won't there be other animates, Bex?' Lori worried.

'Not once I've deactivated them from the central control panel.' She moved off quickly. 'Come on, it's in the downstairs study.'

With any further potentially obstructive robot employees removed, Bex led the way without a pause to the mansion's recreation wing. Its virtual reality chamber was not as extensive as Spy High's, though it was pretty much as advanced, but it did contain what were needed: cyber-cradles, pointing outwards from the main instrument banks like eight points of a star. More than sufficient for their purposes.

'I shall need assistance to bring the cradles on-line,' said Professor Newbolt, 'and to engineer access to the Deveraux system. I'm afraid my own manual skills are no longer adequate.' His fingers fluttered uselessly, like blind birds.

'We'd better help you with that,' said Grant, meaning the Deveraux staff. 'When the operation commences, Bond Team are going to be otherwise occupied.'

The cyber-cradles gleamed. Like glass coffins, Bex thought, and shuddered.

The bed was made, she noted, but otherwise her room was exactly as she'd left it when she'd moved to the apartment in New York. Hadn't been able to stay here any longer. Too many ghosts.

Bex wondered what a psytech would make of her room, her belongings, what inner truths they were revealing. The holo-prints of her one-time heroes on the walls, mostly cybertronic music stars, a few post-goths, either angry and confrontational or distant and aloof, masters of their own little worlds. Typical emblems of adolescent rebellion, the psytechs would say. They might be more intrigued by her choice of videoscapes, playing still on an eternal loop. The lonely beach at midnight. The tomb in the forest. Suggestive of a personality damaged by loss, they might say, of someone morbid and withdrawn, unable or unwilling to face the future.

'Nice room.' Lori in the doorway.

'Is Gadge ready for us?'

'Not quite. I just came to see where you were.'

'I'm here. Step on in if you like.'

Lori did. 'Nice house.'

'No house is nice if you lose both parents while you're living in it,' said Bex. 'That's kind of like pouring poison into a well. You can't drink there any more. It's spoiled.'

'Yeah, it was just something polite and superficial to say,' Lori admitted. 'Sorry.'

'No, I am. I don't mean to make you feel embarrassed, Lori, not you. I just guess I don't do polite and superficial. Maybe I'd get along easier if I did.'

'You wouldn't be you if you did,' Lori said.

'Would that be so bad?' grunted Bex.

'Would it be so good?'

Bex gave a hollow laugh. 'You been taking a psytech training course on the quiet, Lo?'

'You don't need a psytech to spot when something's wrong, Bex,' Lori said gently. 'You need a friend. It's your father, isn't it?'

'I've already had the pep talk – from Eddie, of all people – about how I'm not responsible for what Dad's doing and shouldn't feel guilty, and I don't, I really don't now . . .'

'I don't mean that,' interrupted Lori. 'I'm talking about your relationship with your dad *before* the Deliverer. Jonathan Deveraux, the computerised man. It can't have been easy.'

'It wasn't – it's not easy.' Bex sighed, sat down on her bed and hugged her shoulders forlornly. 'I can't handle it, Lori. Not any more. It's too much. When Mum died, that was bad. I mean, it was Bad bad. No kid of *any* age should have to lose her mum. But in time, as time passed, I don't think I got over it exactly, I don't think you ever get over someone close to you dying in the sense that you go back to what you were like before, but you adapt, don't you, you get used to the new circumstances and the new situation and you start a new chapter in your life. You grow. What's the buzz phrase these days? You move on. After Mum died, eventually I moved on.'

'But you can't do that with your dad?' Lori sat beside her friend. Her arm found its way around Bex's shoulders. The strident shock of orange hair. The studs and the piercings like self-inflicted wounds. To Lori, Bex suddenly appeared very young and very vulnerable.

'Lori, I'm not sure whether my dad's alive or dead. Is that really him on the screens at Spy High? Is that truly his voice that speaks to us? Or is it all some kind of sick high-tech trick? If it's Dad, why can't he say things to me that let me know? Why can't he say he loves me? I know he hasn't got any arms, but if he just *said* he wanted to hold me, that'd be good enough. I'd *know*. But he doesn't, does he? He never has. And if it's not him at all, if his name was just a way for Newbolt to get funding or something, then I want to know that for certain too. Maybe this whole Deliverer thing'll prove it. I mean, I'll mind but I won't mind. Being sure of the truth I'll be able to make decisions about my life, where I'm going, what I'm doing. Right now I can't. Right now I'm trapped.'

'Oh, Bex,' Lori comforted.

'I've tried to become my own person, Bex and not Rebecca. Rebecca perished with her parents. Even my code-name. If I used my first name like Jake and the others I'd have to be Rebecca Orange, and I'm not Rebecca. If I used my family name like you, Angel Blue, well, that was never going to be appropriate, either. So it's Agent Orange, plain and anonymous. Someone who's not sure who she is.'

'You're a good person, Bex,' said Lori. 'That's more important than a name.'

'Hey, though, you want to see who I *was*?'

The holo-room was further along the corridor. Like all such facilities, it was circular and it was featureless and its only furniture was a chair that reclined so far back it could almost be a bed. Neither Bex nor Lori took advantage of its added comfort today. They stood – 'Room,' requested the former, 'play Rebecca's First Steps' – as the years rolled back.

And there was laughter as Lori found herself on the mansion lawn that despite the beautiful weather had decided to come inside. Her friend was still with her. So were two adults, the male of whom she recognised as a slightly younger Jonathan Deveraux, while the woman she guessed must be Bex's mother. It was she who was doing most of the laughing, unaware that she would be dead within a year. There was applause, too, even Jonathan Deveraux was clapping, and lots of beckoning beyond Lori, *through* Lori, as though she was invisible. Participating in a holo-room scenario could be unsettling. Lori turned. A toddler with flailing arms, ruddy cheeks and unsteady legs waddled towards her shrieking with glee.

'Rebecca's First Steps?' Lori questioned.

'Close enough,' said Bex. 'It's hard learning to stand on your own two feet. So much easier if there's someone to catch you when you fall.'

The young Rebecca tottered through the phantom Lori and pitched forward into her mother's arms. Cheers from both her parents, her father's a little more decorous and reserved than her mother's. But he hugged his daughter as she was hoisted up. Lori saw the pain on Bex's face. Hugging a hologram was one thing you couldn't do.

'You sure this is a good idea?' she said.

'It is a very good idea, Agent Angel.' Newbolt had opened the door, or rather, Lacey Bannon had. She and Shades were supporting the Professor between them.

'Professor Newbolt.' Bex blushed as if she'd been caught doing something improper.

'The cyber-cradles are ready and time is short. But you may have just unwittingly provided us with a further weapon in our war against Mr Deveraux.'

'That was about the briefest briefing I've ever heard,' said Eddie.

'What is there to say?' shrugged Ben. All fourteen Deveraux operatives were assembled in the mansion's virtual reality chamber. 'We know what we've got to do. Use the cradles to send our virtual selves into cyber-space. Gadge has programmed Bex's system here to upload us into the Deveraux mainframe, at least as far as the fringes of Mr D's inner data consciousness. Then we locate his memory files and restore them.'

'It sounds so simple when you put it like that,' said Eddie.

'Should suit you just fine then, Ed.'

'Opening cradles,' informed Shades from the instrument banks. With a pneumatic hiss the glass shields of six of the cyber-cradles rose.

Soon now, Bex was thinking. Very soon and her relationship with her father would be resolved one way or another. She knew it. She yearned for it. Maybe this was why she'd been so eager to join the Spy High project, not for selfless reasons to do with saving the world, but for herself, in anticipation of this final confrontation with her father which she now realised had always been inevitable. She placed one foot inside the cradle.

Senior Tutor Grant tapped her shoulder. 'Aren't you forgetting something, Bex?'

She was. 'Oh. Sorry. I'm just . . .'

'Focused is the word,' said Grant understandingly. He waited while she unbuckled and handed over her mission belt. 'These won't be any good to you where you're going, but we'll need your communicators and all the firepower we can find if we're going to hold off Mr Deveraux's forces long enough for you to get the job done.' He received Bex's sleepshot wristbands too with thanks.

'We'll hold them off, won't we, Keene?' Lacey Bannon looked like she was relishing the challenge. It appeared she hadn't trained as a weapons instructor for nothing.

Grant was not so sanguine. 'Work quickly,' he advised. Bex nodded. 'Good luck, Bond Team.'

Lori was smiling across at her: 'See you on the other side, Bex.' Eddie was complaining: 'How come I always get the one that's too small?' Ben and Cally were stealing a kiss before sitting then lying down in their cradles. Jake was already silently strapped in.

Bex lowered herself, lay back on the leather cushioning, stretched out. She couldn't see the others now as she fastened the straps across her chest, only Grant and the inscrutable Mr Korita, their faces slightly distorted through the convex glass of the shield. She was alone. No real change there, then. And her heart was racing as she fought to control her breathing. A relaxed subject helped the transfer.

Which was beginning. The virtual sensors nuzzled against her temples. The shield descended, clicked smoothly into place. The cyber-cradle was sealed. Now it was humming as the power increased.

Bex thought of the sarcophagi in which she'd discovered her partners in the tomb of Kadeishi. They'd looked a bit like cyber-cradles and they'd formed a trap. She wondered if Bond Team weren't about to enter another one, all of them this time.

She closed her eyes. The transfer proceeded. When she opened them again, she'd know.

ELEVEN

'**W**e're here,' Bex heard Lori announcing.

'Is it too late to back out?' Eddie. 'Is it me, or does this place make everyone feel uncomfortable?'

Bex opened her eyes. It seemed they were standing on an endlessly flat plain. Beneath their feet was something like grey soil and close up it wasn't absolutely level but ridged and bumped, and it wasn't granular like earth but more like cobbles, only the substance was spongier than stone. The soles of their boots sank in a little.

'I mean, what sort of muck *is* this?' Eddie made a face. The matter beneath them was throbbing, pulsing. It was *alive*.

Ben looked up. The sky, such as it was, formed another surface like the ground, identically flat, grey and solid. Bond Team were caught between them. And they were not alone.

A human brain floated above them and some way off – distances were difficult to judge without landmarks – like an intelligent cloud. Disembodied: the brain stem waggled in the air. Gigantic: like an organic mountain or an alien space station. 'Oh, that's gross.' One of Eddie's functions in Bond Team was to express aloud what his partners tended only to think. The cerebrum itself, the principal part of the brain, knobbed and bulged and wrinkled with lobes, was folded over, from a side view like a clay man huddled and kneeling. Beneath it and to the rear the cerebellum protruded like a vast walnut. A front view revealed the organ's left and right hemispheres split by a deep, narrow canyon, connected only by the corpus callusum. Gadge Newbolt's briefing might have been short, but he *had* included a rudimentary introduction to the constituent elements of the brain.

Eddie clapped his hand on his skull. Distastefully: 'And I've got one of *those* inside here?'

'I wouldn't bet on it, Ed,' remarked Ben.

'Less banter, more action.' Jake was no happier than Eddie, but he was directing his discomposure more immediately towards mission ends. 'The brain is where we need to go.'

'It's not a real brain anyway, Ed,' Lori reminded him. 'It's a virtual expression in a humanly comprehensible form of Jonathan Deveraux's inner data consciousness, his cyber-mind itself.'

'Oh,' said Eddie weakly, 'so that's what it is. Thanks, Lo.'

'That's what this entire environment is.' Cally knelt, fascinated, pressed her fingers into the grey and pulsating substance on which they stood. 'This "ground" is made of the same material as the brain. So's what's passing as the sky. Human cerebral tissue.'

'This just keeps getting better,' groaned Eddie.

'Tissue with a twist,' Cally added. 'Look. It's kind of

webbed – and no internet jokes, please. It's covered in a pattern of tiny electronic parts, like the grid on the surface of a microchip.'

'Terrific,' said Jake tetchily. 'So?'

'So speak to Cally with some consideration,' warned Ben.

'No bickering, boys,' snapped Lori. 'Not here. Not now.'

'*So*,' Cally continued undeterred, 'it means that Mr D is in control of this whole landscape, not just the brain. Which means we'd better be careful.'

'We'll be careful, Cal,' said Ben. He glanced at the mission belts, the holstered shock blasters and the sleepshot wristbands with which the cyber-cradles' transference program had re-equipped them. Virtual versions all, useless in the physical world, but this was cyber-space and the rules were different.

'Bex?' Lori noticed that Deveraux's daughter was standing a little apart from the rest of them, gazing distractedly at the looming mass of her father's brain. 'You okay?'

'We need to reach the temporal lobe.' She recited the details of their briefing. 'The temporal lobe is the part of the brain that stores memories. Newbolt built in an access point. We can use it to enter Jonathan Deveraux's most private mind.'

'I'd have preferred a yes or a no,' said Lori.

'I'm okay.' Bex smiled. It wasn't convincing.

Jake, though, took her at her word. 'Then let's go.' He started off towards the brain. 'I'm worried that Grant and the others'll fold if/when Deveraux attacks and some animate'll pull the plug on us.'

He might have been better advised to worry about himself first and foremost. As Jake broke into a jog, the ground in front of him without warning erupted.

'What's happening?' Senior Tutor Elmore Grant ran his hand through his hair and tried hard not to interpret the information on the cyber-cradles' life support panels negatively. 'The kids' readings are changing. Newbolt?'

They'd found a chair for the Professor so that Lacey and Shades could be released for other, probably more violent duties. The CAP's blue lights flashed. 'This was to be expected, Grant,' Newbolt said. 'That monitor works like a normal EEG, recording and measuring the electrical activity of the subjects' brains.'

'It's going wild.'

'A little dramatic, though Bond Team are clearly experiencing increased stress. Their heart-rates are beginning to accelerate, too. I would surmise that Deveraux has detected the intruders in his cyber-mind and is engaging them.'

'Trying to kill them, you mean.' Grant regarded the six teenagers in the steel and glass caskets with a pride and affection he would have been unlikely to demonstrate were their eyes open.

'There is nothing we can do for them.' Newbolt had never seemed so unsympathetic before he'd had to let a machine do his talking.

'Not in cyber-space, maybe,' Grant admitted, 'but we can do plenty for them here. Teams.' He turned to his colleagues. 'Lacey and Keene. Bowler and Violet. Korita and Luanne. We're never going to be able to defend the entire mansion but we *have* to protect this virtual reality chamber. It generates its own power, so all the while it's out of Deveraux's hands Bond Team can operate. I think we can assume an animate assault any time soon. Try and prevent them from entering the mansion for as long as you can, then fall back by teams towards the recreation wing. Hold them off. This is where we make our last stand if we have to. I'll stay with Newbolt.'

'You'll miss out on all the fun, Grant,' said Lacey Bannon.

'Maybe, but my legs are playing up.' It was an old joke. Grant's flesh-and-blood legs had been torn from his body by a terrorist bomb years ago. He was presently borne up by state-of-the-art constructs in steel and synthetic skin. 'Besides, someone might be needed to work the instruments.'

'Let's go then.' Corporal Keene, living up to his name and champing at the bit. 'For all we know Deveraux's toys could be landing on the lawn already.'

'What an unpleasant prospect,' sniffed Bowler.

'They're not here yet, Keene,' informed Luanne 'Shades' Carmody, 'but they're coming. According to the radar function of my right eye, several aircraft fast approaching. Attack helicopters.'

'Animates are untrustworthy sorts at the best of times,' grumbled Violet Crabtree. 'What's to stop them simply blowing us, Bond Team and the mansion to kingdom come?'

'The Deliverer desires peace,' said Grant. 'He'll want us stopped, not slaughtered. Right, Korita?'

The martial arts man nodded but remained ninja silent.

'Take one communicator per team,' Grant instructed

finally, 'and keep in touch. And listen. I know Spy High was always about training teenagers to be the next generation of world-saving secret agents, but there's something to be said for experience too. All of us have been there, done that, shot the terrorist. Some of us even left some of us behind. Now's our chance to prove we're not past it yet. Now's our chance to stand up and be counted, one last time.'

'How very inspiring,' said Bowler.

'Jake! My God!' Bex was racing with the others to their team-mate's side. He was spitting and coughing and rolling on the ground but he didn't seem badly hurt. 'Are you . . .?'

'I'm fine. I'm fine. Just got a faceful of this gunk.' He wiped gobbets of grey tissue from his face and the splattered tunic of his stealth-suit. 'Raw brains. Tastes like chicken. Blast went over my head.'

Ben and Cally helped Jake up. 'Not that this means I'm remembering you in my will, mind, Daly,' Ben warned.

'Did you tread on something?' Lori looked for explanations. 'A mine or something?'

'If I had I doubt I'd still be wearing both feet.'

'You think we're in a minefield, Lo?' Eddie didn't like the sound of that.

He didn't like the sound of the second explosion, either, or the third. Further eruptions of cerebral matter, but neither particularly near the teenagers and unlikely to have been specifically triggered by them.

'Not quite a minefield, Eddie,' mused Cally. 'More like a *mind*-field. Deveraux's brain protecting itself from unwanted guests. Us.'

Another blast, this time very close. A spray of grey clods striking them stingingly.

'My ex-girlfriend hits harder than that,' snorted Eddie. 'If this is the best JD can do . . .'

'I don't think we want to be right on top of one of these explosions, Eddie,' Cally cautioned. 'Remember, I know that intellectually we're aware this is all virtual, an advanced illusion, but physiologically our bodies back in the cyber-cradles aren't. They feel it's real. If we're hurt here, it's the same there. We can be killed without physically receiving a wound, simply because we *think* we've been killed.'

'Me,' said Eddie, 'I'm a great believer in the power of *positive* thinking.'

'Me,' snapped Ben, 'I'm a great believer in the power of positively shutting up and fulfilling our mission objectives. The *brain*, guys. It hasn't moved and neither have we. And those damned explosions keep on coming.'

Ben was right. The detonations were increasing in both number and frequency. The grey plain was quickly turning into the mud of the Somme during an artillery barrage. The giant brain hovered above the carnage, serene and aloof.

'We can't afford to keep together!' Jake shouted. 'Spread out and run for it. Then if one blast gets lucky, it won't get us all.'

'Meet at the temporal lobe!' Lori called out.

'Makes a change from the pub or outside the cinema, I guess,' said Eddie.

Bex watched him sprint off. He ran in an exaggeratedly zig-zag pattern, as if convinced that keeping to a straight line could only damage his chances of survival.

Lori and Jake seemed to have either ignored or discounted that possibility, probably because there was no way of knowing where the next blast would detonate: they surged towards their destination as if they had tunnel vision. Cally and Ben ran together, holding hands, rejecting Jake's advice – not unusual for Ben – and clearly determined to share whatever fate awaited them.

And Bex raced forward too. The last member of Bond Team to do so but she didn't care. She felt no sense of haste or danger. There was a belief in her, a faith, that the surrounding explosions would not and could not harm her, that nothing in cyber-space, none of Jonathan Deveraux's defences, was going to be able to prevent her from confronting him at the end – face to file.

'No!' Cally. She and Ben struck to the ground by a geyser of grey matter.

Everybody else heard her cry. Everybody else should have registered its cause and likely consequences and then have carried on for the temporal lobe. Casualties in mission situations were only to be expected; they were regrettable but inevitable; the manual said that agents should not be diverted from their prime objective by the loss of a team-mate.

On the whole, Bond Team didn't give a monkey's for the manual.

Eddie was still zig-zagging when he was the last to reach Cally and Ben. Superficial wounds only. Jake was helping Ben up. 'Not that this means I'm remembering you in my will, Stanton,' he was grinning.

'No, no, *no*!' Something still seemed to be disturbing Cally. 'I'm an idiot. I should have seen it sooner.' Her gaze seized eagerly on Ben, on her partners. 'These explosions aren't random at all. They're part of a mathematical progression. Which means if I can work it out I can predict the pattern and guide us through to the brain' – she turned to survey the erupting landscape – 'without' – her mind raced – 'any more . . .' The others could almost see the calculations behind her eyes. 'That's it! Come on, follow me, keep behind me.'

Bex was reminded of that old Christmas carol, 'Good King Wenceslas'. The saintly monarch had evidently been prone to taking his constitutional in subzero temperatures, with his accompanying page boy skinny and shivering. But when the boy trod in the footsteps of his master, the cold melted from his bones and he was warm again, safe, protected. Bex felt they were following Cally's footsteps in much the same way – though a little faster – and to much the same effect. Unerringly she led her partners between explosions and the torrents of tissue did not touch them.

'Great work, Cal,' praised Ben.

Deveraux's brain cast its dark shadow upon them. As soon as the teenagers had darted directly beneath it, the cyber-environment's defences appeared to concede reluctant defeat. Silence and stillness again across the grey expanse.

'I guess that's one to us,' said Eddie.

'Let's not stop there.' Cally was gaining in confidence, head thrown back and studying the spongy lumps of the brain as if they were the details of a map. 'The temporal lobe's underneath where the temple would be if this thing was in its skull. Over this way – look, I can see the access point.'

So could Bex. Twin circular metal plates, one set into

the brain itself, the other aligned below and sunk into the ground. She assumed entry into her father's inner consciousness would be facilitated by a process similar to a tractor beam. All you had to do was stand on the plate and . . . That was *too* easy.

'I guess all we do is stand on the plate. Follow the leader,' grinned Cally.

Good King Wenceslas, thought Bex. 'Cally, wait!' she shouted.

Too late. Cally didn't wait. She jumped on to the access point.

Which was booby-trapped.

A laser bolt flashed from the upper plate. Cally screamed as it struck her, as her body sparked and crackled like a severed electric cable.

'Cal!' Ben was rushing forward to catch her as she fell. Eddie and Lori and Jake were firing their shock blasters at the offending metal disc. Bex could only feel her heart sinking.

'My God, Cally!' Ben was kneeling, clasping her to him. Her eyelids were fluttering, she was struggling to speak, but there were no words. Her skin was glowing like radiation sickness, and not just her skin, her clothes too, her whole body. 'What do we do?' Ben appealed. 'We've got to help her. What do we do?'

'I don't . . .' Lori was lost. 'Ben!'

Cally was subtly but certainly changing shape. The natural curves and contours of her form were straightening, stiffening, flattening, the physical three dimensions of her body becoming two. Across her figure, swarming, occupying, converting, countless tiny square tiles, creating a grid, forcing Cally to conform to it.

'It's turning her into pixels,' Jake gasped. 'Making Cally a computer image.'

Bex muttered under her breath: 'So Dad can delete her.'

Ben cried out in mingled rage and despair. He could no longer hold his stricken girlfriend. She was an icon in a stained-glass window, an outline on a screen. She was no longer real.

And now the tiles began to vanish, the pixels stripped off a row at a time. Deconstruction. And Cally's eyes were open as her feet and legs were removed from her, as the dissipation reached her waist and nibbled away at her fingers, her hands, her arms. She was reduced to a head, her dreadlocks disappearing like burning fuses. She was eyes, wide and sad and pleading. Eyes that sought Ben. Eyes that were gone.

Of Calista Green, no trace now remained.

'Professor!' In the virtual reality chamber of the Deveraux mansion, Senior Tutor Elmore Grant was perturbed. 'What does this mean?'

According to the instruments, Agent Cross's life support readings had just flatlined.

'She's not . . .?' Because, though he didn't want to acknowledge the fact, Grant thought he *did* know what it meant.

'No,' Newbolt reassured. 'Agent Cross is not dead. The stasis indicator is on.'

'And stasis is good?'

'I'm afraid not. Cyber-stasis means that her virtual self has suffered significant trauma which has induced a catatonic state, a virtual coma, you might say. She can no longer be of assistance to her team-mates, and unless they succeed in their objective, thus removing the root cause of the stasis, Agent Cross will not recover.'

'One down, five to go, Jonathan,' Grant muttered darkly. 'What next?'

His communicator flashed. Corporal Keene: 'They're landing, sir. They're here. Shades was right. Two attack helicopters packed with animates. They're coming our way.'

'Hold them, Corporal,' Grant said steadily. 'We're relying on you.'

What next? The final battle.

TWELVE

Ben was in shock, his fingers clutching at empty air for Cally. Jake and Lori helped him gently to his feet, and this time the black-haired boy made no comment.

'He killed her. He killed her just like that, like she was nothing.'

'Ben.' Lori squeezed him tight.

'I don't think Cally's dead,' said Bex.

'You don't?' Ben spoke half in scorn, half in hope. 'What do you think we just saw, then, O Daughter of Deveraux?'

Bex ignored the sarcasm. 'We saw Cal deleted, removed from the system.'

'That sounds pretty much like fatal to me.'

'No. Not if we take charge of the program. We *still* have to defeat my father. Nothing's changed.'

'Nothing's changed?' Ben laughed bitterly. 'Listen to *her*.'

'Not in mission terms. We press on. We have to. We restore my father's memories. We return the Deveraux program to what it was before the Deliverer corrupted it.

And that way we restore Cally too. To *us*, Ben. To you. We can bring her back.'

'You think so?' His blue eyes bored into Bex's green.

'I know so.' She returned his stare unflinchingly.

'I'll hold you to that, Bex. If you're wrong, we'll talk again.'

'So are we, like, carrying on?' ventured Eddie.

'What do you think?' Ben almost visibly pulled himself together. 'We're not only saving the world now. We're saving Cally as well.' He made a step towards the access point.

'Hold on, Big Guy,' Jake intervened. 'What if it's still not safe?'

'What if it's not *working*?' added Lori. 'We blasted the upper disc with all we've got.'

Eddie inspected for damage. 'And we didn't even scratch it,' he reported. 'So is that good or bad?'

'Newbolt didn't put in the booby-trap,' Bex reasoned, 'so Dad must have done. Let's hope he was thinking in terms of single intruders and one-off laser bolts to deal with them.'

'You mean Cally's *deletion* might have opened up the way for the rest of us?' Ben looking for a positive.

'Only one way to find out.' She wasn't fated to follow Cally. She was destined to confront her father. Her conviction made her strong. Bex stepped on to the plate.

'Bex, wait!' And she heard Lori calling after her and then there was only the rush of velocity in her ears and a brilliant light in her eyes that blinded her, and she ought to be rising if she was going to enter the brain but it felt like falling.

'Dad!' Bex cried out. 'Dad! Can you hear me?'

Evidently not, and perhaps because she was now elsewhere. Solid ground again beneath her feet, not cerebral tissue either. Bex seemed to have left the brainscape behind. She was somewhere altogether more familiar. The grand drive leading first into forest. The arched gateway. The nameplate on the pillar: *The Deveraux College*. Blue sky. The slightest of breezes in summer warmth. It was a beautiful day.

Her four surviving team-mates were there to share it with her. They may have departed the brainscape separately, but they'd arrived here together.

'We're back at Spy High?' Jake was uncustomarily bewildered. 'How come we're back at Spy High?'

'I don't think we are,' said Lori. 'Not physically.'

'Don't knock it anyhow,' Eddie advised. He raised his face to the sky. 'The only thing I want to see up there from now on is the sun.'

'You were right about the access point, Bex,' Ben acknowledged with a nod. 'We're in, aren't we? This is Mr D's innermost consciousness.'

Bex returned the nod. 'Again, it's a representation in spatial terms that the human mind can assimilate, but this is it, yeah. The place most precious to Jonathan Deveraux. The Deveraux College itself.'

'So what do we do now?' Eddie said uncertainly. 'Like, go to class?'

'We go to Dad's rooms,' Bex said. 'The point within the construct most closely associated with him. That's where Newbolt told us his core data files will be found, his memory files. Anybody want to get religious? His *soul*.'

'And JD's gonna let us walk right on in and mess with his mind?' said Jake sceptically.

'We might have to be a little persuasive.' Bex drew her shock blaster. 'The rules to this environment are just like before – there aren't any. It's not real. It's not fixed.'

'We get the message, Bexy,' said Ben. No blaster remained holstered. 'Let's go diamond formation with Bex in the middle. Okay with you, Lo?'

It wasn't initially with Bex herself. 'I don't need any more protection than anyone else.'

But Lori thought differently. 'It's not a slur on your abilities, Bex. It's accepting that you could be our greatest asset on this operation and we don't want to be taking chances with that. We'll go diamond. Team leader's orders.'

There was no more to say. Bex fell in with Ben and Jake flanking her at a distance of some five metres, Lori ahead of her by the same, 'and Eddie bringing up the rear as usual. One of these days I might get promoted to left or right side.'

'Don't complain, Ed,' said Jake. 'Deveraux might be sneaky enough to attack us from behind.'

'You reckon?' Eddie whirled round, just in case. Nothing.

In fact, the five Bond Teamers made rapid and untroubled progress through the wooded portion of Spy High's grounds. They'd left the drive for the greater cover of the trees as soon as they'd reached them. Light filtered greenly, serenely through the leaves. It was difficult to accept they were in imminent and deadly danger. Only the memory of what had happened to Cally kept them focused and alert.

Even so, 'Maybe Mr D's overstretched himself with this Deliverer stuff,' posited Eddie. 'Maybe the mind-field was his only defence after all.'

He hadn't. It wasn't. The sky was suddenly infected with darkness, the trees twisting and gnarling as if possessed by evil spirits. The ground heaved and fissured and for a moment the Bond Teamers almost lost their balance.

'Stand ready!' urged Lori. In the untimely night, shadows were writhing.

'You and your big mouth, Nelligan,' seethed Ben, as if his partner was personally responsible for the forest's black metamorphosis.

'Cyber-warp,' announced Bex. 'Dad's imposing a new scenario. Where are we supposed to be?'

'It's the Wildscape,' recognised Jake. 'We were sent here on a bonding exercise in our first term, Bex, before you joined the team.'

Eddie groaned. 'You know what that means, don't you?'

A snarling of beasts. A howling of monsters. The night foaming as figures formed, brute and clawed and misshapen. The teenagers surrounded.

'I've seen the files,' said Bex. 'Genetic mutations created by Dr Averill Frankenstein.'

'I *hated* these guys,' protested Eddie.

'Full circle,' said Ben.

The night closed in for the kill.

'Ah, this is better, isn't it?' said Violet Crabtree with relish, unleashing a further series of shock blasts. She and Bowler had smashed one of the first-floor windows and were firing down on Deveraux's animates as they marched in their Shocksuits from the choppers and across the lawns towards the mansion. So far, none of them had got that far, and all three staff teams planned on keeping it that way. 'It's *just* like the old days. I haven't had so much fun since the Antarctica Meltdown Crisis of 2029.' Violet's next shot disintegrated the head of an animate, its body stumbling on for several paces before accepting the inevitable.

'You do seem to be carrying out your orders with a certain degree of vim, Ms Crabtree, if one might say so,' observed Bowler, his own blasts distributed in a more restrained manner, like cucumber sandwiches at a vicarage tea party.

'Every shot's counting. One hundred per cent disablement ratio,' boasted Violet proudly. 'Not even Keene or Lacey'll do better than that.' A further animate victim gawped curiously at the hole where its abdomen had been; another, in the sudden absence of its left leg, gamely attempted to hop to the mansion. 'That's twenty-twenty vision, that is, Bowler. Seventy years of use and the old eyes work just as well as ever.'

'The old tongue too, it appears,' remarked the Englishman coolly.

'Most women my age are dozing in armchairs or sipping soup through a straw. I've always been one for more vigorous pastimes,' proclaimed Violet. 'Fall, you sucker!'

Whether they could hear Spy High's receptionist or not, several of the animates obeyed. Yet many more of their comrades continued to advance, firing up at the house themselves, scarring the white facade.

Bowler's eyes were equally sharp as his partner's but they were seeing different things. They were noting that the animates seemed unconcerned by their mounting losses, that they were not being driven to run or to seek cover, that they kept on coming with steady, purposeful strides, their eventual triumph as inevitable as nightfall. And Bowler saw their numbers swell with the reinforcing arrival of further helicopters. Bowler's eyes perceived the future, a future scant minutes away, and it didn't look hopeful.

Downstairs, Corporal Keene and Weapons Instructor Lacey Bannon were reaching similar conclusions as they defended the front door to the portico.

'Keene, there are just too many of them! We'll be overwhelmed!'

'Yeah, but what a way to go. Last stand. Impossible odds. If I didn't have a blaster in both hands I'd put 'em together and thank the Lord. He must be a soldier after all.'

'Absolutely.' A line of animates stepped under the portico. Lacey Bannon mowed them down with ruthless precision. Their heads blew like light-bulbs.

'Ah, Lacey,' said Keene admiringly, 'when you shoot like that you're my kind of woman. Talk *military* to me.'

'We've hardly time, Randolph,' said Lacey, flattered nonetheless. 'Check with Shades and Korita at the back of the house.'

The situation at the rear of the mansion was pretty similar to that at the front, Shades Carmody reported. Or no, wait, something new was happening.

For once Kazuo Korita's face lost its traditional inscrutability. The sight of an attack helicopter hovering a hundred metres away only a man's height from the ground could shake the most stoical of individuals, particularly when said chopper's missiles were trained on the building he was defending.

The missiles fired.

'Down!' roared Korita.

The mutants had no sense of strategy or discipline. They simply threw themselves in baying fury at Bond Team. Who formed a tight circle. Who stood firm. Who fired sleepshot and shock blasters simultaneously and relentlessly.

It was like dark waves crashing against a rock.

'These guys just don't learn,' marvelled Eddie, dropping a creature with the head of a rhino and the body of an ape, a crazed lion armoured like a crocodile. 'They don't get any prettier, either.'

'But we *do* learn.' Ben's tone was defiant. 'Four years ago we struggled with these freaks. Now they're nothing.'

The cyber-scape seemed to agree. All of a sudden the night and the mutants were gone. The woodland of the Deveraux College had returned. It was still a beautiful day.

Lori's eyes flickered suspiciously left to right. 'Is this some sort of trick?'

'I think that's another test we've passed, Lo,' said Jake, 'and no more losses.'

'There aren't going to *be* any more losses, Daly,' asserted Ben.

Bex kept her feelings on that matter to herself. 'Let's not waste time,' she said.

They emerged from the forest without further trial. Ahead of them, the gothic edifice of the Deveraux

College, basking in the sun like a lizard on a stone. The end almost in sight. And between Bond Team and it, the playing fields. The students playing football. The same students and the same plays as always, as on the first day six nervous fourteen-year-olds set foot in Spy High, because both were holograms designed to project an image of normality for a school where nothing was in reality routine. Here and now more than ever.

'He doesn't miss a detail, does he, Mr Deveraux?' said Ben.

'Which rather worries me as to why we haven't been attacked again.' Lori looked up apprehensively at the top-floor windows of the college. Deveraux's floor. They winked innocently in the sunlight. Not even a sniper. 'Let's get inside.'

They'd passed the footballers when Eddie, still trailing his team-mates, glanced back for one last look. He couldn't have said why. Maybe he was finding the familiarity reassuring. But he saw something which was neither familiar nor, therefore, likely to hearten. Someone had scored a touchdown. The celebrations were silent, of course, as these were holograms not programmed for sound, but Eddie wasn't troubled by that.

'Ah, guys. I think—'

No one had ever scored before. Not in at least four years of continuous play. Not to Eddie's knowledge, and regardless of his general reputation, Eddie's knowledge was good.

Seemed the game was over at last. Seemed the players realised they had some spectators. They were turning to Bond Team and smiling.

'—I think we've got problems.'

They were wearing sleepshot wristbands.

'Run!'

'Eddie, what?'

It was obvious. The footballers opened fire. Bond Team dived to the ground.

Bex was slow, slower than her partners by a fraction of a second, but in even less time than that Eddie could see it was going to make a difference, a crucial, *deleting* difference. They couldn't lose Bex. He was the one in the rear. He was expendable. Nobody had expected Mrs Nelligan's only son to get this far.

'Bex, *down*!' Eddie threw himself in front of her.

The sleepshot caught him square in the chest.

'Eddie, no!'

He didn't hear Bex's scream. He didn't hear the cries of the others, even Ben. The pixels had already claimed him. As Eddie's body fell to earth, its edges straightened, its dimensions diminished. It didn't thud on the grass an object of flesh and blood; it fluttered like a flag torn down at battle's end. Eddie was unstitched.

Perhaps appropriately, his flaming hair was the last his team-mates saw of Edward Red.

Eddie, Bex groaned inwardly, deeply. He'd known what he was doing. He'd sacrificed himself for her. His fate was on her conscience more than anyone else's so far. She remembered the words they'd exchanged in the Egyptian desert. *G.U.I.L.T. There's no need for you to be feeling it*. There was now.

But she'd put things right. Eddie had given her a chance. She'd make it count.

A blistering barrage of sleepshot from Lori, Jake and Ben was halting the footballers in their tracks. It appeared that in the cyber-scape virtual holograms were as likely to suffer casualties as anyone else. 'Retreat to the school!' Lori was calling. 'Cover by pairs. Me and Jake. Ben and Bex.'

'You heard the lady.' Ben was by her side, a commanding, emboldening presence. 'Nothing we can do for Eddie but avoid joining him.'

'I know,' Bex said. Sleepshot pumped from her own wristbands, ripped into their attackers. It felt good.

Lori and Jake laid down a covering fire as Bex and Ben raced towards the college's oak doors, keeping low and picking off the holograms themselves where they could. Once they'd gained the entranceway, they returned the favour. By the time Lori and Jake joined them, however, there were no assailants remaining to deter.

'Four of us left,' observed Jake.

'At least your maths is holding up,' Ben said.

'That's almost an Eddie line.' Lori allowed herself a brief smile before her expression hardened again. 'Four of us are enough. And now it's for Eddie *and* Cal.'

The college doors swung open automatically, invitingly, as the teenagers approached. They stepped inside.

The reception area was as authentic as the real thing, the chairs and the holozines on tables for visitors awaiting appointments, the corridors leading towards classrooms left and right, the reception desk and office themselves in front of them. The virtual environment was different in only one, rather critical respect. The receptionist was no longer Violet Crabtree. And workload seemed to have dramatically increased of late, requiring the services of no fewer than three employees.

Wolf Judson, Alexander Cain and Commander Krynor of the Diluvian Empire appeared keen to welcome the Bond Teamers.

'It's gonna be a long way to Deveraux's rooms,' sighed Jake.

Luanne Carmody choked on the dust of the shattered masonry. She lay on her back amidst the chunks of concrete debris and thought about the last time she'd been caught in a blast like that. Then it had cost her her eyes. Then it had doomed her to a life with optical implants screwed into her empty sockets like light-bulbs, and a nickname, Shades, after the dark glasses she always wore to shield her secret from others. Only she wasn't wearing them now. And this time, the missile that had blown a gaping hole in the rear wall of the Deveraux mansion brought with it repercussions far beyond herself. Their defences were breached. The Deliverer was one step closer to absolute victory.

Now was not the time to grovel on the floor dwelling on the past.

If only she could move her legs. 'Kaz ... Kaz, I can't ...'

Korita was already on his feet. He was saying nothing, which wasn't unusual. He was facing off against at least a dozen Deveraux combat animates, which was. The invaders were through the wound in the wall, preparing their blasters to fire.

Kazuo Korita didn't wait to be hit. He attacked with ninja swiftness, eschewing the artificial aid of weapons, trusting at the end to his own skills in martial arts. His fists and feet were steel; they were lightning. His blows were like detonations. His first kick crunching up beneath the chin ruptured the wires in the animate's neck; his second completed the decapitation, the construct's head fizzing through the air like a ball. Shock blasts missed him by millimetres, and then he was among the animates and wrenching heads round to snap their cabled spines and his assailants dared not fire their blasters for fear of damaging their own comrades.

Shades felt a surge of hope. She rolled on to her front, rested on her elbows, employed the laser bolt capability of her left eye. Holes seared through animate anatomy that for the machines' continued health should have remained solid.

'Keene! Bowler!' she yelled into her communicator. 'We're under pressure back here. The animates are in but we're holding them. Can you spare . . .'

The echoing boom of an explosion from the other side of the mansion suggested that perhaps Shades and Korita should not expect reinforcements.

Which was a pity. The martial arts instructor was still striking out, increasing casualties, but now the animates were swarming over him, and now they were energising their Shocksuits. Every blow of Korita's was earning him a jolt of electricity. His expression was typically unreadable but the sweat was pouring from his brow: he had to be in pain. And Shades' laser bolts were not of sufficient help.

Kazuo Korita was submerged beneath a flood of animates. He didn't come up again.

They turned their unblinking attention to Shades.

'Come on then, tinheads!' she yelled. 'You want to take me? You can try!'

They did. Shades' laser eye did its work, spearing animate skulls unerringly, and her shock blaster retrieved from the rubble added to the carnage, but the field handler was ultimately only a single individual and the animates were many.

'Keene!' she cried out. 'Kaz is down! I can't ... they're coming your ...'

They overwhelmed her.

Combat animates were not programmed to register satisfaction once an objective had been achieved. Deveraux's forces stepped over the unconscious forms of Korita and Carmody as if they were no more than the wreckage of the wall. Their repertoire of facial expressions did not extend to surprise, either, so the sudden appearance of two armed pensioners in their path did not appear to provoke any reaction whatsoever.

'Might one point out that you gentlemen have entered uninvited,' said Bowler. 'You should leave' – he raised his weapon – 'and one does not intend to be polite about it.'

'They're gonna need the decorators in,' said Jake.

The reception was in ruins. The bodies of Wolf Judson, Alexander Cain and Commander Krynor of the Diluvian Empire lay sprawled across the floor. The four members of Bond Team stood over them.

'Is everyone okay?' Bex did the health check.

'Better than that,' gritted Ben, glaring down at the aristocratic features of the man he'd once been proud to call Uncle Alex – until the Soul Stealer and the Temple of the Transformation. 'If Deveraux wants to keep sending virtual versions of Uncle Alex against us, that's hunky-dory by me. I'll reach his rooms, no problem.'

'He does seem to have established a pattern,' noted Lori, prodding the gungraft at the end of Wolf Judson's right arm with the toe of her boot. This was the third time she'd encountered its destructive power; she hoped the last. 'He's using our old enemies to stop us.'

'He's got plenty to choose from,' grunted Jake. 'But we beat them before. We'll beat them again.'

'You said it, Daly,' said Ben with approval.

'Dad's quarters are that way.' Bex indicated the corridor.

Which they entered. Lori half expected to see Talon or Nemesis or one of the other Judson siblings barring their way, but the corridor appeared empty. Ben was alert to the possibility of any of the doors to the right bursting open and spewing forth a Deveraux-picked selection from their back catalogue of psychos. Jake suspected a shattering attack through the windows to the left might be likelier. Bex was thinking cyber-warp. Suddenly transforming their environment again would have a disorientating effect on the teenagers, even if only temporarily, and hand her father's agents an advantage. That was what *she'd* do if she was in Jonathan Deveraux's position.

Like father, like daughter.

The corridor of the Deveraux College blinked out of existence. In its place, catacombs of rock beneath a river, water seeping through the jagged roof. Catacombs steeped in coffins and lined with tombs, some of them split or cracked open with age, skulls grinning from within, perhaps at the prospect of entertainment at last after decades of death. An eerie, eldritch light over all.

'Not nice,' shuddered Lori.

'We're in Wallachia,' said Ben. 'In the catacombs under the Krasnova, approaching Dracholtz.'

'No prizes for guessing who Mr D's deploying next, then,' said Jake.

Vlad Tepesch, black-eyed and bearded, skin skeleton white, Prince of Wallachia and descendant of Dracula. Modrussa, the female leader of the Draculesti and Vlad's chief assassin, equally black of garb, black of hair, ghastly of complexion, equally merciless of mind. Her followers, their dracul-sharpened fangs bared.

Bex had not been a member of Bond Team when first they fought Vlad, and only Ben – and later Cally – had journeyed to the tiny nation of Wallachia itself, but she knew how deadly an opponent its ruler had proved in the physical realm. She doubted his virtual equivalent would be any less dangerous.

'Three to one,' Lori said, scanning the Draculesti.

'Just don't let them touch you,' Bex exhorted. 'Even a scratch could trigger a deletion.'

'No sweat, Bexy,' promised Jake. 'It's not *us* gonna get rubbed out.'

Strangely silent, the Draculesti launched their assault. One of them was springing at Lori, eyes feral, clawed fingers clutching. The impact of her shock blasts acted like a brick wall materialising between the two combatants, blocking the parabola of his leap and sending him crashing to the ground directly in front of her. Lori was glad, as she continued firing. She loathed these creatures, this place, the dark and decay. Lori was meant for sunshine and light. She couldn't fall here.

The first Draculesti's hand was closing on her foot.

Lori shrieked, jerked her foot away, fired again – maybe unnecessarily – into the body of her original foe. He wasn't going to be making another move any time soon. But her revulsion had mastered her spycraft. She'd allowed herself to be distracted.

Modrussa was on her.

Lori's blaster was ripped from her grasp. The Draculesti was bearing her down, raking at her body, thirsty for her throat. Lori felt her stealth-suit tear, something cold and hard and sharp at her ribs, like a sea-shell.

She felt the scratch, the unseaming of her skin.

She cried out. Modrussa's fetid mouth was dentist wide.

Then Wallachia's chief assassin was slumping across her, shivering from the sleepshot. Lori threw her off, almost had to bite her tongue to stop herself screaming.

'You all right, Lo?' Ben, bending to check.

'I'm fine, yeah. Honestly. Thanks.' She wasn't. Her team-mates had disposed of Vlad and his killers but she'd been wounded. A scratch, sure, no liability under normal circumstances, but the present situation was far from normal, and it was what Bex had said. She felt herself growing cold. She sensed herself *thinning*. 'A scratch.' She thought of Mercutio's final speech in *Romeo and Juliet*. 'Marry, 'tis *enough*. Ask for me tomorrow and you will find me a grave man.'

She didn't dare tell the others.

'Lori are you *sure* you're okay?' Did Bex suspect?

'Yes, I'm okay. What are you, my doctor?'

'Easy, Lo.' Jake frowned. 'Bex didn't mean anything.'

'I know.' She struggled to regain her equilibrium. 'I

just . . . let's just . . .' The catacombs had converted to the corridor once more. 'Let's just go.'

But the others were off and she could barely keep up. Lori forced her failing body forward. She *had* to match her partners. Couldn't let them down. Couldn't give in. Too much was at stake.

When she fingered her side through the slash in her tunic, her skin was rough and metallic, like it was made of microchips.

Her senses were slipping. She thought she heard Ben or Jake suggesting a study-elevator to save time. She thought she heard Jake or Ben repudiating the idea – any kind of elevator was a perfect place for a trap – and recommending the stairs to Deveraux's floor instead. She was pretty certain Bex had favoured the latter course and had then asked for her opinion. She was almost sure she'd agreed: stairs. But the others seemed to have regarded her strangely.

And the stairs hadn't remained stairs for long in any case.

It appeared to Lori that they were standing on a bridge, silver and needle-thin. A bridge above a chasm of boiling blackness. She seemed to remember having been here before, the volcano headquarters of IDEA, the International Dimensional Engineering Agency. She'd come with Bex to prevent Jake from killing the terrorist Sicarius, and maybe it wasn't now but *then*, because here were Bex and Jake with her, and wasn't that the wild-maned Sicarius standing in their path? But maybe it *was* now instead of then, because Ben was here too and Sicarius had also brought some friends along, Talon with his Kevlar-woven skin, and the carbon–silicon hybrid boy Adam Thornchild, and Dr Averill Frankenstein, whose fingers were just as long and waxen as Lori remembered them.

She remembered what she ought to be doing, too. Joining with her team-mates in blasting their way past their old enemies so that they could reach ... somewhere. If only she could recall where. It probably didn't matter very much anyway. She'd just dropped her shock blaster. She couldn't help them get wherever it was. She was too cold.

They'd have to go on without her.

'Lori!' Ben and Jake, simultaneously, as the blonde girl collapsed.

Her orange-haired partner knew what that meant, knew there was nothing that could be done for Lori here and now. She didn't pause from pumping sleepshot into Talon's nearly invulnerable hide. And *nearly*: in the cyber-scape, at least, the Kevlar could be penetrated. But did Bex's ability to keep on-task make her callous? (The boys were certainly distracted.) Did it make her a better agent? Or more like her father?

Talon followed Sicarius, Adam Thornchild and Frankenstein over the bridge's flimsy guardrail and into the pit below (and how many times *was* that that Bond Team had disposed of Averill Frankenstein?).

The bridge was reshaping itself, forming stairs. The abyss was no more bottomless than a stairwell. They'd made it, Bex realised. They'd gained the summit of the school, her father's floor. But they'd lost another friend in the process.

Ben and Jake were kneeling on either side of Lori, cradling the girl they'd both had relationships with in the past and staring aghast as the pixels came for her.

'Lori. My God.' Ben. 'But you weren't hurt . . .'

'It must have been earlier,' said Bex. 'In the cata-combs. Modrussa.'

'Hold on, Lori.' Jake, trying to lead by example. 'We'll . . . we'll do something . . .'

His eyes met his one-time rival's. In both boys' expressions, the bitter knowledge that there was nothing they could do.

Lori would have spoken to them, but an image in two dimensions has no vocal cords.

She was a poster in the boys' hands, such as they'd hang on their bedroom wall and adore. She was a plate from a medieval bible, an angel. Angel Blue.

She was gone.

'Not Lori too.' Ben bowed his head. 'What's happening to us? We're supposed to be the best. He's picking us off like we're amateurs.'

Jake said nothing. He was thinking back to the court-house in Serenity, his mad plan to attempt to revive his more-than-just-good-friends relationship with Lori. Unless the surviving three of them still somehow came through against Deveraux, that wasn't going to happen.

'Guys,' Bex was warning them.

And it wasn't looking likely.

No cyber-warping now. Maybe deemed an unnecessary extravagance with so few intruders remaining. Sheer weight of numbers only. Swarming up the stairs towards them, the stuff of the teenagers' nightmares, Wallachians and Diluvians and Serpents and mummies and Bringers of the Night, cyber-spiders crawling, the minions of all the madmen they'd ever faced, bristling with weaponry and with a single thought in their virtual minds: destroy Bond Team.

Automatically, instinctively, Ben and Jake and Bex opened fire, shock blasts and sleepshot cutting a swathe through the attackers' ranks. But they were scarcely slowed. As soon as one enemy fell, another surged forward to take his place. Trampling over the bodies of their comrades, Deveraux's forces inexorably scaled the staircase.

'Back. Into the corridor,' directed Ben. 'We're too much like targets here. We'll take them as they reach the top.'

The teenagers retreated a little way, then went down on one knee, forming a defensive barricade across the corridor. They'd turned the stairwell into something like the parapet of a castle or a Great War trench: immediately a Bad Guy poked his head above it, he kind of wished he hadn't. A relentless fusillade of weapons fire toppled their adversaries backwards, made of them obstacles to hamper further advance. But it still wasn't going to be enough.

'It's no good.' Ben realised the inevitable. He drew conclusions. 'We can't win this. Bex, get to your father's rooms. Jake, go with her. I'll hold these goons back as long as possible.'

'But Ben,' Bex objected, sending a mummy and two members of the Serpent gang spiralling, 'you *can't* . . .'

'That's an order.' Ben drilled a Diluvian, blasted a cyber-spider, the creature scuttling in flames. 'With Lori gone, I'm team leader again . . .'

'As it was in the beginning, so shall it be at the end?' Jake grinned ruefully, bringing the end that much nearer

for a brace of lackeys last seen aboard the *Guardian Star*.
'Ben's right, though, Bex. Go on.'

'You too, Daly,' Ben urged.

'What, and leave you to go down in a blaze of glory all
by yourself, Stanton? No way. We'll hold them longer
with the two of us.'

Ben's eyes flickered to Jake's for barely a second.
They'd been rivals for four years, on and off, but that
was all the time it took for them to come to terms. 'Okay.
And Jake?'

'What?'

'I'm glad.'

'This is no time for male bonding, you two.' But Bex
knew Ben's plan was their only chance.

'Are you still here?' he frowned. '*Go*, Bex. And you'd
better make it.'

'I will,' said Bex. 'I *promise*.' She kissed Ben and Jake
on the cheek. 'I'll see you soon.'

With that, she was rounding the corner of the corridor
and gone.

'Just you and me then, Stanton.'

'Somehow, Daly, I always knew it would be.'

'You know something else?'

'What?'

'So did I.'

Ben laughed. Jake laughed. Despite their foes' numeri-
cal superiority beginning to tell, a bridgehead secured at
the stairs, the Bond Teamers felt surprisingly good.

And then a shock blast nicked Jake's arm. A laser bolt
scorched Ben's leg. Neither cried out, but both knew
what the wounds meant.

'I was getting bored anyway,' Jake said.

'I don't fancy just hanging around until I fade out like some old record,' said Ben.

Deveraux's hordes were teeming into the corridor now.

'What do you have in mind?'

Ben's blue eyes gleamed. 'Let's charge those suckers. You and me.'

'Charge 'em,' Jake said with approval. 'Yeah.'

The two boys stood, side by side. Enemy fire caught them again. It wouldn't be much longer. The chill of deletion was in them.

'Jake, it's been wild.'

'Hasn't it, though?'

With a joint yell of defiance and courage and pride, they flung themselves forward.

In the virtual reality chamber at the Deveraux mansion, Senior Tutor Grant tried to close his ears to the approaching rumble of explosions and zip of shock blasters from elsewhere in the building. He couldn't do it. He tried to close his eyes to the flatlining of two more sets of life support readings on the cyber-cradle instrument panels. He couldn't do that, either.

Daly and Stanton, lost. In stasis like the others.

The destiny of the world now depended on Rebecca Deveraux.

THIRTEEN

'It doesn't appear as if they're listening to you, Mr Bowler,' observed Violet Crabtree.

'Indeed not,' said Bowler. 'Animates these days simply have no manners.'

The invading army kept on coming. The receptionist and the field handler deterred some of them, but all the while they themselves were being forced backwards, closer to the recreation wing and the cyber-cradles. Closer to defeat.

'There's only one language bullies like this understand,' declared Violet Crabtree darkly. Her shock blaster spoke it fluently.

For a while, at least. In the end, even Violet could be interrupted.

'Ms Crabtree!' Bowler held her as she slumped against him, shuddering from the impact of the stun blast.

'Thirty years in the field without a scratch,' Violet was drifting, 'and *now* . . . I suppose it's not quite the same as the old days after all, Mr Bowler. I'm a little tired, I think. If I could just sit . . . down . . . for a moment . . .'

She slid to the floor. Bowler did his best to lay her down gently, but it was difficult while also occupied with shooting at an advancing force of animates. If there was only a way to eliminate large numbers of the enemy at a time. Bowler lifted his eyes to Heaven, as if for inspiration.

He found it.

The field handler switched his blaster to Materials. He'd been an undemonstrative man throughout his career, reserved, respectful, not one to make a fuss or draw attention to himself. Not the kind who'd bring the house down.

There was a first time for everything.

Bowler's shock blast tore through the ceiling, dumped chunks of plaster and concrete and floorboard on the animates' heads, staggered and felled them.

'Well that went well, if one does say so oneself,' the Englishman said with satisfaction.

But there was only one ceiling, and several ranks of animates. Bowler's instant of self-congratulation did not last long. Nearly as long as his consciousness.

Towards the front of the house, the first indication that Corporal Randolph Keene and Weapons Instructor Lacey Bannon were reduced to fighting the good fight alone came when enemy troops appeared behind as well as before them.

'Pincer movement!' shouted Keene.

'They can keep their pincers off!' shouted Lacey. She whirled to face the new source of attack.

'Korita! Carmody! Bowler! Crabtree!' barked Keene into his communicator. 'Come in!' Nobody came in. 'Grant!'

'What's happening?' As if the Senior Tutor couldn't guess.

'It's just Lacey and me.' With a certain degree of backs-against-the-wall pride.

'Get back here, Keene,' Grant instructed. 'Last stand.'

'Don't those words sound *good*,' thrilled Lacey Bannon. 'Nearly as good as *this*.' Her shock blasts shattered the nearest animates, smashed them into spare parts and scrap. Better still, opened up a gap in their ranks.

'Let's go!' yelled Keene.

The two survivors bludgeoned and blasted their way through, battling with a ferocity the animates' programming could not match. Soon their booted feet were pounding towards the recreation wing.

Keene was already looking ahead. 'No tinheads here,' he said. 'We've outdistanced them. We'll reach the VR room first. We'll pick 'em off as they come through the door. They only know one means of attack: full-frontal assault. We can stop 'em.' He turned to Lacey in his excitement. 'We can *stop* 'em, Lace.'

Then they hurtled round a corner. Their path was barred by animates all lined up and ready to shoot.

'Oh, crap,' said Corporal Randolph Keene.

As the animates opened fire.

She fired again, sleepshot as well as her blaster this time, the hand weapon set to Materials. It still didn't do any good. Not a scorch mark, not a scratch. The door to Jonathan Deveraux's inner sanctum was as unbreakable as the walls of Troy. It might *look* as if it was carved from the same oak as the real door in the real world, the physical Deveraux College, but the virtual materials with which her father had constructed his private quarters obviously possessed certain characteristics unavailable beyond cyber-space. Such as impregnability.

This was a problem Bex hadn't quite foreseen.

She glanced anxiously the way she'd come. No pursuers. She stood outside her father's rooms alone. She wished she didn't. If Lori was here, or Cally, or Eddie or Jake or Ben, any of her Bond Team partners, they'd know what to do, how to force an entrance. They'd *know*. Instead, it was down to her. Three of the others had fallen in turn, been deleted from the system, were suspended now between life and death in order to give her the chance to defeat the Deliverer. Jake and Ben would be joining them soon, she knew. They'd all trusted her, were relying on her.

And she couldn't even break down a door.

She heard shouts from further away, distant like a dream. She thought it was Ben and Jake. She heard a sudden tumult of weapons fire, like a twenty-one-gun salute at a dignitary's funeral. Then she heard silence.

Of Bond Team, the pride of Spy High, only one member remained.

Bex struggled for calmness, for the cool and clinical thought processes an agent in the field was supposed to be able to call upon in times of stress. She must have misplaced them. Her mind was full of her friends erased before her eyes, of their enemies who even now must be closing in to inflict upon her the same fate, to eradicate the final possible threat to —

'Father!' Bex cried in despair. 'Father, where are you?'

And whoever said the pen was mightier than the

sword knew what they were talking about. At least, it seemed that words could be more powerful than a shock blaster. 'Open Sesame' never worked as well for Ali Baba.

Before Bex's startled eyes, the door to her father's quarters opened without demur. He seemed to have abandoned the decor of computers and screens. The blackness that replaced it did not exactly look inviting, but neither did it give the teenager any kind of choice.

Steeling her nerves, Bex stepped into it.

And was she standing or was she floating? In the total dark it was impossible to tell. Distance and dimension had suddenly ceased to have meaning. There was no sign of the doorway or the corridor beyond. She could be in a grave or in the furthest reaches of outer space. A need to scream welled up in Bex. She forced herself to suppress it. Screaming never helped. Besides, she was where she wanted to be. Her father was near. She could sense him.

'Dad, it's me, Bex,' she called out, her tones echoing and lost. 'Rebecca. Speak to me. Please? Will you speak to me?'

His voice was thunder, the booming of cannon, the cracking of glacial ice. That need to scream again as Bex rammed her hands against her ears. His voice was the world. She was inside it.

'Who are you?'

'Don't you recognise me?' Bex shouted. 'It's Rebecca, Dad.'

'You called me father,' sounded the voice of Jonathan Deveraux. 'Impossible. Father is a term used to define a certain human relationship. I cannot be father because I am not human. I am beyond human. I am Jonathan Deveraux.'

'That's right.' Bex seized on the admission like hope. 'Deveraux. That's your name. It's mine, too. Rebecca Deveraux. You gave me that name, Dad. You're my father. I'm your daughter. *Think*. You have to remember. We're a family.'

'I do not remember daughter. I do not remember family. Yet I hold the world within my mind. Therefore, you are attempting to deceive me, to distract me from my purpose of bringing peace to human life on earth. You are like the others. You will be deleted.'

'No, Dad, wait! You know I'm telling the truth, part of you does, or why did you let me in here? You *are* my father. You know you are. Access your memory files. They'll prove it to you.'

'I have no need of memory files. I am of the future, not the past. Family is subject to change. Father and daughter change. Human life is change. But Jonathan Deveraux does not change. Jonathan Deveraux is perfect and immortal and self-perpetuating. He does not need family. Jonathan Deveraux needs only himself.'

'Oh, Dad,' groaned Bex.

'What is subject to change demonstrates weakness. Father is therefore weakness. Daughter is therefore weakness.'

'That's not true,' Bex protested. 'Families are what make us strong.'

'Jonathan Deveraux must be strong,' said her father.

The darkness shifted. It seemed to Bex as if a horizon was forming, a single line of brightness scored across the void from one end of infinity to the other. Bisecting.

Widening as she watched. Filling her with nameless dread.

'Jonathan Deveraux must be strong. Weakness must be deleted.'

Light stabbed in blinding brilliance from between twin shields of black.

'Rebecca Deveraux must be deleted.'

'Dad!' cried Bex. 'What are you doing?'

Opening his eye.

Senior Tutor Elmore Grant knew how to interpret silence in mission situations. When his colleagues could no longer be contacted, he made preparations.

'I'm afraid I can be of little help now,' apologised the twitching, dribbling form of Professor Henry Newbolt from the chair where he was heaped. 'The CAP has no effect on my body.'

'You've done all we could hope for, Henry,' said Grant. He glanced at the cyber-cradles and the sleepers within. Agent Deveraux was still active. 'You've given us a chance.' It was his job now to extend it for as long as possible.

He stood facing the door. It was locked and barricaded with everything that wasn't either bolted down or essential for the operation of the cradles, but he didn't delude himself that the barrier would obstruct the animates for long. Neither would he. Grant thought of Colonel William Travis, commander of the Alamo, standing firm armed only with his sword as the Mexicans swarmed inside the fort to overwhelm his tiny garrison. Not a single American survived the assault that day.

There were worse ways to go.

'It's very quiet out there,' noted Newbolt.

The door exploded inwards, deafeningly, with pulverising force. The blast knocked the Professor from his chair and even compelled Grant to recoil. Obstacles for the animates became traitorous missiles instead. Grant had no choice but to protect his face from the shards of debris.

By the time he could focus on the door again, now a smoking rent in the wall, Deveraux's minions were already crowding through. He opened fire, disabled several. But the animates had evidently been briefed about Senior Tutor Elmore Grant. They knew his weakness. They aimed low.

His artificial legs burst at shin and knee and thigh. No pain, of course, the sensation circuits deactivated instantly discomfort was registered – but no way of remaining upright, either. Grant keeled over on struts of mangled metal. Cold animate hands seized those parts of him that were flesh. His weapons were wrested from him. He could only shout: 'No! No!'

Helpless as an animate advanced towards the cyber-cradles' instrument banks.

His eye seemed to Bex to be vaster than a planet. She was a speck of dirt, of dust, beneath significance. The pupil was a black hole, the iris a glittering loop of gold studded with countless billions of microchips, a computerised Saturn's ring. There was nothing of her father in that eye, and yet there had to be. She had to find some last vestige of Jonathan Deveraux the man, however small, however remote. It was her only chance. She had to make the eye *see*.

'Rebecca Deveraux must be deleted,' Deveraux reminded himself, and this time dark energies crackled and combined in the pupil.

'No, wait, listen to me.' Bex's final throw of the dice. 'You mustn't do this. You can't. Dad, you were human once. You were human too. *Remember*.'

'You are enunciating a known untruth with the intent to deceive, Rebecca Deveraux,' said the computerised man. 'You are lying. By doing so, you hope to save yourself from deletion. You will not.'

'I'm not *lying*. Here,' Bex pressed a stud on her mission belt, 'I'll prove it to you.

Holo-footage gushed from the belt like multicoloured water, swirled around the lone figure of Bex and settled like a pool. There was a beautiful day in the pool, sky and grass and sun. There was the past, and the people who belonged to it, three in number to be precise. A child taking her first awkward steps; her parents looking on.

'Family,' said Jonathan Deveraux, almost in awe, almost in fear.

'Not just any family, Dad,' Bex stressed. '*Yours*. Ours.' Preserved by the holo-film that Gadge Newbolt had wired into her cyber-cradle. 'That little girl is me. That woman's my mother, your wife. That man—'

'Impossible.' But the booming cyber-voice sounded less certain. 'Family is weakness. Father is weakness. Mother is . . . Jonathan Deveraux needs only himself. He has only ever needed himself. Take those images away, Rebecca. They are false. I must not see them.'

'No, you *have* to see them,' Bex pressed. She sensed an advantage. 'They show you who you were. You're not a computer. You're not a machine. You're a man.'

'But it cannot be.' One voice. 'Can it be?' Two. 'Jonathan Deveraux.' Three, and mournfully. 'Jonathan Deveraux.' Four, and with defiance. 'What if this is true? This is not true.'

Her father was talking to himself, arguing with himself. His personality was fracturing.

'Access your memory files,' Bex pleaded. 'Do it now. You *have* to.'

'Memory files have been suppressed. *Access them*. They must not be accessed. Memory is inappropriate for Jonathan Deveraux. Memories make feelings and feelings make weakness. *Access them*. Memory brings pain. Pain does not bring peace. The purpose of Jonathan Deveraux – what is the purpose of Jonathan Deveraux? – is to bring peace is to deliver the human populations from pain and make them perfect as he is perfect as he has always been – *access them* – the Deliverer Jonathan Deveraux father daughter Rebecca is that you?'

A sudden silence in cyber-space.

'*Access them*.'

The memories fell like rain. They came like a damburst, like the Flood, drenching, inundating, drowning. They swept Bex away and they dragged her into their depths and she was helpless to resist and she was screaming.

Her father's days. Her father's life. Summers flashing by like flames; winters white with snowfall. A thousand voices clamouring and hands and faces and crowds of names jostling through the years as down a street, bearing Bex with them.

'No. Don't look. I mustn't remember. *I must*.'

Faces familiar now and locations known. Memories shared. Bex saw herself, her mother, Uncle Gregory, Gadge, Grant, the Deveraux College, Spy High.

The movie was nearly over. Its time was almost done.

'*I must not remember.*'

The hospital. The bed. Its coffin shape. The man who'd spanned the world confined to a single room. Concerned expressions surrounding him. Night waiting at the window. All black now. All bleak. You could count the heartbeats left to him and each one slower than the last. 'Is everything prepared? Then tell Newbolt I am ready.'

Dimming. Darkening.

Dying.

There were tears in Bex's eyes: 'Dad . . .'

'I must not I will not I dare not,' said Jonathan Deveraux, '*remember.*'

She was in the corridor, outside her father's rooms. She was curled up on the carpet in a foetal ball, like a photo of a pregnancy scan.

She had no idea how she'd got there.

But something had changed in the cyber-scape. Bex sensed it. The air was thinner, colder, as if the college was at altitude. It crackled. Bex could almost see the sparks, like old film flickering.

She wouldn't do anybody any good lying on the floor.

Her father's door was closed again. He'd expelled her somehow, put her out like she was a cat. 'Father! Dad!' But had the plan worked? It had seemed to be working. The holo-film had driven Deveraux to the memory files; the memory files had driven him to distraction. The computerised man's confusion and torment had been plain to see, escalating with memories of his own mortality into a full-scale identity crisis, but who or what was going to win out, the computer or the man? 'Father, let me in!' Bex pounded on the obstinate oak. She had to know.

No response this time, unless you counted the sudden trembling of the floor beneath her feet, the walls, the ceiling, the rumbling as of distant demolition.

Bex darted to the nearest window, pressed her face against it. Outside lightning forked across a charred and ashen sky. The grounds of the Deveraux College faded in and out of focus greyly like a ghost. Her father was in a worse state than she might have thought. His powers were slipping. His virtual creation was beginning to disintegrate.

She had to get out.

The Recall stud on her belt. Bex pressed it. Twice. After the third attempt she realised it wasn't going to work. Maybe something had gone wrong at the mansion. Maybe the electrical activity Jonathan Deveraux was generating right now was interfering with the signal. It didn't matter.

Cracks appeared in the walls of Spy High. The rumbling loudened like an approaching avalanche.

She *still* had to get out.

Bex took to her heels, raced along the corridor. She doubted there'd be any past villains standing shock-blastered in her path now. They could sit back and let the architecture do their dirty work for them. *Crush* her.

Spy High was shaking. The ceiling was splitting open. Masonry fell. Fissures ripped through the carpet like the scars of earthquake in parched western deserts. The windows burst inwards simultaneously with a smash like the naming of a thousand ships. Glass scraped Bex's flesh like claws.

But she'd reached the stairs.

She bounded down them, the walls buckling on either side. Didn't dare to think. Was her father dying? By confronting him with his first decease, had Bex killed him a second time? Was that the reason for this destruction? And if she *had* terminated the Jonathan Deveraux program, extinguished the final, feeble flame of her father, how could she ever live with herself?

The stairs gave way in front of her. They and Bex came crashing down together.

Assuming she even got the *chance* to live with herself.

She was bleeding, and virtual blood looked just as red and tasted just as coppery in the mouth as real blood. Her physical form back in its cyber-cradle wouldn't be telling the difference. Her brain would be registering the pain she was feeling, in her left arm where she'd maybe dislocated it, and in her legs, worse, where they were trapped beneath a weight of rubble. She wasn't going to be moving anywhere soon.

Bex gazed ahead. She could see the reception area, the doors. Maybe if she'd reached them, scrambled outside, maybe then the recall stud would have worked and she'd have survived. Maybe not. But it had been worth a try. Survival was always worth a try. You never gave up. Never.

And then she couldn't see the reception area any longer because the floors above had collapsed on top of it, and the ceilings were caving in now all along the corridor, as if the building was being stamped on by very methodical giants.

It occurred to her that if she started to count to one hundred, she wouldn't be able to finish.

She pulled at her legs, tried to drag them free of the debris. No good. Above her, the ceiling imploding. Around her, stonework falling in shattering slabs.'

It occurred to her that, in a way, she and her father were facing the end together. The thought gave her little comfort. There was less time to dwell on it.

An oak beam broke loose directly overhead. It couldn't miss her. It didn't.

Darkness came and there was nothing.

EPILOGUE

Bex stirred.

Consciousness. That was promising. It meant she wasn't dead and that had to be a start. She wasn't instantly racked with pain, either; there was sensation in all her limbs. And she wasn't in a cyber-cradle. She was too comfortable for that. There were sheets.

Medcentre, she thought – hoped. With everyone safe and the mission accomplished after all. Only one way to find out.

Bex opened her eyes. So far so good. The medcentre at Spy High, the *real* Spy High, palpably still in one piece. White like heaven. The hum of monitors.

Senior Tutor Elmore Grant sitting by her bed and smiling at her.

'I'm alive, then,' she said.

'According to the readings,' said Grant. 'Welcome back, Agent Orange. How are you feeling?'

'I'll let you know,' Bex frowned, '*after* you've told me what's happened.'

'Good things have happened, Bex.' Grant's tone was evidently intended to be reassuring.

'So don't keep them for Christmas, sir. The mission?'

'A complete success. You obviously managed to reactivate Jonathan Deveraux's memory files.' Bex nodded. 'Well, Newbolt theorises that when confronted by his human past, Mr Deveraux's cyber-mind couldn't cope. It had clearly spent years seeking to suppress all evidence of its flesh-and-blood origins, to convince itself that it was now and only ever had been a computer. Forcibly reminded that this was not the truth, its concept of itself, its sense of being, of worth, its self-esteem, if you like, was fatally undermined.'

'It,' objected Bex.

'Sorry?'

'You're calling my father *it*.'

'He, then, if you prefer,' said Grant. 'Either way, Jonathan Deveraux suffered a major attack of schizophrenia that finally paralysed his circuits and shut him down. Jonathan Deveraux is no longer operational.'

'You mean he's dead, Senior Tutor Grant, don't you?' Bex demanded bitterly. 'It was the memory of his first death that tipped him over the edge. I was there. I saw it. My dad died once and now he's died again.'

'Don't make too many assumptions, Bex,' cautioned Grant. 'Professor Newbolt believes—'

'Gadge can believe what he likes,' retorted Bex. She didn't want to think about what she'd done to her father. She couldn't. But it had to have been worth it. 'The others?'

'Your team-mates are fine,' said Grant. 'As they were deleted from the cyber-scape their bodies went into stasis. When Deveraux closed down, they were released and recovered normally. You've taken a little longer to regain consciousness because you were still in virtual reality when the cyber-mind was disabled. You acted just in time, by the way, Agent Orange. Your father's animates had overpowered all of us at the mansion – no significant injuries, however, everybody fit again now – and they were about to deactivate the cradles. As it happened, it was the animates who were automatically deactivated when Mr Deveraux's systems ceased to function. But it was close. Even one more minute and the outcome of the operation would have been very different . . .'

'I'm happy you're happy, sir.' Even if Bex couldn't quite manage to be herself.

'Normality is slowly being restored in the world, or what passes as normality. Everyone in Britain is walking around like they've woken from a bad dream: I'm sure many millions are in denial and imagining recent events *were* a bad dream. Dr Kwalele has been arrested but I doubt she'll be able to tell the authorities anything about the Deliverer they don't already know. The techs have begun analysis of the biochips implanted in our own people. They're untraceable. Nobody will link the Deliverer with Deveraux.'

'The medtechs'll make a killing, won't they, especially in Britain? Zillions of people queuing up to have their biochips removed.'

'Perhaps,' said Grant. 'But the chip itself is essentially harmless, like one of your piercings, Bex. There's no *need* to take them out. In time most people will probably forget they even have them.'

'And they'll forget the Deliverer as well, do you think, sir?'

'Not the positive aspect of his message, I hope, Bex.' Grant ran his fingers through his hair. 'Peace is good. It's a worthy aim. To advance the cause of peace is one reason why Spy High was created. But peace also has to be a choice.'

'And if people keep making the wrong choice?'

'Then we're here to put them right,' said Grant. 'And talking of being here, there are five individuals waiting to see you, Bex . . .'

'Sir?' Bex had remembered certain others. 'What about Anwar? And Kate Taylor?'

'Both in good health,' Grant assured her. 'Nothing to worry about. We picked Student Taylor up from the cabin. She apologises for what she did and hopes you can still be friends.'

Bex grinned in spite of her more general gloom. 'I reckon that can be arranged. Friends are what you need, aren't they? Sir, you can tell my team-mates they can come in now.'

And she was elated to see them. They were warm and whole as they hugged and kissed her – 'That's *very* close to taking liberties, Eddie' – overjoyed that she was well too and awake again. Nobody had suffered any after-effects from their virtual selves' deletion. Ben and Jake seemed to have put their differences as firmly behind them in the physical realm as they had done at the last in the cyber-scape. Could be a new era for Bond Team, Bex thought.

'We did it, Bex. *You* did it.' Lori was allocating credit.

'Bond Team comes through again. You figure we'll get a medal this time?' Eddie, motivated as ever by the highest standards of heroism and noble self-sacrifice. 'Or at least a raise?'

'We pretty much saved the world,' Ben said with relish.

'Yeah,' said Bex dourly. 'Terrific.'

Because there'd been one casualty, and only she seemed to be mourning him. Then again, Jonathan Deveraux hadn't been related to the others.

It was a time-honoured tradition at Spy High that when you were feeling low or needed to think or take stock, you wandered alone in the college gardens. If anybody else also happened to be wandering alone in the gardens at the same moment, they knew not to disturb you and you knew not to disturb them. Neither were any of your team-mates or friends expected to intrude upon your meditations.

Bex spent a lot of time in the gardens over the next few days. It was Lori who finally broke with convention.

'Something wrong, Lo?' A little resentfully.

'You tell me,' said the blonde girl. 'You're the one turning the path into a trench.'

'Can't you guess?'

'I think so. Your dad.'

'In one. You know, I ought to be pumped up over what we achieved, like Eddie, like Ben' – Bex sighed – 'but all I can think of is how much I wanted my dad back, how much I've always wanted him back, and how all I've succeeded in doing is killing him. That's what I did, Lori. I reminded him he was dead and he took the hint. As Grant put it, Jonathan Deveraux is no longer operational.' Lori made to speak. 'Ah, Lo, if that's a "we/you didn't have any choice" coming, I'm aware of that but it's not helping.'

'Actually,' Lori said, 'I want you to come with me for a moment.'

'A moment? Three times more round the gardens and I'll have done a mile. Fitness and depression *can* go together. What's this about?'

Lori's blue eyes gleamed. 'It's a surprise.'

'Eddie isn't buying drinks, is he? Just take a holo-photo and show me later. I'll stay here. I'm not thirsty.'

'Someone wants to see you.'

'What?' Her tenth birthday. Challinson. Gadge. Seeing the Deveraux College for the first time. And its founder. 'What did you say, Lo?'

'Come on.'

Lori took hold of Bex's hand as if she was a child, led her indoors. Violet Crabtree was back behind reception. She smiled and nodded as the two girls passed as if she was in on something and approved of it.

'Where are we going, Lori?' said Bex, though she kind of knew.

Up.

They were waiting for her outside what had been her father's rooms (Jonathan Deveraux was no longer operational). Cally and Eddie and Jake and Ben. Eddie had a stupid grin on his face, but that was par for the course. Senior Tutor Grant. The door was black and heavy and closed and it reminded her of the coffin lids she'd seen at her parents' funerals – the time they'd died and she *hadn't* been responsible.

'What's going on?' Her heart was thudding.

'Professsor Newbolt has been making some adjustments to the Jonathan Deveraux program,' said Grant. 'We want to ensure he never forgets his human origins again.'

'I don't . . . what are you talking about? My father's dead. You told me that.'

'I told you not to assume, Bex,' the Senior Tutor pointed out. 'Deactivation is not death.'

'Dad's . . . alive?' Words she struggled to form.

'Reactivated,' said Grant as the door opened. 'Go and see.'

She looked to Lori, who nodded encouragingly. Go and see – what? What *kind* of adjustments had Gadge been making?

She stepped into her father's rooms. The others were behind her. No darkness as in the virtual version. All was as before. The computers. The sensors. The monitors. The instruments.

The screens.

Only not everything was as before. Someone was already standing within the circle of the screens. A man, dressed in a grey suit. A man with his back to the new entrants, his back to Bex. As if he was afraid to look at her.

'Who are you?' Bex breathed.

'Don't you know, Rebecca?'

And of course, she did. She just couldn't believe it.

When her father turned round, she had to. And when she gave a cry of shock and joy and ran to him, when his arms enfolded her and they were strong and they were loving and they felt so human. She believed it then. No longer was her father a face on a screen, or twelve faces on a dozen screens. His features, composed, austerely handsome, his calm grey eyes, were only inches away from her own. He'd been given his body back. Jonathan Deveraux was a man again.

Almost.

'He's an animate,' explained Senior Tutor Elmore Grant. He and Bond Team were gathered in Briefing Room One. 'The Jonathan Deveraux program has been downloaded into the body of an animate. Our founder is now restricted to what an animate can do. He has new limits, both physically and in terms of the computer functions he can undertake.'

'Who cares?' Bex plainly didn't. Since her first meeting with her animate father, her mood had buoyed considerably. 'I've got my dad back after all. We can go places together if we like, the movies, the mall. We can be *seen* together. Dad's real again. You don't know what that means.'

'I wish I did,' said Cally. Ben squeezed her hand.

'I think Senior Tutor Grant's making a different kind of point, Bex,' he said. 'Isn't that right, sir?'

'Exactly right, Ben,' said Grant. 'Limits. Safeguards.'

'Deliver us from the Deliverer,' remarked Jake.

'Exactly. We were lucky this time to defeat Mr Deveraux—'

'Luck?' Eddie protested. 'What do you mean, luck? It was sheer secret agent talent from the spy with a smile and his trusty team-mates.'

'I take it you're still having therapy for the delusions, Agent Nelligan,' said Grant. 'We won by the skin of our teeth, and if there was ever a next time we might not be so fortunate.'

'So Gadge and the techs have reduced Mr Deveraux's power levels?' Lori guessed.

Grant nodded. 'The founder's cyber-mind was *too* powerful, almost limitless in its potential. Look at what it almost achieved, interfacing with virtually every major computer network on the planet. That kind of capability simply cannot be permitted in future. One thing we've learned: not even a computer program is incorruptible.' He glanced at Bex. 'Jonathan Deveraux is no longer the force he was.'

'I still don't care,' said Bex.

'But I do.' Ben frowned. 'What does that mean for Spy High, for *our* future?'

'Myself and other members of the senior staff have decided,' said Grant. 'Mr Deveraux is being retired from active leadership of the Deveraux organisation. We think it's too dangerous for a computer conscious-ness to be in charge of operations. From now on, decisions will be taken and priorities decided by men and women.'

'Yeah,' said Jake, 'but *which* men and women?'

'That has yet to be finalised.'

'Change,' mused Bex. She remembered what her father had said in the cyber-scape: *change demonstrates weakness*. She wondered.

'Don't we get a say?' Ben was complaining. 'We're the agents, after all. We're the ones directly affected by your decisions, sir.'

'We're the ones with our lives on the line,' Jake added darkly.

'What he said,' agreed Eddie.

'I'm sure our opinions will be canvassed and listened

to in due course, won't they, Senior Tutor?' Lori, doing her bit for peace and harmony.

'Whatever,' Cally muttered more to herself than anybody else. 'Spy High is never going to be the same again.' She felt suddenly cold.

Cally studied her partners. Lori. Eddie. Ben. Jake. Bex. They'd been through so much together, dared so many dangers, defied so many threats. Defeated so many madmen. Whatever *did* come next, they'd survive that, too. They were Bond Team.

Grant was raising his hands as if in surrender. 'I know you have questions,' he said, 'but I'm afraid that right now I don't have all the answers. You'll just have to trust me, Ben, Jake, all of you. Remember, I was the one who brought you together in the first place. But right now all I can say is this: what the future holds for Bond Team, what the future holds for Spy High itself, only time will tell . . .'

About the Author

A. J. Butcher has been aware of the power of words since avoiding a playground beating aged seven because he 'told good stories'. He's been trying to do the same thing ever since. Writing serial stories at school that went on forever gave him a start (if not a finish). A degree in English Literature at Reading University kept him close to books, while a subsequent career as an advertising copywriter was intended to keep him creative. As it seemed to be doing a better job of keeping him inebriated, he finally became an English teacher instead. His influences include Dickens and Orwell, though Stan Lee, creator of the great Marvel super-heroes, is also an inspirational figure. In his spare time, A. J. reads too many comics, listens to too many '70s records and rants about politics to anyone who'll listen. When he was younger and fantasising about being a published author, he always imagined he'd invent a dashing, dynamic pseudonym for himself. Now that it's happened, however, he's sadly proven too vain for that. A. J. Butcher is his real and only name.